# THE HISTORY OF
# RASSELAS,
# PRINCE OF ABISSINIA

**broadview editions**
series editor: L.W. Conolly

Portrait of Samuel Johnson by Sir Joshua Reynolds (1756–1757), courtesy of National Portrait Gallery, London.

# THE HISTORY OF RASSELAS, PRINCE OF ABISSINIA

Samuel Johnson

*edited by Jessica Richard*

broadview editions

**Library and Archives Canada Cataloguing in Publication**

Johnson, Samuel, 1709–1784.
    The history of Rasselas, Prince of Abissinia / Samuel Johnson ; edited by Jessica Richard.

(Broadview editions)
Includes bibliographical references.
ISBN 978-1-55111-601-3

    I. Richard, Jessica.    II. Title.    III. Series.

PR3529.A2R52 2008        823′.6        C2007-906335-7

**Broadview Editions**
The Broadview Editions series represents the ever-changing canon of literature in English by bringing together texts long regarded as classics with valuable lesser-known works.

Advisory editor for this volume: Jennie Rubio

Broadview Press is an independent, international publishing house, incorporated in 1985. Broadview believes in shared ownership, both with its employees and with the general public; since the year 2000 Broadview shares have traded publicly on the Toronto Venture Exchange under the symbol BDP.

We welcome comments and suggestions regarding any aspect of our publications—please feel free to contact us at the addresses below or at broadview@broadviewpress.com.

*North America*
Post Office Box 1243, Peterborough, Ontario, Canada K9J 7H5
2215 Kenmore Avenue, Buffalo, NY, USA 14207
Tel: (705) 743-8990; Fax: (705) 743-8353;
email: customerservice@broadviewpress.com

*UK, Ireland, and continental Europe*
NBN International, Estover Road, Plymouth PL6 7PY UK
Tel: 44 (0) 1752 202300   Fax: 44 (0) 1752 202330
email: enquiries@nbninternational.com

*Australia and New Zealand*
UNIREPS, University of New South Wales
Sydney, NSW, 2052 Australia
Tel: 61 2 9664 0999; Fax: 61 2 9664 5420
email: info.press@unsw.edu.au

www.broadviewpress.com

This book is printed on paper containing 100% post-consumer fibre.

Typesetting and assembly: True to Type Inc., Claremont, Canada.

PRINTED IN CANADA

For Norris Richard Blackburn

# Contents

# Acknowledgements

I wish to thank the Wake Forest University English Department, especially successive department chairs Gale Sigal and Eric G. Wilson and administrative assistants Connie Green and Peggy Barrett, for supporting my work on this project and for funding the stellar work of my research assistants Olivia Garnett, Audrey Looker, and Andrew Burchiel. I gratefully acknowledge support from the Wake Forest University Graduate School of Arts and Sciences Publication & Research Fund. Graduate students in my Fall 2003 graduate seminar on "Eighteenth-Century British Fiction: The Oriental Tale" were instrumental in developing my ideas for this edition and suggesting texts for the Appendices; I wish particularly to acknowledge B. Hunter Ginn, Dorothy Hans, and Spence Brooks O'Neill. Jack Lynch made crucial suggestions for the Appendices and Introduction. Srinivas Aravamudan generously shared his forthcoming work on the oriental tale with me. Marah Gubar, Claudia Thomas Kairoff, and Carlotta Richard made incisive comments on the Introduction. I am grateful for Claudia L. Johnson's support of this project. Thanks to Julia Gaunce, Leonard Conolly, and Jennie Rubio at Broadview. I would not have completed this edition without the excellent child care Stacy Martorana, Celia Rowlson-Hall, and Melissa Williams provided for baby Norris. Timothy C. Blackburn daily disproves Nekayah's gloomy assessment of marriage, giving me the happiest "choice of life."

# Introduction

When Jane Eyre arrives at Lowood Institution early in Charlotte Brontë's novel, she strikes up a conversation with "a girl sitting on a stone bench near; she was bent over a book, on the perusal of which she seemed intent: from where I stood I could see the title—it was 'Rasselas;' a name that struck me as strange, and consequently attractive."[1] But "a brief examination convinced me that the contents were less taking than the title: 'Rasselas' looked dull to my trifling taste; I saw nothing about fairies, nothing about genii; no bright variety seemed spread over the closely-printed pages." Jane expects a book with the "strange," "attractive" title of *Rasselas* to be part of the immensely popular eighteenth-century genre, the oriental tale.

English interest in cultures broadly defined as "oriental"—in the eighteenth century, the "orient" denoted the Near and Far East, as well as North Africa—had been increasing as merchants returned with exotic wares that became the centerpieces of fashionable English attire, interior design, and gardening. In 1704, Antoine Galland began publishing *Mille et une Nuits*, a French translation of a collection of tales of Arabic, Persian, Turkish, Indian, and Egyptian origins known as *Alf Layla wa-Layla*; an anonymous English translation from the French soon followed under the title *Arabian Nights' Entertainments*.[2] The *Arabian Nights* developed the oriental vogue in the literary sphere and led to genuine translations of additional oriental tales as well as many pseudo-translations and imitations.[3] Booksellers brought out

---

1  Charlotte Brontë, *Jane Eyre*, ed. Richard J. Dunn (New York: W.W. Norton, 2001) 41–42.

2  See C. Knipp, "The *Arabian Nights* in England: Galland's Translation and its Successors," *Journal of Arabic Literature* 5 (1974): 44–54 and Duncan B. MacDonald, "A Bibliographical and Literary Study of the First Appearance of the *Arabian Nights* in Europe," *Literary Quarterly* 2 (1932): 387–420.

3  As Lynn Meloccaro notes, there are examples of literary orientalism in England and France before the appearance of the *Arabian Nights* by writers such as Marlowe, Dryden, and de Scudéry, but as a collection of apparently genuine tales from the East, the *Arabian Nights* represents an important point of departure for eighteenth-century orientalism. "Orientalism and the Oriental Tale: Gender, Genre, and Cultural Identity in Eighteenth-Century England," diss., Rutgers University, 1992, 61.

such titles as *The Thousand and One Days, or the Persian Tales*; *Chinese Tales*; *Mogul Tales*; and *Turkish Tales*. Popular periodicals such as the *Tatler* (1709–11), the *Spectator* (1711–14), the *Rambler* (1750–52), the *Adventurer* (1752–54), and the *Idler* (1758–60) sometimes used "oriental" settings, themes, and character types to inculcate moral lessons in essays and short tales. Longer oriental tales published as independent volumes include Voltaire's *Zadig* (1749), John Hawkesworth's *Almoran and Hamet* (1761), Frances Sheridan's *History of Nourjahad* (1767), Horace Walpole's *Heiroglyphic Tales* (1785), and William Beckford's *Vathek* (1786). Following Giovanni Marana's *Letters Writ by a Turkish Spy* (1687) and Montesquieu's *Lettres persanes* (1730), Eliza Haywood's *The Adventures of Eovaai* (1735), Oliver Goldsmith's *Citizen of the World* (1760–61), Elizabeth Hamilton's *Translations of the Letters of a Hindoo Rajah* (1796), and others use the device of an imagined oriental visitor's letters home to criticize European culture. All of these indicate the breadth of the British literary orientalism into which Jane Eyre instinctively expects to place *Rasselas*.

Yet instead of an exotic story from the *Arabian Nights* with "fairies" or "genii," Jane finds *Rasselas*, after a cursory glance, "dull." When *The History of Rasselas, Prince of Abissinia* first appeared in two small volumes, on 19 April 1759, some critics expressed a view not unlike Jane Eyre's. For the critic Owen Ruffhead, writing in the *Monthly Review* in May 1759 (see Appendix B1), *Rasselas* lacks the "sprightliness of imagination," the "ease and variety of expression" necessary for "the romantic way of writing" the oriental tale required. While some readers thus explicitly criticized the book for not being oriental enough, most have assumed that the oriental setting is merely incidental to Johnson's primary purposes. The appendices to this edition provide texts that indicate the reception of *Rasselas* and its place in Johnson's œuvre while encouraging students to consider *Rasselas* in the context of the eighteenth-century vogue for the oriental tale.

If the story of "the rise of the novel" in eighteenth-century England narrates the ascendance of realism, how do we account for the popularity of the fantastic oriental tales modelled on the *Arabian Nights* that appeared profusely throughout the century? If one of fiction's functions was (in the novelist Frances Burney's words) "to mark the manners of the times," and if readers used fiction as (in Johnson's words) "lectures of conduct, and introductions into life," what were the purposes and uses of oriental tales?[1] Despite their popularity, neither the oriental tale in general nor *Rasselas* in particular has been adequately accounted for in our histories and theories of eighteenth-century fiction; both have been treated as exotic oddities left over after the story of the rise of the British novel of manners has been told.[2] While providing students with contextual material that will enrich their understanding of *Rasselas* and its place in Johnson's work and time, this edition also aims to reposition *Rasselas* not just as a philosophical but also as an oriental tale, and thus contribute to a developing discussion of the oriental tale in eighteenth-century fiction. Such a discussion might posit the excesses of the oriental tale—its magical plots, dazzling settings, despotic viziers, and gorgeous princesses—as central rather than peripheral to the arts of fiction in this period. Examining oriental excess both in *Rasselas* and in the figure of Johnson himself (rather than emphasizing the neoclassically balanced periods of the great lexicographer and moralist) reveals the utility of the oriental tale for exploring English enjoyment of—and concern about—the material luxuries and existential contingencies of an increasingly global culture.

## Johnson's Life and the Composition of *Rasselas*

Samuel Johnson lived from 1709 to 1784. He was born in Lichfield, Staffordshire, where his father was a struggling bookseller. He suffered various ailments during early childhood, including

---

1 Frances Burney, *Evelina*, ed. Susan Kubica Howard (Peterborough: Broadview, 2000) 95; Rambler No. 4 (see Appendix A3).

2 Scholarly accounts from the early twentieth century, such as Ernest A. Baker's *The History of the English Novel: The Novel of Sentiment and the Gothic Romance* Vol. 5. (London: H.F. & G. Witherby: 1929), devote chapters to the oriental tale, but the form is all but ignored by major historians of the novel such as Ian Watt, Michael McKeon, and Margaret Doody. See Srinivas Aravamudan, "In the Wake of the Novel: The Oriental Tale as National Allegory," *Novel* 33.1 (1999): 5–31. See Ros Ballaster's study of the oriental tale in England, *Fabulous Orients* (Oxford: 2005). For accounts of teaching *Rasselas* in a university course on eighteenth-century British fiction, see Melvin New, "*Rasselas* in an Eighteenth-Century Novels Course," *Approaches to Teaching the Works of Samuel Johnson*, eds. David R. Anderson and Gwin J. Kolb (New York: MLA, 1993) 121–27; Tita Chico, "*Rasselas* and the Rise of the Novel," *Johnsonian News Letter* 56.1 (March 2005): 8–11; and George Justice, "*Rasselas* in 'The Rise of the Novel,'" *The Eighteenth-Century Novel* 4 (2005): 217–31.

vision and hearing impairments and scrofula (a form of tuber-culosis infecting the lymph nodes of the neck). As a boy, Johnson augmented his education with hours spent reading in his father's shop; later he could afford to attend Pembroke College, Oxford, for only one year. He married a widow, Eliza-beth Porter, in 1735 and briefly ran a school near Lichfield. In 1737, Johnson moved to London and made his living by mis-cellaneous hack writing, including pieces for *Gentleman's Mag-azine*, sermons, and reports on parliamentary debates. He pub-lished the well-received poems *London* (1738) and *The Vanity of Human Wishes* (1749). His tragedy *Irene* was produced and pub-lished in 1749. His periodical the *Rambler* (1750–52) and his *Dictionary of the English Language* (1755), along with *Rasselas*, brought him fame as England's chief man of letters; a govern-ment pension of £300 in 1762 brought him financial security at long last. Johnson's later publications include an extensively annotated eight-volume edition of Shakespeare's plays (1765), *A Journey to the Western Islands of Scotland* (1775), and a series of fifty-two literary biographies commonly known as *The Lives of the English Poets* (1779–81). He was awarded honorary degrees by Trinity College, Dublin in 1763 and by Oxford Uni-versity in 1775.

Johnson was famous not only for his writing but also for his conversation; his nervous, idiosyncratic demeanor accentuated by tics was offset by his incisive, epigrammatic talk. This talk was recorded most extensively by James Boswell in *The Life of Samuel Johnson* (1791), a massive biography that came to be read, in the nineteenth century at least, more widely than many of Johnson's own works and that made the figure of "Dr. Johnson" familiar to readers as a dogmatic, opinionated arbiter of literary and moral values. As Philip Davis notes, "Many of Johnson's contempo-raries ... wrote accounts" of Johnson's life and conversation "not only because of Johnson's memorable impressiveness but as if there was something vitally left-over in him that demanded to be saved and converted into writing."[1] In his friends' view, there was more to him than his published works; he had an excess of vital-ity and almost alarming corporeality that could hardly be repre-sented even in a biography like Boswell's—a book that rivals the *Arabian Nights* both in length and as an episodic collection of oral

---

1 Philip Davis, "Extraordinarily Ordinary: The Life of Samuel Johnson," *The Cambridge Companion to Samuel Johnson*, ed. Greg Clingham (Cam-bridge: Cambridge UP, 1997) 9.

anecdotes.[1] Johnson's nickname, the "Great Cham of literature," specifically represents his abilities in terms of oriental excess ("cham" is a form of the word "khan," a title given to Tartar, Mongol, and Chinese rulers); calling Johnson the "Great Cham of literature" implies his absolute, far-reaching, perhaps ruthless dominance in the realm of letters.[2] But while his friends celebrated the aspects of Johnson that somehow exceeded his writing, Johnson himself was plagued by the anxiety that, as he wrote in his diary, "my life has stolen unprofitably away," that he had not done justice to the abilities God had given him.[3] He aspired to be a scholar-poet in the Latin European humanist tradition, not an English hack-writer and critic.[4] Physical and intellectual excess marked his singularity in London society but, to some degree at least, these attributes also burdened him.

Johnson's biographers note the occasion of his mother's death as the immediate impetus for the composition of *Rasselas*. Boswell claims that Johnson composed the tale in the evenings of one week (see Appendix B3). Letters from this period, 13 to 27 January 1759, show Johnson's increasing concern over his mother's deteriorating health and his efforts to send her money that might ease any financial worries exacerbating her illness. He wrote her a farewell letter on 20 January:

> Dear honoured Mother,
> Neither your condition nor your character make it fit for me to say much. You have been the best mother, and I believe the best woman in the world. I thank you for your indulgence to me, and beg forgiveness of all that I have done ill, and all that I have omitted to do well. God grant you his Holy Spirit, and receive you to everlasting happiness, for Jesus Christ's sake.

1  Even the left-overs of Johnson's body outlived him as autopsy anecdotes and exemplary organs. See Helen Deutsch, "Dr. Johnson's Autopsy, or Anecdotal Immortality," *Eighteenth Century: Theory and Interpretation* 40.2 (Summer 1999): 113–16.

2  James Boswell, *Life of Johnson*, ed. R.W. Chapman and J.D. Fleeman (Oxford: Oxford UP, 1970) 247.

3  Samuel Johnson, *Diaries, Prayers, and Annals*, ed. E.L. McAdam, Jr., *Yale Edition of the Works of Samuel Johnson* Vol. I (New Haven: Yale UP, 1958) 225.

4  See Robert DeMaria, Jr., *The Life of Samuel Johnson: A Critical Biography* (Cambridge, MA: Blackwell, 1993) xxii.

Amen. Lord Jesus receive your spirit. Amen. I am, dear, dear
Mother, your dutiful Son,
Sam. Johnson

On the same day, he wrote to the printer William Strahan for
immediate cash against the imminent sale of his book, then titled
"The choice of Life"; desperate to supplement his mother's care
and comfort, he urged in a post-script "Get me the money if you
can."[1] His mother died and he used this money to pay her debts
and funeral expenses.

For many readers, the melancholic occasion of his mother's
death explains what some perceive as inconsolable gloominess in
*Rasselas*, a tale in which the characters are unable to find a
"choice of life" that leads to happiness.[2] Some scholars, however,
have warned against giving this occasion too much weight and
thus overlooking the tale's comic form.[3] Not only is *Rasselas* carefully structured, as Gwin J. Kolb and Emrys Jones have each
shown (and thus not hastily or thoughtlessly rattled off the top of
Johnson's head), but its moral and didactic purpose is achieved
through ironic satire, exposing hypocrisies and flawed philosophical systems unstintingly. Indeed, the tale's structure creates its
satiric, comic effects, so that, as Srinivas Aravamudan and others
point out, Imlac's "Dissertation upon Poetry" in Chapter X
(often mistaken as Johnson's straightforward *ars poetica*) parallels
the inventor's "Dissertation on the art of flying" in Chapter VI.[4]
Both men's rhapsodies on their art are undermined. The inventor falls into a lake on his first attempt at flight; Rasselas cuts off
Imlac's lengthy catalogue of the knowledge necessary for poetry
with a curt "Enough! Thou hast convinced me, that no human
being can ever be a poet" (64). Though *Rasselas* is full of anti-

1 Bruce Redford, ed., *The Letters of Samuel Johnson* Vol. 1: 1731–1772
    (Princeton: Princeton UP, 1992) 177–79.
2 See James Clifford, *Dictionary Johnson* (NY: McGraw-Hill, 1979)
    215–17 and Gwin J. Kolb, "The Reception of *Rasselas*, 1759–1800,"
    *Green Centennial Studies*, ed. Paul J. Korshin and Robert Allen (Char-
    lottesville: U of Virginia P, 1984) 217–49 for accounts of published and
    private responses to *Rasselas*.
3 Alvin Whitley, "The Comedy of *Rasselas*," *ELH* 23.1 (1956): 48–70.
4 Srinivas Aravamudan, *Tropicopolitans* (Durham: Duke UP, 1999)
    207–08. See also DeMaria, Jr. 207–08.

thetical epigrams that are easy to quote out of context (such as "Marriage has many pains, but celibacy has no pleasures"), Alvin Whitley stresses the crucial role context plays in the tale, and exhorts us to notice the "irony which arises from our realization that something has been said in a special way by a particular character in specific circumstances" (50). Jones suggests that the tale's epigrams should not be taken as "Johnson's weighty conclusions on life" but that the precise point is to notice what is left over, unencapsulated by his neat formulations. While we enjoy their wit, we must also acknowledge how "comically insufficient ... such rhetorical devices are." The comment on marriage and celibacy, for example, leads us—and Rasselas himself—"into a baffling cul-de-sac"; it seems both witty and wise, but is no help (398). In Rasselas's response, Johnson highlights the insufficiency of such epigrams to provide moral guidance. Rasselas stubbornly refuses to believe the results of Nekayah's research and clings to a romantic vision of marriage. His romanticism seems foolish, but despair would be wrong. *Rasselas*'s comedy highlights its characters' hopefulness in excess of any evidence to support that hope.

Jones argues that attention to the overall structure of the tale illuminates both Johnson's skepticism of neat systems and his comic optimism. Jones sees the tale falling into three sections of sixteen chapters each, with the final chapter serving as a coda. In the first section, Rasselas determines to escape the Happy Valley and make his choice of life. In the second section, Chapters XVII–XXXII, Rasselas, Nekayah, Pekuah, and Imlac begin their "experiments upon life" (76), investigating many stations and modes of life and looking unsuccessfully for happiness. The third section, Chapters XXXIII–XLVIII, begins with Pekuah's abduction at the Pyramids and concludes with the party's visit to the catacombs; this section shows "the travellers living fully in the world, no longer at leisure to contemplate the spectacle of life, but buffeted by circumstances, and themselves becoming actively involved with other men" (Jones 397).

### *Rasselas* as an Oriental Tale

*Rasselas* begins in a classic scene of oriental excess, the Happy Valley in Abyssinia (now Ethiopia), where the children of the emperor are confined in luxury. The setting is a fascinating nexus of many sources, as Donald M. Lockhart and others have shown.[1] While it may have taken final form in the evenings of one traumatic week, *Rasselas* builds on Johnson's extensive reading of histories and travel books and on his prior reading and writing of oriental tales. We can date his early exposure to the region in which he sets his tale to his first book-length publication, a translation from the French of a travel book by a Jesuit missionary, Father Jerome Lobo's *Voyage to Abyssinia* (1735). Abyssinia was primarily known to eighteenth-century Europeans as the site of "Portuguese imperial and commercial ambition" carried out through Jesuit missionaries.[2] Johnson's translation shows his disapproval of the missionaries' efforts to bring the Abyssinian Christian Church in conformity with Rome, from which it had separated in 451 when it rejected the Council of Chalcedon; rather than portray them as "heretics" and "schismatics" with unorthodox beliefs, as they appeared from the Roman Catholic perspective, Johnson describes the Abyssinians as "People that adhered to the Religion of their Ancestors" and the Jesuits as trespassers who attempted to "seduce them from the true Religion."[3] Johnson appears to have read widely in the controversial histories of Abyssinia that debated the Catholic view of the Abyssinian Church as a "debased, Judaized form of Christianity" and found instead "striking parallels between the Abyssinian practices ... and modern Protestantism" (Greene 71); these histories are the sources for many of the details of *Rasselas*'s Happy Valley, including the prince's and Imlac's names.

---

1 See Donald M. Lockhart, "'The Fourth Son of the Mighty Emperor': The Ethiopian Background of Johnson's *Rasselas*," *PMLA* 78 (December 1963): 516–28; Gwin J. Kolb, "The 'Paradise' in Abyssinia and the 'Happy Valley' in *Rasselas*," *Modern Philology* 56.1 (Aug 1958): 10–16; Arthur J. Weitzman, "More Light on *Rasselas*: The Background of the Egyptian Episodes," *Philological Quarterly* 48.1 (January 1969): 42–58; and Thomas M. Curley, *Samuel Johnson and the Age of Travel* (Athens: U of Georgia P, 1976) 147–82.

2 Donald Greene, *The Politics of Samuel Johnson*, 2nd ed. (Athens: U of Georgia P, 1990) 69.

3 Quoted in Joel J. Gold, "Johnson's Translation of Lobo," *PMLA* 80.1 (March 1965): 51–61. See also Samuel Johnson, *A Voyage to Abyssinia*, ed. Joel J. Gold, *Yale Edition of the Works of Samuel Johnson* Vol. XV (New Haven: Yale UP, 1985).

In addition to indicating Johnson's early interest in Abyssinia, his version of Lobo can also illuminate Imlac and Rasselas's discussion of imperialism in Chapter XI. Joel J. Gold argues that Johnson's translation of Lobo shows his objections to "the long exploitation of the Africans by the Portuguese"; Donald Greene believes the work testifies to Johnson's "strong suspicion that projects of colonization and proselytization often cloak motives of aggrandizement and commercial gain" (Gold 61; Greene 72). Johnson's Preface to Lobo's *Voyage* (see Appendix A1) indicts the Jesuits for being "cruel," "insolent," and "oppressive," for "continually grasping at dominion over souls as well as bodies," and for "procuring to themselves impunity for the most enormous villanies" (Johnson, *A Voyage to Abyssinia* 4). Against this scathing critique, Imlac's bland enumeration of European superiorities darkens; while European "armies are irresistible," Johnson by no means approves of the uses to which this strength has been put (64). Clement Hawes notes that in Chapter XI Johnson does not ultimately explain European power in terms of inherent, divinely ordained superiority, though he seems to at first.[1]

"By what means," said the prince, "are the Europeans thus powerful? or why, since they can so easily visit Asia and Africa for trade or conquest, cannot the Asiaticks and Africans invade their coasts, plant colonies in their ports, and give laws to their natural princes? The same wind that carries them back would bring us thither."

"They are more powerful, Sir, than we," answered Imlac, "because they are wiser; knowledge will always predominate over ignorance, as man governs the other animals. But why their knowledge is more than ours, I know not what reason can be given, but the unsearchable will of the Supreme Being." (64-65)

Imlac's first reference to European wisdom seems to imply inherent superiority, but this quickly becomes "knowledge," a practical attribute that can be acquired by anyone and may very well reverse directions as Rasselas proposes. Indeed, the fearsome dominance of the Ottoman empire in the seventeenth century

---

1  Clement Hawes, "Johnson and Imperialism," *The Cambridge Companion to Samuel Johnson*, ed. Greg Clingham (Cambridge: Cambridge UP, 1997) 118–19.

was recent enough to remind eighteenth-century European imperialists that conquest could go from east to west.[1] Later Imlac names exotic Egypt (not classical Greece) as the source of modern civilization, eastern and western; Egypt is "a country where the sciences first dawned that illuminate the world" (98). Imlac uses the analogy of man governing animals for European dominance over Asians and Africans, but his reference to the divine emphasizes "contingency rather than inevitability"; this is simply the way things happen to be at one moment in history (Hawes 119). Thus in his version of Lobo and in *Rasselas*, Johnson demonstrates a complicated view of the relationship between East and West, criticizing European abuses of power and reminding Europeans of the oriental foundations of their knowledge and the merely provisional nature of their current dominance.

Hawes argues that Johnson never suggests that Europeans are inherently superior and thus "refuses any sort of racial essentialism by way of accounting for the imbalance" of power between East and West (119). Indeed, Johnson has been criticized from his day to our own for not making his characters seem different enough from Europeans, for neither adhering to stereotypes from oriental tales nor attempting to represent actual Ethiopians.[2] Instead, *Rasselas* is grounded in an Enlightenment universalism that emphasizes common humanity across cultures and geographic regions. As Johnson wrote in his Preface to Lobo's *Voyage*, "wherever human nature is to be found, there is a mixture of vice and virtue, a contest of passion and reason ... the Creator doth not appear partial in his distributions."[3] While demonstrating common humanity, however, Johnson's universalism does not erase cultural differences. Details of life in North Africa—from the Abyssinian royal seclusion to the rich variety of urban Cairo

---

1  As Kevin Berland points out, "The primary difference between eighteenth-century and later British orientalism lies in ... the fact that throughout the seventeenth century the balance of power between east and west is the reverse of the configuration [Edward] Said premises. The Ottoman Turks (and other forces from the Islamic world, such as the Barbary pirates) were an extremely powerful presence." "The Paradise Garden and the Imaginary East: Alterity and Reflexivity in British Orientalist Romances," *The Eighteenth-Century Novel* 2 (2001): 138. See also Byron Porter Smith, *Islam in English Literature* (Beruit, Lebanon: American Press, 1939) 100.

2  See Aravamudan, (*Tropicopolitans*) 203; and Lynn Meloccaro, introduction, *The History of Rasselas; Dinarbas* (London: Everyman, 1994) xxxi.

3  Johnson *A Voyage to Abyssinia* 3–4.

to the dangers faced by tourists at the Pyramids—are carefully rendered. Johnson's detailed universalism reminds readers that far from functioning simply as an exotic Other, the ancient civilizations of North Africa were in many ways foundations for the modern civilizations of Europe (Hawes 117). As Imlac explains, "The ruins of their architecture are the schools of modern builders" (98).

Johnson's careful attention to accurate cultural detail in *Rasselas* may come from skepticism he expresses in his Preface to Lobo's *Voyage* of the "romantick absurdities or incredible fictions" sometimes found in supposedly factual travel narratives. Johnson praises Lobo for avoiding the rhetorical hyperbole of other accounts: "he meets with no basilisks that destroy with their eyes, his crocodiles devour their prey without tears, and his cataracts fall from the rock without deafening the neighbouring inhabitants" (139). Just as he praises Lobo for having "copied nature from the life" in his non-fictional narrative, in his *Rambler* essay No. 4 (1750; see Appendix A3), Johnson values fiction that "exhibit[s] life in its true state, diversified only by accidents that daily happen in the world, and influenced by passions and qualities which are really to be found in conversing with mankind" (153). Did Johnson fully adhere to his own injunctions in *Rasselas*? He draws on historical sources for cultural detail, his characters do not speak in an unduly elevated style, and numerous incidents in the tale—from the visit to the shepherds in Chapter XIX to Pekuah's description of harem life in Chapter XXXVIII— serve to deflate the "romantick absurdities" of fiction.[1] Yet oriental fiction is as important a source for *Rasselas* as Abyssinian travel narratives; Johnson mines the conventions of the oriental tale as much as he undermines them. "Why," asks one critic, noting the many romance sources for a paradise in Abyssinia, "did Johnson prefer fancy to fact in *Rasselas*?"[2]

We might answer this question by examining what "fancy" made possible for Johnson. The oriental tale as it had developed by the mid-eighteenth century functioned in England both as a vehicle for moral teaching and as a repository for the fantastic. Galland's version of the *Arabian Nights* set the pattern for this duality. He suggests in his preface that "if those who read these

1   See Stephen S. Power, "Through the Lens of *Orientalism*: Samuel Johnson's *Rasselas*," *West Virginia University Philological Papers* 40 (1994): 6–10.
2   Kolb "The 'Paradise' in Abyssinia" 16. See also Berland.

Stories have but any Inclination to profit by the Examples of Vertue and Vice, which they will here find exhibited, they may reap an advantage by it, that is not to be reap'd in other Stories, which are more proper to corrupt than to reform our Manners."[1] This didactic frame domesticates these strange tales, giving them a familiar purpose; Galland proposes the *Arabian Nights* as an ur-novel of manners.[2] Indeed, Arthur J. Weitzman suggests that Galland played up the didacticism of the tales to appeal to his European readers and "added moral digressions to some of the stories for which no authority exists."[3] Weitzman goes so far as to argue that most of the European oriental tales inspired by the *Arabian Nights* were primarily didactic and not particularly "wild, fantastic, or extravagant." Yet many of the tales in the *Arabian Nights* have no clear instructive purpose; reading vertiginous clusters of proliferating tales within tales within tales, one revels in the seemingly endless possibilities of narrative, and this fecundity was just as inspiring for imitators as the oriental tale's didactic opportunities. Martha Pike Conant explains the oriental tale's popularity as an escape valve releasing energies that are otherwise inexpressible in neoclassical forms; while this may be an unfair characterization of neoclassicism, Conant seems right to emphasize the appeal of the oriental tale's open-ended playfulness.[4] As Horace Walpole, himself the author of oriental tales, describes the *Arabian Nights*, "there is a wildness in them that captivates."[5] The popularity of oriental tales derives from their dual function as moral tales and as pure pleasure. We can see this peculiar combination of the didactic and the fantastic in one of the most famous

---

1   *Arabian nights entertainments: consisting of one thousand and one stories, told by the Sultaness of the Indies, ... Translated into French from the Arabian MSS. by M. Galland, ... and now done into English ...* (London: Andrew Bell, 1713).

2   The idea that the oriental tale could reform European manners was the foundation for tales, mentioned above, by Marana, Montesquieu, Goldsmith, and Hamilton featuring an oriental visitor's comments on European society.

3   Arthur J. Weitzman, "The Oriental Tale in the Eighteenth Century: a Reconsideration," *Studies on Voltaire and the Eighteenth Century* 58 (1967): 1843.

4   Martha Pike Conant, *The Oriental Tale in the Eighteenth Century* (New York: Columbia UP, 1908; New York: Octagon Books, 1966) 12.

5   Horace Walpole, *Letters*, Vol. XIV, ed. Mrs. Paget Toynbee (Oxford: Clarendon, 1903–18) 140. Quoted in Robert L. Mack, Introduction, *Oriental Tales* (Oxford: Oxford World's Classics, 1992) xix.

English oriental tales, Joseph Addison's *Spectator* essay "The Vision of Mirzah" (see Appendix C1); many writers followed Addison's example and used the oriental tale to present moral instruction in a trendy and appealing guise. But for Johnson, the wild possibilities of the oriental tale are not merely instrumental; they form a central component of the instruction *Rasselas* conveys.

By using the conventions of the oriental tale, *Rasselas* shows the insufficiency of any·one "choice of life" to fulfill human desire. The luxurious excesses of a paradisical retreat, the tyrannical power of a greedy bassa, the sexual decadence of a harem, the teeming possibilities of an ancient market city: all these are typical of the *Arabian Nights* and its progeny, and are also prominent features of *Rasselas*. In his *Rambler* Nos. 204 and 205 (see Appendices A4, A5), Johnson experimented with the oriental tale as a vehicle for exploring desire and happiness; as Hawkins notes in his biography (see Appendix B2), the success of these essays influenced his choice of form in *Rasselas*.[1] When Seged, emperor of Ethiopia, decides to "try what it is to live without a wish unsatisfied," the excesses standard in the oriental tale give him a vast range of resources to draw on. "All that could solace the sense, or flatter the fancy, all that industry could extort from nature, or wealth furnish to art, all that conquest could seize, or beneficence attract, was collected together, and every perception of delight was excited and gratified" (159). None of this can guarantee Seged happiness or insulate him from misfortune, but it does provide the reader with an oriental spectacle of excess that is, at least momentarily, very satisfying. Similarly, in the first section of *Rasselas*, Johnson uses standard oriental luxuries to show that the restlessness of human desire cannot be sated by all that power, money, and imagination can provide; we see that unhappiness is not due merely to lack of resources while we take pleasure in the narrative description of those resources.

In addition to providing a template for depicting unfulfilled desire, the oriental tale provided an episodic form especially congenial to Johnson's purposes in *Rasselas*. Just as characters tell each other stories in the *Arabian Nights*, the travellers in *Rasselas*

---

1 Oriental tales can be found in *Rambler* Nos. 38, 65, 120, 190, 204, and 205. After *Rasselas*, Johnson wrote oriental tales for the *Idler* Nos. 75, 99, and 101. Johnson's friend John Hawkesworth wrote at least eight oriental tales for his periodical *The Adventurer* before *Rasselas* was published.

report on their research into different modes of life and hear the accounts of those they meet. *Rasselas* is not merely a collection of essays in the mode of Johnson's *Rambler*, as has sometimes been thought. As a series of interrelated stories it conforms closely to its oriental models. The episodic form also facilitates the travellers' free movement as they consider the choice of life;[1] rather than following any unity of place, the oriental tale ranges from one locale to another, collecting narratives along the way.

Chance is an important feature of the episodic oriental tale; in "The Story of Cogia Hassan Alhabbal" from the *Arabian Nights*, for example, a poor merchant's attempts to improve his economic situation are subject, both for ill and for good, to chance events: a kite snatches the turban where the merchant had stashed his money, his wife finds a diamond in a fish. Similarly, Johnson's travellers meet characters, like the stoic in Chapter XVIII unphilosophically grieving at his daughter's untimely death, whose careful attempts to regulate their lives according to intellectual systems are undone by chance events. Rasselas finds fault with the mindless frivolity of the young men of Cairo in Chapter XVII, but his reasoning is flawed because he wants to eliminate chance: "He thought it unsuitable to a reasonable being to act without a plan, and to be sad or chearful only by chance. 'Happiness,' said he, 'must be something solid and permanent, without fear and without uncertainty'" (76-77). But this definition of happiness is impossible to fulfill. Similarly, Rasselas suggests in Chapter XXIX that late marriages carefully and prudently deliberated are more likely to be happy than a marriage based on nothing more solid than "a youth and maiden meeting by chance"; but Nekayah points out that this attempt to cheat chance will be ineffective given that older people find it difficult to change their habits to adapt to another's (96).

As Rasselas and Nekayah argue about how to account for chance events in their calculus of happiness, Imlac warns them not to sequester themselves entirely from chance: "while you are making the choice of life, you neglect to live" (98). Their ensuing tour of the Pyramids grounds them simultaneously in history and in the unpredictable present. They go there to study the timeless "monuments of industry and power before which all European magnificence is confessed to fade away" and end up learning a lesson about their own vulnerability (98). As the travellers con-

---

1 Mary Lascelles, "*Rasselas* Reconsidered," *Essays and Studies* n.s. 4 (1951): 43.

sider the Pyramids "a monument of the insufficiency of human enjoyments," and a testament to the timelessness of "that hunger of imagination which preys incessantly upon life," Pekuah's abduction initiates them into a different kind of unhappiness (102). Subjecting themselves to chance by living instead of theorizing, the travellers experience civic and personal evils excluded or unacknowledged in the Happy Valley: violence, robbery, abduction, and the inability of government to redress these crimes, as well as the pain of a dear friend's loss. While Imlac speculates that a king's restless desires led him to have the Pyramids built so that he could watch thousands laboring for him, Pekuah's disappearance shows Nekayah how difficult it is to enjoy whatever limited "satisfaction this world can afford" alone, "without a partner" (107).

This third section of *Rasselas* builds on both the historical and the fictional elements of its oriental foundations. Weitzman shows that Johnson used both ancient accounts of the Pyramids, such as those of Herodotus and Pliny (who, like Imlac, saw them as an example of monarchical vanity), and contemporary reports, including those by Aaron Hill, Richard Pococke, and John Greaves, which probably provided Johnson with details of the interiors of the Pyramids, unknown to ancient writers. The Pyramids near Al-Jîzah were a popular tourist attraction; it was common for visitors to measure their dimensions, as Johnson's travellers do, but rare to gain access, as they do, to the interiors of the ancient structures. The details of Pekuah's abduction closely follow an adventure Aaron Hill reports in his *Present State of the Ottoman Empire* (1709; Egypt was an Ottoman province from 1517), in which Arab assailants try to enclose the tourist Hill in the catacombs at Saqqârah (a site visited by Johnson's travellers in Chapter XLVII) and steal the goods he had left outside; luckily for Hill, his assailants are stopped in time by a troop of Janissaries.[1]

While the event itself may be based in part on historical texts, Pekuah's abduction both builds on and dismantles conventions of literary orientalism. Stereotypes of oriental fiction inform Nekayah's initial response to Pekuah's abduction; she laments that she had not exercised the dictatorial power available to her as an oriental princess by frightening Pekuah from voicing her own desire to remain outside while the others toured the pyramid's interior. "'Had not my fondness,' said she, 'lessened my authority,

---

1   Weitzman, "More Light on *Rasselas*" 44–45.

Pekuah had not dared to talk of her terrours. She ought to have feared me more than spectres. A severe look would have overpowered her; a peremptory command would have compelled obedience'" (105). Imlac, however, counsels Nekayah to resist the temptation of tyranny. Like the *Arabian Nights'* murderous Schahriar captivated by Scheherazade's tales, the roving Arab marauder is also a courteous gentleman charmed by Pekuah's intelligence as well as the monetary reward she promises for her fair treatment. Indeed, even though critics describe Pekuah's account of the harem as an "antidote to the 'Oriental' infection in storytelling which made the most of the exotic and erotic elements of Moslem marriage and concubinage,"[1] Johnson seems to take the license afforded by the wide-ranging oriental tale to conflate his historical sources, for the Arab Rover is less a "Bedouin chieftan" than "a picture of an aristocratic Turk" and his fortress is "more like a grand seigneur's harem than the tents of a roving sheik."[2]

Pekuah's description of the Arab's harem is an important part of Johnson's interaction with the conventions of literary orientalism in *Rasselas*, for a harem or seraglio was an expected feature and source of much fascination in English oriental tales. Pekuah, like Lady Mary Wortley Montagu in her *Turkish Embassy Letters* (written in 1717 and published in 1763; see Appendix C2), reports an insider view of the exclusive female world of the harem and the bath-house. Yet Montagu's empirical realism itself becomes a form of orientalism, as her account to some degree further exoticizes the women she describes. Although she derides the representations of women in eastern travel narratives (given that male authors could not have directly witnessed the seraglio as she has), her portrayal nonetheless imagines the women as figures in a painting. She gazes at the luxuries of the harem and baths through a lens colored by the *Arabian Nights* and other images of the exotic east.[3] At the same time, however, Montagu

---

1  Weitzman, "More Light on *Rasselas*" 51.
2  Weitzman 51–52.
3  See Joseph W. Lew, "Lady Mary's Portable Seraglio," *Eighteenth-Century Studies* 24.4 (Summer 1991): 432–50; Teresa Heffernan, "Feminism against the East/West Divide: Lady Mary's *Turkish Embassy Letters*," *Eighteenth-Century Studies* 33.2 (Winter 2000): 201–15; Lisa Lowe, *Critical Terrains: French and British Orientalisms* (Ithaca: Cornell UP, 1991); Felicity Nussbaum, *Torrid Zones: Maternity, Sexuality, and Empire in Eighteenth-Century English Narratives* (Baltimore: Johns Hopkins UP, 1995); and Aravamudan, *Tropicopolitans* 159–89.

reverses that gaze to point out freedoms enjoyed by the women of Sophia and to defamiliarize English customs. She calls their comfortable nudity in the baths "being in the state of nature" and when she uses her corset as an excuse for not joining them in nakedness, imagines that they interpret that apparatus as a "machine" in which her husband had locked her.

Like Montagu's critique of male travel narratives and like Johnson's critique in his Preface to Lobo's *Voyage*, Pekuah's adventure also posits empirical realism against European fantasy. The Arab laughs when Pekuah expects to find the mermaids and tritons that "European travellers have stationed in the Nile" (115). The harem itself is a site of stultifying boredom rather than luxurious pleasure. Johnson debunks orientalist fantasies of the harem by showing the Arab women engaged in nothing more exotic than needlework. But like Montagu, he implies criticism of English women as well, for they are likely to pass their time as foolishly as the Arab women Pekuah encounters. Indeed, the kind of frank, equal conversation that Pekuah and her Arab kidnapper enjoy might have been just as unusual in England as it seems to be in Egypt.

## Oriental Conclusions

Such deflation of the usual oriental tropes might explain why Jane Eyre is dissatisfied with *Rasselas*, although, as I have argued elsewhere, Brontë herself follows in a line of women writers who were both provoked and inspired by *Rasselas*.[1] Indeed, the oriental tale was a particular favorite of women writers.[2] British women found allegorical uses for a form featuring tyrannical male authority and harems of women defined solely by their sexuality; at the same time, prototypes of powerful women (both natural, like the storytelling Scheherazade, and supernatural, like the Fairy Pari Banou) in the *Arabian Nights* inspired women writers. Johnson's oriental tale is unusual in its gender blindness. He licenses both Rasselas's and Nekayah's restless desires and Nekayah and Pekuah participate equally with Rasselas and Imlac

---

1  See Jessica Richard, "'I am equally weary of confinement': *Rasselas* and Women Writers from *Dinarbas* to *Jane Eyre*," *Tulsa Studies in Women's Literature* 22.2 (2003): 335–56.

2  See, for example, Frances Sheridan's *The History of Nourjahad* (1767), Clara Reeve's *The History of Charoba, Queen of Ægypt* (1785), and Maria Edgeworth's *Murad the Unlucky* (1804).

in the choice-of-life inquiry. Recent research has illuminated Johnson's relations with women writers both as mentor and colleague.[1] Appendix B features two sequels by women writers that *Rasselas* inspired; *Dinarbas* (1790), by Ellis Cornelia Knight, and *The Second Part of the History of Rasselas* (1835), by Elizabeth Pope Whately, take as their point of departure the hint in Hawkins's biography that Johnson "had meditated a second part [to *Rasselas*], in which he meant to marry his hero, and place him in a state of permanent felicity" (172).

*Dinarbas* was evidently a popular work; it went through at least ten editions by 1820, and was bound together with *Rasselas* throughout the nineteenth century, both in England and the United States.[2] Knight describes Abyssinia as a country ruled by tyranny, engaged in border wars and eventually in civil wars. In such a setting, the choice of life inquiry that Rasselas and his party undertake becomes more explicitly political, and explicitly threatening to the established order. In fact, Rasselas learns in *Dinarbas* that his escape from the Happy Valley directly caused his country's civil war. Thus, the discourse of liberty that motivates the original Rasselas's project is shown to have far-reaching, disruptive consequences. *Dinarbas* disables the dangerous discourse of liberty and inquiry that drives Johnson's narrative and replaces it with the safer, less threatening rhetoric of duty and resignation. When the characters have learned that resignation rather than restless inquiry is the appropriate response to the vanity of human endeavor, when they cease to question their lot in the established order, they are rewarded with marriage and all the power that order protects.

*The Second Part of the History of Rasselas* (reprinted for the first time since its original publication–see Appendix B5), by Elizabeth Pope Whately, a writer of children's tracts and other religious works, and the wife of Archbishop Richard Whately, makes

---

1   See James G. Basker, "Dancing Dogs, Women Preachers and the Myth of Johnson's Misogyny," *The Age of Johnson* 3 (1990): 63–90; James G. Basker, "Myth Upon Myth: Johnson, Gender, and the Misogyny Question," *The Age of Johnson* 8 (1997): 175–87; Annette Wheeler Cafarelli, "Johnson and Women: Demasculinizing Literary History," *The Age of Johnson* 5 (1992): 61–114; and Isobel Grundy, "Samuel Johnson as Patron of Women," *The Age of Johnson* 1 (1987): 59–77.

2   Claude Rawson, "The Continuation of *Rasselas*," *Bicentenary Essays on Rasselas*. Ed. Magdi Wahba (Cairo: Société Orientale de Publicité, 1959) 86.

evangelical Christianity the explicit answer to the travellers' choice-of-life inquiry. Whately proposes that if the characters are supplied with "christian hopes and christian motives,—the whole scene would change without effort, and a better and happier conclusion naturally arise" (185). Johnson's detailed universalism describes human commonalities (both good and bad) without collapsing cultural difference, but Christianity in Whately's *Second Part* requires the characters to repudiate their previous cultural practices. Whately's *Second Part of the History of Rasselas* Christianizes Johnson's discourse of liberty so that his heterodox tale can more clearly serve the established order. Writing in an era of imperial expansion, Whately draws characters who are confident that Christian order will eventually spread over the globe.

Knight and Whately wrote continuations of *Rasselas* because there seemed to be something left over, something more to be said. Like its larger-than-life creator, *Rasselas* cannot be contained in its slim volume. Although Knight and Whately's attempts to provide conclusive answers to the choice of life inquiry may seem to misunderstand Johnson's aims, Johnson himself did not uncritically celebrate the restlessness of human desire with which he inconclusively concludes *Rasselas*. Before we get to that point, he provides the travellers with a case study in Chapter XLIV of the "dangerous prevalence of imagination" in the astronomer (122). After telling his companions about the astronomer's deluded belief that he controls the weather, Imlac posits a disturbing universalism: "Perhaps, if we speak with rigorous exactness, no human mind is in its right state." We are all mad, in varying degrees, and Imlac describes this "insanity," in which "fancy" dominates "reason," in distinctly oriental terms: "airy notions" "tyrannise" the mind, which "feasts on the luscious falsehood"; the "reign of fancy" is "despotick"; "the mind dances from scene to scene, unites all pleasures in all combinations, and riots in delights which nature and fortune, with all their bounty, cannot bestow." The taste for oriental tales inspired Johnson's depiction of insatiable desire; here that taste is the mind's undoing: "To indulge the power of fiction, and send imagination out upon the wing, is often the sport of those who delight too much in silent speculation" (122-23). As in *Rambler* No. 4, Johnson worries about the effects of imaginative indulgence, but he does not proscribe it.

Imlac describes the path to madness in terms that sound very much like the choice-of-life inquiry itself: the fantasist "expatiates in boundless futurity, and culls from all imaginable conditions that which for the present moment he should most desire, amuses his desires with impossible enjoyments, and confers upon his pride unattainable dominion." The travellers recognize themselves in this portrait; each sheepishly admits to having indulged a "fantastick delight" of the imagination. Nekayah has been acting out a pastoral fantasy, complete with borrowed shepherdess costume, even though the group had witnessed the unhappiness of shepherds in Chapter XIX, while Rasselas has been imagining himself at the head of a "perfect government" though his father and brothers' deaths must precede his succession (124). Despite this implicit death wish, Rasselas (unlike Pekuah and Nekayah) does not renounce his fantasy; rather, he reiterates it in the novel's final chapter. Even as Johnson warns of the oriental dangers of the despotic imagination, he refuses to condemn his characters for indulging in such pleasures.

The astronomer is cured of his delusion by interpersonal engagement, especially by the gentle and intelligent conversation of Pekuah and Nekayah. Such a social resolution is fitting in this third section of *Rasselas*, in which the travellers become active participants in life. But the third section is also framed by monuments, the pyramids and the catacombs, meant to preserve bodies after life ends.[1] Death, unacknowledged in the artificial paradise of the Happy Valley, surrounds the travellers. They have come far enough in their inquiry, however, to recognize the futility of efforts to subvert death's effects; "living fully in the world" includes facing death (Jones 397). Aravamudan provocatively suggests that "the escapees have made a choice of death" by leaving the Happy Valley to pursue the choice of life, an action that may be punishable by death.[2]

Some readers have taken Nekayah's comment, made at the conclusion of the visit to the catacombs and ensuing discussion of the nature of the soul, as the true moral of the story: "'To me,' said the princess, 'the choice of life is become less important; I hope hereafter to think only on the choice of eternity'" (137). Boswell writes, "Johnson meant, by shewing the unsatisfactory nature of things temporal, to direct the hopes of man to things

---

1   Alan Liu, "Toward a Theory of Common Sense: Beckford's *Vathek* and Johnson's *Rasselas*," *Texas Studies in Literature and Language* 26.2 (Summer 1984): 183–217.

2   Aravamudan, *Tropicopolitans* 204. As Aravamudan points out, Knight recognizes "the transgressive implications" of Rasselas's escape, which leads in *Dinarbas* to civil war.

eternal" (174) and calls *Rasselas* an enlarged prose version of Johnson's poem *The Vanity of Human Wishes* (see Appendix A2). Yet Nekayah's comment does not end the book; instead the infamous "conclusion, in which nothing is concluded" shows the travellers forming plans for their choice of life even though "of these wishes that they had formed they well knew that none could be obtained" (137). Jones suggests that this "coda" disrupts the closed tripartite structure of the book in order to reassert the comic forces of life that "refuse to be contained within a neat literary form" (401). Rather than be disheartened by their research in the book's second section or by the specter of death in the third section, the travellers continue to indulge their hopes and desires. Johnson's characters learn the vanity of their wishes, but he allows them to continue to wish and does not mock them for doing so. From beginning to end, *Rasselas* licenses our desires even as it shows us that their fulfillment will only ever be partial at best.

This radically unstable ending has been the subject of much controversy. Johnson's contemporaries wanted a more orthodox, Christian conclusion, while twentieth- and twenty-first-century critics have asked whether Imlac's and the astronomer's desires "to be driven along the stream of life without directing their course to any particular port" (137) are included among "these wishes" that could not be obtained. Is Johnson indicting their desire to opt out of the choice of life as well as the more active schemes of the younger characters?[1] In other words, does the tale advocate going with the flow, as Imlac and the astronomer want to do, or is this just as impossible to achieve as Rasselas's perfect government? The final sentence of the book tells us the travellers will "return to Abissinia" after the seasonal flooding of the Nile; does this mean they will return to the Happy Valley?[2] Answering this question may mean deciding whether one reads the tale as comic—the travellers will continue to live "fully in the world," their desires always exceeding the possibility of fulfillment as they desire and are disappointed and desire again in Abyssinia—or as tragic—they will return chastened to the artificial, controlled

---

1 See Mahmoud Manzalaoui, "*Rasselas* and some Medieval Ancillaries," *Bicentenary Essays on "Rasselas*," ed. Magdi Wahba (Cairo: 1959) 59–73; and Gwin J. Kolb, "Textual Cruxes in *Rasselas*," *Johnsonian Studies*, ed. Magdi Wahba (Cairo: 1962) 257–63.

2 See George Sherburn, "Rasselas Returns—to What?" *Philological Quarterly* 38 (1959): 383–84.

excesses of the enclosed world of the Happy Valley, cloistered from the vicissitudes of desire.[1] Either way, the excesses of the oriental tale, the narrative form that inspired Johnson, remain central to interpreting *Rasselas*.

---

1   See Nicholas Hudson, "'Open' and 'Enclosed' Readings of *Rasselas*," *Eighteenth Century: Theory and Interpretation* 31.1 (Spring 1990): 47–67.

# Samuel Johnson: A Brief Chronology

| | |
|---|---|
| 1709 | Born at Lichfield, Staffordshire (7 September), eldest of two sons of Michael Johnson, bookseller, and Sarah Ford Johnson. |
| 1712 | Taken by his mother to London to be touched by Queen Anne in hopes of curing his scrofula. |
| 1717 | Studies at Lichfield grammar school. |
| 1726 | Enters King Edward VI School at Stourbridge, West Midlands; Johnson leaves school the same year because of illness. |
| 1728 | Enters Pembroke College, Oxford; leaves a year later without a degree. |
| 1731 | Death of Johnson's father. |
| 1733 | Translates into English Joachim Le Grand's French version of Jerónimo Lobo's *Voyage to Abyssinia* (published 1735). |
| 1735 | Marries Elizabeth Porter, a widow twenty years his senior. After a few short stints teaching and tutoring, opens a school at Edial, near Lichfield, which closes a year later. |
| 1737 | Death of Johnson's brother Nathaniel. Johnson moves to London with pupil David Garrick (who becomes an immensely successful actor). Johnson is unable to get his play, *Irene*, produced. |
| 1738 | Publishes *London: a Poem in Imitation of the Third Satire of Juvenal*, his first London literary success. Writes a wide variety of pieces for *Gentleman's Magazine*. |
| 1740–44 | Writes reports of parliamentary debates for *Gentleman's Magazine*. |
| 1739 | Publishes political satires. |
| 1744 | Publishes *An Account of the Life of Richard Savage*, which transformed the genre of biography. |
| 1745 | Publishes *Miscellaneous Observations on the Tragedy of Macbeth*, a pamphlet meant as the beginning of an edition of Shakespeare, which was stalled by publishing rivalries. |
| 1747 | Publishes *The Plan of a Dictionary of the English Language*, the prospectus for the project completed in 1755. |

| 1749 | *Irene* published and performed for nine nights (with mixed reviews) when Garrick became manager of Drury Lane Theatre. Publishes poem *The Vanity of Human Wishes*. |
|---|---|
| 1750–52 | The *Rambler*, a series of 208 essays published twice a week, almost all written by Johnson. |
| 1752–54 | Contributed at least thirty essays to John Hawkesworth's *Adventurer*. |
| 1754 | Death of Johnson's wife. |
| 1755 | Receives the MA degree from Oxford in recognition of the forthcoming *Dictionary*. |
| 1755 | Publishes, after nine years' labor, *A Dictionary of the English Language*, the first dictionary of the English to use extensive quotations (all selected by Johnson) illustrating actual usage and various gradations of meaning. The quotations, drawn only from writers whose language and piety Johnson approved, also outline a moral canon. |
| 1756 | Becomes editor of the *Literary Magazine*, for which he writes a variety of reviews. Publishes *Proposals for Printing the Dramatic Works of William Shakespeare*. |
| 1758–60 | The *Idler*, over 100 essays originally appearing in the *Universal Chronicle*. The most famous are Nos. 60 and 61, in which critics are caricatured in the figure of Dick Minim. |
| 1759 | Death of Johnson's mother. Publishes *The History of Rasselas, Prince of Abissinia*. |
| 1762 | Granted royal pension of £300 a year for life. |
| 1763 | Awarded honorary Doctor of Laws degree by Trinity College, Dublin. Meets James Boswell. |
| 1764 | Founding member of the Literary Club, a regular gathering of men of letters in a variety of disciplines, in which Johnson's wide-ranging intellect and superb conversational skills shone. |
| 1765 | Publishes *The Plays of William Shakespeare*, a significant work of textual editing and critical commentary. Befriends Henry and Hester Lynch Thrale, whose home at Streatham, ten miles south of London, became an important retreat for Johnson. |
| 1770 | Publishes *The False Alarm*, a political pamphlet on a struggle between parliament and the MP John Wilkes. |

| 1771 | Publishes *Thoughts on the Late Transactions respecting Falkland's Islands*, a political pamphlet on a dispute between Britain and Spain. |
|---|---|
| 1773 | Takes a three-month tour of Scotland with Boswell. |
| 1774 | Publishes *The Patriot*, a political pamphlet on the further developments of the Wilkes affair. |
| 1775 | Publishes *A Journey to the Western Islands of Scotland*. Publishes *Taxation no Tyranny*, a political pamphlet on the impending American revolution. Awarded honorary degree of Doctor of Civil Laws by Oxford University. |
| 1779–81 | Publishes a series of fifty-two literary biographies commonly known as *The Lives of the English Poets*, setting a new standard in the art of literary biography. |
| 1784 | Dies in London (13 December). Buried at Westminster Abbey. |

# A Note on the Text

This edition has been prepared from the British Library copy of the second edition of *The History of Rasselas, Prince of Abissinia* (1759), microfilmed for *The Eighteenth Century* (Research Publications, Reel 155 No. 8). The second edition was published two months after the first and contains minor textual changes attributed by scholars to Johnson.[1] This edition reprints the text as it appears in the original except in the following instances:

- Long s has been modernized
- Quotation marks follow modern North American conventions
- Misnumbering of chapters listed in the Contents of the Second Volume of *Rasselas* has been corrected

Words or senses of words likely to be unfamiliar to an undergraduate reader are defined whenever possible using Samuel Johnson's *Dictionary of the English Language* (4th edition, 1773), abbreviated in the footnotes as *Dictionary*. Where necessary, I have also used the *Oxford English Dictionary* (*OED*). Readers interested in the way particular ideas in *Rasselas* resonate throughout Johnson's œuvre are encouraged to consult the extensive footnotes in Gwin J. Kolb's edition, *Rasselas and Other Tales* (1990), vol. 26 in the *Yale Edition of the Works of Samuel Johnson*.

---

1   See O.F. Emerson, "The Text of Johnson's *Rasselas*," *Anglia* 22 (Dec. 1899): 499–509 and R.W. Chapman, ed., *The History of Rasselas, Prince of Abissinia, A Tale* (Oxford: Clarendon, 1927) xviii–xx.

# THE
# PRINCE
OF
# ABISSINIA.

A
# TALE.

IN TWO VOLUMES.

VOL. I.

THE SECOND EDITION.

LONDON:

Printed for R. and J. DODSLEY, in Pall-Mall;
and W. JOHNSTON, in Ludgate-Street.
M DCC LIX.

# CONTENTS OF THE FIRST VOLUME

CONTENTS OF THE SECOND VOLUME

# CHAPTER I
## Description of a palace in a valley

YE who listen with credulity to the whispers of fancy, and persue with eagerness the phantoms of hope; who expect that age will perform the promises of youth, and that the deficiencies of the present day will be supplied by the morrow; attend to the history of Rasselas prince of Abissinia.[1]

Rasselas was the fourth son of the mighty emperour, in whose dominions the Father of waters[2] begins his course; whose bounty pours down the streams of plenty, and scatters over half the world the harvests of Egypt.

According to the custom which has descended from age to age among the monarchs of the torrid zone, Rasselas was confined in a private palace, with the other sons and daughters of Abissinian royalty, till the order of succession should call him to the throne.

The place, which the wisdom or policy of antiquity had destined for the residence of the Abissinian princes, was a spacious valley in the kingdom of Amhara,[3] surrounded on every side by mountains, of which the summits overhang the middle part. The only passage, by which it could be entered, was a cavern that passed under a rock, of which it has long been disputed whether it was the work of nature or of human industry. The outlet of the cavern was concealed by a thick wood, and the mouth which opened into the valley was closed with gates of iron, forged by the artificers[4] of ancient days, so massy that no man could without the help of engines[5] open or shut them.

From the mountains on every side, rivulets descended that filled all the valley with verdure and fertility, and formed a lake in the middle inhabited by fish of every species, and frequented by every fowl whom nature has taught to dip the wing in water. This lake discharged its superfluities by a stream which entered a dark

---

1 The country in north-east Africa on the Red Sea, predominantly Christian in the eighteenth century, now known as Ethiopia.
2 According to Lobo's *Voyage to Abyssinia*, "natives" call the Nile "*Abavi*, that is, the Father of Waters." See Appendix A1.
3 A central, mountainous region of Ethiopia, home to the Amhara, one of the country's dominant ethnic groups.
4 An artist; a manufacturer; one by whom any thing is made. *Dictionary*.
5 Any mechanical complication, in which various movements and parts concur to one effect. *Dictionary*. A mechanical contrivance, machine, implement, tool. *OED*.

cleft of the mountain on the northern side, and fell with dreadful noise from precipice to precipice till it was heard no more.

The sides of the mountains were covered with trees, the banks of the brooks were diversified with flowers; every blast shook spices from the rocks, and every month dropped fruits upon the ground. All animals that bite the grass, or brouse[1] the shrub, whether wild or tame, wandered in this extensive circuit, secured from beasts of prey by the mountains which confined them. On one part were flocks and herds feeding in the pastures, on another all beasts of chase frisking in the lawns; the sprightly kid was bounding on the rocks, the subtle monkey frolicking in the trees, and the solemn elephant reposing in the shade. All the diversities of the world were brought together, the blessings of nature were collected, and its evils extracted and excluded.

The valley, wide and fruitful, supplied its inhabitants with the necessaries of life, and all delights and superfluities were added at the annual visit which the emperour paid his children, when the iron gate was opened to the sound of musick; and during eight days every one that resided in the valley was required to propose whatever might contribute to make seclusion pleasant, to fill up the vacancies of attention, and lessen the tediousness of time. Every desire was immediately granted. All the artificers of pleasure were called to gladden the festivity; the musicians exerted the power of harmony, and the dancers shewed their activity before the princes, in hope that they should pass their lives in this blissful captivity, to which these only were admitted whose performance was thought able to add novelty to luxury. Such was the appearance of security and delight which this retirement afforded, that they to whom it was new always desired that it might be perpetual; and as those, on whom the iron gate had once closed, were never suffered to return, the effect of longer experience could not be known. Thus every year produced new schemes of delight, and new competitors for imprisonment.

The palace stood on an eminence raised about thirty paces above the surface of the lake. It was divided into many squares or courts, built with greater or less magnificence according to the rank of those for whom they were designed. The roofs were turned into arches of massy stone joined by a cement that grew harder by time, and the building stood from century to century, deriding the solstitial rains and equinoctial hurricanes, without need of reparation.

---

1  To eat branches, or shrubs. *Dictionary*.

This house, which was so large as to be full
but some ancient officers who successively inh
of the place, was built as if suspicion herself
plan. To every room there was an open and sec
square had a communication with the rest, eith
stories by private galleries, or by subterranean
lower apartments. Many of the columns had unsuspected cavities, in which a long race of monarchs had reposited their treasures. They then closed up the opening with marble, which was
never to be removed but in the utmost exigencies of the kingdom;
and recorded their accumulations in a book which was itself concealed in a tower not entered but by the emperour, attended by
the prince who stood next in succession.

## CHAPTER II
### The discontent of Rasselas in the happy valley

HERE the sons and daughters of Abissinia lived only to know
the soft vicissitudes of pleasure and repose, attended by all that
were skilful to delight, and gratified with whatever the senses can
enjoy. They wandered in gardens of fragrance, and slept in the
fortresses of security. Every art was practiced to make them
pleased with their own condition. The sages who instructed
them, told them of nothing but the miseries of publick life, and
described all beyond the mountains as regions of calamity,
where discord was always raging, and where man preyed upon
man.

To heighten their opinion of their own felicity, they were daily
entertained with songs, the subject of which was the *happy valley*.
Their appetites were excited by frequent enumerations of different enjoyments, and revelry and merriment was the business of
every hour from the dawn of morning to the close of even.

These methods were generally successful; few of the Princes
had ever wished to enlarge their bounds, but passed their lives in
full conviction that they had all within their reach that art or
nature could bestow, and pitied those whom fate had excluded
from this seat of tranquility, as the sport of chance, and the slaves
of misery.

Thus they rose in the morning and lay down at night, pleased
with each other and with themselves, all but Rasselas, who, in the
twenty-sixth year of his age, began to withdraw himself from their
pastimes and assemblies, and to delight in solitary walks and
silent meditation. He often sat before tables covered with luxury,

,orgot to taste the dainties that were placed before him: he ,se abruptly in the midst of the song, and hastily retired beyond the sound of musick. His attendants observed the change and endeavoured to renew his love of pleasure: he neglected their officiousness, repulsed their invitations, and spent day after day on the banks of rivulets sheltered with trees, where he sometimes listened to the birds in the branches, sometimes observed the fish playing in the stream, and anon cast his eyes upon the pastures and mountains filled with animals, of which some were biting the herbage, and some sleeping among the bushes.

This singularity of his humour[1] made him much observed. One of the Sages, in whose conversation he had formerly delighted, followed him secretly, in hope of discovering the cause of his disquiet. Rasselas, who knew not that any one was near him, having for some time fixed his eyes upon the goats that were brousing among the rocks, began to compare their condition with his own.

"What," said he, "makes the difference between man and all the rest of the animal creation? Every beast that strays beside me has the same corporal necessities with myself; he is hungry and crops the grass, he is thirsty and drinks the stream, his thirst and hunger are appeased, he is satisfied and sleeps; he rises again and is hungry, he is again fed and is at rest. I am hungry and thirsty like him, but when thirst and hunger cease I am not at rest; I am, like him, pained with want, but am not, like him, satisfied with fullness. The intermediate hours are tedious and gloomy; I long again to be hungry that I may again quicken my attention. The birds peck the berries or the corn, and fly away to the groves where they sit in seeming happiness on the branches, and waste their lives in tuning one unvaried series of sounds. I likewise can call the lutanist and the singer, but the sounds that pleased me yesterday weary me to day and will grow yet more wearisome to morrow. I can discover within me no power of perception which is not glutted with its proper pleasure, yet I do not feel myself delighted. Man has surely some latent sense for which this place affords no gratification, or he has some desires distinct from sense which must be satisfied before he can be happy."

After this he lifted up his head, and seeing the moon rising, walked towards the palace. As he passed through the fields, and saw the animals around him, "Ye," said he, "are happy, and need

---

1   General turn or temper of mind. Present disposition. *Dictionary*.

not envy me that walk thus among you, burthened with myself; nor do I, ye gentle beings, envy your felicity; for it is not the felicity of man. I have many distresses from which ye are free; I fear pain when I do not feel it; I sometimes shrink at evils recollected, and sometimes start at evils anticipated: surely the equity of providence has balanced peculiar sufferings with peculiar enjoyments."

With observations like these the prince amused[1] himself as he returned, uttering them with a plaintive voice, yet with a look that discovered him to feel some complacence in his own perspicacity,[2] and to receive some solace of the miseries of life, from consciousness of the delicacy with which he felt, and the eloquence with which he bewailed them. He mingled cheerfully in the diversions of the evening, and all rejoiced to find that his heart was lightened.

## CHAPTER III
### The wants of him that wants nothing

ON the next day his old instructor, imagining that he had now made himself acquainted with his disease of mind, was in hope of curing it by counsel, and officiously sought an opportunity of conference, which the prince, having long considered him as one whose intellects were exhausted, was not very willing to afford: "Why," said he, "does this man thus intrude upon me; shall I never be suffered to forget those lectures which pleased only while they were new, and to become new again must be forgotten?" He then walked into the wood, and composed himself to his usual meditations; when before his thoughts had taken any settled form, he perceived his persuer at his side, and was at first prompted by his impatience to go hastily away; but, being unwilling to offend a man whom he had once reverenced and still loved, he invited him to sit down with him on the bank.

The old man, thus encouraged, began to lament the change which had been lately observed in the prince, and to enquire why he so often retired from the pleasures of the palace, to loneliness and silence. "I fly from pleasure," said the prince, "because pleasure has ceased to please; I am lonely because I am miser-

---

1 To entertain with tranquillity; to fill with thoughts that engage the mind, without distracting it. *Dictionary*.
2 Quickness of sight. *Dictionary*. Clearness of understanding or insight; great mental penetration; discernment. *OED*.

able, and am unwilling to cloud with my presence the happiness of others." "You, Sir," said the sage, "are the first who has complained of misery in the *happy valley*. I hope to convince you that your complaints have no real cause. You are here in full possession of all that the emperour of Abissinia can bestow; here is neither labour to be endured nor danger to be dreaded, yet here is all that labour or danger can procure or purchase. Look round and tell me which of your wants is without supply: if you want nothing, how are you unhappy?"

"That I want nothing," said the prince, "or that I know not what I want, is the cause of my complaint; if I had any known want, I should have a certain wish; that wish would excite endeavour, and I should not then repine to see the sun move so slowly towards the western mountain, or lament when the day breaks and sleep will no longer hide me from myself. When I see the kids and the lambs chasing one another, I fancy that I should be happy if I had something to persue. But, possessing all that I can want, I find one day and one hour exactly like another, except that the latter is still more tedious than the former. Let your experience inform me how the day may now seem as short as in my childhood, while nature was yet fresh, and every moment shewed me what I never had observed before. I have already enjoyed too much; give me something to desire."

The old man was surprised at this new species of affliction, and knew not what to reply, yet was unwilling to be silent. "Sir," said he, "if you had seen the miseries of the world, you would know how to value your present state." "Now," said the prince, "you have given me something to desire; I shall long to see the miseries of the world, since the sight of them is necessary to happiness."

## CHAPTER IV
### The prince continues to grieve and muse

AT this time the sound of musick proclaimed the hour of repast,[1] and the conversation was concluded. The old man went away sufficiently discontented to find that his reasonings had produced the only conclusion which they were intended to prevent. But in the decline of life shame and grief are of short duration; whether it be that we bear easily what we have born long, or that, finding ourselves in age less regarded, we less regard others; or, that we

---

1   A meal; act of taking food. *Dictionary*.

look with slight regard upon afflictions, to which we know that the hand of death is about to put an end.

The prince, whose views were extended to a wider space, could not speedily quiet his emotions. He had been before terrified at the length of life which nature promised him, because he considered that in a long time much must be endured; he now rejoiced in his youth, because in many years much might be done.

The first beam of hope, that had been ever darted into his mind, rekindled youth in his cheeks, and doubled the luster of his eyes. He was fired with the desire of doing something, though he knew not yet with distinctness, either end or means.

He was now no longer gloomy and unsocial; but, considering himself as master of a secret stock of happiness, which he could enjoy only by concealing it, he affected to be busy in all schemes of diversion, and endeavoured to make others pleased with the state of which he himself was weary. But pleasure never can be so multiplied or continued, as not to leave much of life unemployed; there were many hours, both of the night and day, which he could spend without suspicion in solitary thought. The load of life was much lightened: he went eagerly into the assemblies, because he supposed the frequency of his presence necessary to the success of his purposes; he retired gladly to privacy, because he had now a subject of thought.

His chief amusement was to picture to himself that world which he had never seen; to place himself in various conditions; to be entangled in imaginary difficulties, and to be engaged in wild adventures: but his benevolence always terminated his projects in the relief of distress, the detection of fraud, the defeat of oppression, and the diffusion of happiness.

Thus passed twenty months of the life of Rasselas. He busied himself so intensely in visionary bustle, that he forgot his real solitude; and, amidst hourly preparations for the various incidents of human affairs, neglected to consider by what means he should mingle with mankind.

One day, as he was sitting on a bank, he feigned to himself an orphan virgin robbed of her little portion[1] by a treacherous lover, and crying after him for restitution and redress. So strongly was the image impressed upon his mind, that he started up in the maid's defence, and run forward to seize the plunderer with all the eagerness of real persuit. Fear naturally quickens the flight of

---

1  Part of an inheritance given to a child; a fortune. *Dictionary*.

guilt. Rasselas could not catch the fugitive with his utmost efforts; but, resolving to weary, by perseverance, him whom he could not surpass in speed, he pressed on till the foot of the mountain stopped his course.

Here he recollected himself, and smiled at his own useless impetuosity. Then raising his eyes to the mountain, "This," said he, "is the fatal obstacle that hinders at once the enjoyment of pleasure, and the exercise of virtue. How long is it that my hopes and wishes have flown beyond this boundary of my life, which yet I never have attempted to surmount!"

Struck with this reflection, he sat down to muse, and remembered, that since he first resolved to escape from his confinement, the sun had passed twice over him in his annual course. He now felt a degree of regret with which he had never been before acquainted. He considered how much might have been done in the time that had passed, and left nothing real behind it. He compared twenty months with the life of man. "In life," said he, "is not to be counted the ignorance of infancy, or imbecility of age. We are long before we are able to think, and we soon cease from the power of acting. The true period of human existence may be reasonably estimated as forty years, of which I have mused away the four and twentieth part. What I have lost was certain, for I have certainly possessed it; but of twenty months to come who can assure me?"

The consciousness of his own folly pierced him deeply, and he was long before he could be reconciled to himself. "The rest of my time," said he, "has been lost by the crime or folly of my ancestors, and the absurd institutions of my country; I remember it with disgust, yet without remorse: but the months that have passed since new light darted into my soul, since I formed a scheme of reasonable felicity, have been squandered by my own fault. I have lost that which can never be restored: I have seen the sun rise and set for twenty months, an idle gazer on the light of heaven: In this time the birds have left the nest of their mother, and committed themselves to the woods and to the skies: the kid has forsaken the teat, and learned by degrees to climb the rocks in quest of independent sustenance. I only have made no advances, but am still helpless and ignorant. The moon by more than twenty changes, admonished me of the flux of life; the stream that rolled before my feet upbraided[1] my inactivity. I sat

---

1 To bring reproach upon; to shew faults by being in a state of comparison. *Dictionary*.

feasting on intellectual luxury, regardless alike of the examples of the earth, and the instructions of the planets. Twenty months are past, who shall restore them!"

These sorrowful meditations fastened upon his mind; he past four months in resolving to lose no more time in idle resolves, and was awakened to more vigorous exertion by hearing a maid, who had broken a porcelain cup, remark, that what cannot be repaired is not to be regretted.

This was obvious; and Rasselas reproached himself that he had not discovered it, having not known, or not considered, how many useful hints are obtained by chance, and how often the mind, hurried by her own ardour to distant views, neglects the truths that lie open before her. He, for a few hours, regretted his regret, and from that time bent his whole mind upon the means of escaping from the valley of happiness.

## CHAPTER V
### The prince meditates his escape

HE now found that it would be very difficult to effect that which it was very easy to suppose effected. When he looked round about him, he saw himself confined by the bars of nature which had never yet been broken, and by the gate, through which none that once had passed it were ever able to return. He was now impatient as an eagle in a grate.[1] He passed week after week in clambering the mountains, to see if there was any aperture which the bushes might conceal, but found all the summits inaccessible by their prominence. The iron gate he despaired to open; for it was not only secured with all the power of art, but was always watched by successive sentinels, and was by its position exposed to the perpetual observation of all the inhabitants.

He then examined the cavern through which the waters of the lake were discharged; and, looking down at a time when the sun shone strongly upon its mouth, he discovered it to be full of broken rocks, which, though they permitted the stream to flow through many narrow passages, would stop any body of solid bulk. He returned discouraged and dejected; but, having now known the blessing of hope, resolved never to despair.

---

1   A partition made with bars placed near to one another, or crossing each other: such as are in cloysters or prisons. *Dictionary.* A barred place of confinement for animals, also, a prison or cage for human beings. *OED*, which uses this sentence from *Rasselas* to illustrate this meaning.

In these fruitless searches he spent ten months. The time, however, passed chearfully away: in the morning he rose with new hope, in the evening applauded his own diligence, and in the night slept sound after his fatigue. He met a thousand amusements which beguiled his labour, and diversified his thoughts. He discerned the various instincts of animals, and properties of plants, and found the place replete with wonders, of which he purposed to solace himself with the contemplation, if he should never be able to accomplish his flight; rejoicing that his endeavours, though yet unsuccessful, had supplied him with a source of inexhaustible enquiry.

But his original curiousity was not yet abated; he resolved to obtain some knowledge of the ways of men. His wish still continued, but his hope grew less. He ceased to survey any longer the walls of his prison, and spared to search by new toils for interstices[1] which he knew could not be found, yet determined to keep his design always in view, and lay hold on any expedient that time should offer.

## CHAPTER VI
### A dissertation on the art of flying

AMONG the artists that had been allured into the happy valley, to labour for the accommodation and pleasure of its inhabitants, was a man eminent for his knowledge of the mechanick powers, who had contrived many engines both of use and recreation. By a wheel, which the stream turned, he forced the water into a tower, whence it was distributed to all the apartments of the palace. He erected a pavillion in the garden, around which he kept the air always cool by artificial showers. One of the groves, appropriated to the ladies, was ventilated by fans, to which the rivulet that run through it gave a constant motion; and instruments of soft musick were placed at proper distances, of which some played by the impulse of the wind, and some by the power of the stream.

This artist was sometimes visited by Rasselas, who was pleased with every kind of knowledge, imagining that the time would come when all his acquisitions should be of use to him in the open world. He came one day to amuse himself in his usual manner, and found the master busy in building a sailing chariot:

1 Space between one thing and another. *Dictionary*.

he saw that the design was practicable upon a level surface, and with expressions of great esteem solicited its completion. The workman was pleased to find himself so much regarded by the prince, and resolved to gain yet higher honours. "Sir," said he, "you have seen but a small part of what the mechanick sciences can perform. I have been long of opinion, that, instead of the tardy conveyance of ships and chariots, man might use the swifter migration of wings; that the fields of air are open to knowledge, and that only ignorance and idleness need crawl upon the ground."

This hint rekindled the prince's desire of passing the mountains; having seen what the mechanist had already performed, he was willing to fancy that he could do more; yet resolved to enquire further before he suffered hope to afflict him by disappointment. "I am afraid," said he to the artist, "that your imagination prevails over your skill, and that you now tell me rather what you wish than what you know. Every animal has his element assigned him; the birds have the air, and man and beasts the earth." "So," replied the mechanist, "fishes have the water, in which yet beasts can swim by nature, and men by art. He that can swim needs not despair to fly: to swim is to fly in a grosser[1] fluid, and to fly is to swim in a subtler.[2] We are only to proportion our power of resistance to the different density of the matter through which we are to pass. You will be necessarily upborn by the air, if you can renew any impulse upon it, faster than the air can recede from the pressure."

"But the exercise of swimming," said the prince, "is very laborious; the strongest limbs are soon wearied; I am afraid the act of flying will be yet more violent, and wings will be of no great use, unless we can fly further than we can swim."

"The labour of rising from the ground," said the artist, "will be great, as we see it in the heavier domestick fowls; but, as we mount higher, the earth's attraction, and the body's gravity, will be gradually diminished, till we shall arrive at a region where the man will float in the air without any tendency to fall: no care will then be necessary, but to move forwards, which the gentlest impulse will effect. You, Sir, whose curiosity is so extensive, will easily conceive with what pleasure a philosopher, furnished with wings, and hovering in the sky, would see the earth, and all it's

---

1  Thick; bulky. *Dictionary.*
2  Subtile: Thin; not dense; not gross. *Dictionary.*

inhabitants, rolling beneath him, and presenting to him successively, by its diurnal[1] motion, all the countries within the same parallel. How must it amuse the pendent[2] spectator to see the moving scene of land and ocean, cities and desarts! To survey with equal security the marts of trade, and the fields of battle; mountains infested by barbarians, and fruitful regions gladdened by plenty, and lulled by peace! How easily shall we then trace the Nile through all his passage; pass over to distant regions, and examine the face of nature from one extremity of the earth to the other!"

"All this," said the prince, "is much to be desired, but I am afraid that no man will be able to breathe in these regions of speculation[3] and tranquility. I have been told, that respiration is difficult upon lofty mountains, yet from these precipices, though so high as to produce great tenuity[4] of the air, it is very easy to fall: therefore I suspect, that from any height, where life can be supported, there may be danger of too quick descent."

"Nothing," replied the artist, "will ever be attempted, if all possible objections must be first overcome. If you will favour my project I will try the first flight at my own hazard. I have considered the structure of all volant[5] animals, and find the folding continuity of the bat's wings most easily accommodated to the human form. Upon this model I shall begin my task to morrow, and in a year expect to tower into the air beyond the malice or pursuit of man. But I will work only on this condition, that the art shall not be divulged, and that you shall not require me to make wings for any but ourselves."

"Why," said Rasselas, "should you envy[6] others so great an advantage? All skill ought to be exerted for universal good; every man has owed much to others, and ought to repay the kindness that he has received."

"If men were all virtuous," returned the artist, "I should with great alacrity[7] teach them all to fly. But what would be the security of the good, if the bad could at pleasure invade them from the

---

1  Performed in a day; daily; quotidian. *Dictionary.*
2  Supported above the ground. *Dictionary.*
3  Examination by the eye; view. *Dictionary.*
4  Thinness; exility; smallness; minuteness; not grossness. *Dictionary.*
5  Flying; passing through the air. *Dictionary.*
6  To grudge; to impart unwillingly; to withold maliciously. *Dictionary.*
7  Cheerfulness, expressed by some outward token; sprightliness; gayety; liveliness; cheerful willingness. *Dictionary.*

sky? Against an army sailing through the clouds neither walls, nor mountains, nor seas, could afford any security. A flight of northern savages might hover in the wind, and light at once with irresistible violence upon the capital of a fruitful region that was rolling under them. Even this valley, the retreat of princes, the abode of happiness, might be violated by the sudden descent of some of the naked nations that swarm on the coast of the southern sea."

The prince promised secrecy, and waited for the performance, not wholly hopeless of success. He visited the work from time to time, observed its progress, and remarked many ingenious contrivances to facilitate motion, and unite levity with strength. The artist was every day more certain that he should leave vultures and eagles behind him, and the contagion of his confidence seized upon the prince.

In a year the wings were finished, and, on a morning appointed, the maker appeared furnished for flight on a little promontory: he waved his pinions a while to gather air, then leaped from his stand, and in an instant dropped into the lake. His wings, which were of no use in the air, sustained him in the water, and the prince drew him to land, half dead with terrour and vexation.

## CHAPTER VII
### The prince finds a man of learning

THE prince was not much afflicted by this disaster, having suffered himself to hope for a happier event, only because he had no other means of escape in view. He still persisted in his design to leave the happy valley by the first opportunity.

His imagination was now at a stand; he had no prospect of entering into the world; and, notwithstanding all his endeavours to support[1] himself, discontent by degrees preyed upon him, and he began again to lose his thoughts in sadness, when the rainy season, which in these countries is periodical,[2] made it inconvenient to wander in the woods.

The rain continued longer and with more violence than had been ever known: the clouds broke on the surrounding moun-

---

1  To endure any thing painful without being overcome. *Dictionary*.
2  Lobo's *Voyage to Abyssinia* describes daily rain from June to September. Samuel Johnson. *A Voyage to Abyssinia*, ed. Joel J. Gold, *Yale Edition of the Works of Samuel Johnson* Vol. XV (New Haven: Yale UP, 1985), 55–56.

tains, and the torrents streamed into the plain on every side, till the cavern was too narrow to discharge the water. The lake overflowed its banks, and all the level of the valley was covered with the inundation. The eminence, on which the palace was built, and some other spots of rising ground, were all that the eye could now discover. The herds and flocks left the pastures, and both the wild beasts and the tame retreated to the mountains.

This inundation confined all the princes to domestick[1] amusements, and the attention of Rasselas was particularly seized by a poem, which Imlac rehearsed upon the various conditions of humanity. He commanded the poet to attend him in his apartment, and recite his verses a second time; then entering into familiar talk, he thought himself happy in having found a man who knew the world so well, and could so skillfully paint the scenes of life. He asked a thousand questions about things, to which, though common to all other mortals, his confinement from childhood had kept him a stranger. The poet pitied his ignorance, and loved his curiosity, and entertained him from day to day with novelty and instruction, so that the prince regretted the necessity of sleep and longed till the morning should renew his pleasure.

As they were sitting together, the prince commanded Imlac to relate his history, and to tell by what accident he was forced, or by what motive induced, to close his life in the happy valley. As he was going to begin his narrative, Rasselas was called to a concert, and obliged to restrain his curiosity till the evening.

## CHAPTER VIII
### The history of Imlac

THE close of the day is, in the regions of the torrid zone, the only season of diversion and entertainment, and it was therefore midnight before the musick ceased, and the princesses retired. Rasselas then called for his companion and required him to begin the story of his life.

"Sir," said Imlac, "my history will not be long: the life that is devoted to knowledge passes silently away, and is very little diversified by events. To talk in publick, to think in solitude, to read and to hear, to inquire, and answer inquiries, is the business of a scholar. He wanders about the world without pomp or terrour, and is neither known nor valued but by men like himself.

---

1   Private; done at home. *Dictionary.*

"I was born in the kingdom of Goiama,[1] at no great distance from the fountain[2] of the Nile. My father was a wealthy merchant, who traded between the inland countries of Affrick and the ports of the red sea. He was honest, frugal and diligent, but of mean[3] sentiments, and narrow comprehension: he desired only to be rich, and to conceal his riches, lest he should be spoiled[4] by the governours of the province."[5]

"Surely," said the prince, "my father must be negligent of his charge, if any man in his dominions dares take that which belongs to another. Does he not know that kings are accountable for injustice permitted as well as done? If I were emperour, not the meanest of my subjects should be oppressed with impunity. My blood boils when I am told that a merchant durst not enjoy his honest gains for fear of losing them by the rapacity of power. Name the governour who robbed the people, that I may declare his crimes to the emperour."

"Sir," said Imlac, "your ardour is the natural effect of virtue animated by youth: the time will come when you will acquit your father, and perhaps hear with less impatience of the governour. Oppression is, in the Abissinian dominions, neither frequent nor tolerated; but no form of government has been yet discovered, by which cruelty can be wholly prevented. Subordination supposes power on one part and subjection on the other; and if power be in the hands of men, it will sometimes be abused. The vigilance of the supreme magistrate may do much, but much will still remain undone. He can never know all the crimes that are committed, and can seldom punish all that he knows."

"This," said the prince, "I do not understand, but I had rather hear thee than dispute. Continue thy narration."

"My father," proceeded Imlac, "originally intended that I should have no other education, than such as might qualify me for commerce; and discovering in me great strength of memory, and quickness of apprehension, often declared his hope that I should be some time the richest man in Abissinia."

"Why," said the prince, "did thy father desire the increase of

---

1 A region of Abyssinia, now the province Gojam.
2 The head or first spring of a river. *Dictionary.*
3 Low-minded; base; ungenerous; spiritless. *Dictionary.*
4 To plunder, to strip of goods. *Dictionary.*
5 The corruption of rulers was a standard motif in oriental tales.

his wealth, when it was already greater than he durst discover or enjoy? I am unwilling to doubt thy veracity, yet inconsistencies cannot both be true."

"Inconsistencies," answered Imlac, "cannot both be right, but, imputed to man, they may both be true. Yet diversity is not inconsistency. My father might expect a time of greater security. However, some desire is necessary to keep life in motion, and he, whose real wants are supplied, must admit those of fancy."

"This," said the prince, "I can in some measure conceive. I repent that I interrupted thee."

"With this hope," proceeded Imlac, "he sent me to school; but when I had once found the delight of knowledge, and felt the pleasure of intelligence and the pride of invention, I began silently to despise riches, and determined to disappoint the purpose of my father, whose grossness[1] of conception raised my pity. I was twenty years old before his tenderness would expose me to the fatigue of travel, in which time I had been instructed, by successive masters, in all the literature[2] of my native country. As every hour taught me something new, I lived in a continual course of gratifications; but as I advanced towards manhood, I lost much of the reverence with which I had been used to look on my instructors; because, when the lesson was ended, I did not find them wiser or better than common men.

"At length my father resolved to initiate me in commerce, and, opening one of his subterranean treasuries, counted out ten thousand pieces of gold. 'This, young man,' said he, 'is the stock with which you must negociate. I began with less than the fifth part, and you see how diligence and parsimony[3] have increased it. This is your own to waste or to improve. If you squander it by negligence or caprice, you must wait for my death before you will be rich: if, in four years, you double your stock, we will thenceforward let subordination cease, and live together as friends and partners; for he shall always be equal with me, who is equally skilled in the art of growing rich.'

"We laid our money upon camels, concealed in bales of cheap goods, and travelled to the shore of the red sea. When I cast my eye on the expanse of waters my heart bounded like that of a prisoner escaped. I felt an unextinguishable curiosity kindle in my

---

1  Intellectually coarse. *Dictionary.*
2  Learning; skill in letters. *Dictionary.*
3  Frugality; covetousness; niggardliness; saving temper. *Dictionary.*

mind, and resolved to snatch this opportunity of seeing the manners of other nations, and of learning sciences[1] unknown in Abissinia.

"I remembered that my father had obliged me to the improvement of my stock, not by a promise which I ought not to violate, but by a penalty which I was at liberty to incur; and therefore determined to gratify my predominant desire, and by drinking at the fountains of knowledge, to quench the thirst of curiosity.

"As I was supposed to trade without connexion with my father, it was easy for me to become acquainted with the master of a ship, and procure a passage to some other country. I had no motives of choice to regulate my voyage; it was sufficient for me that, wherever I wandered, I should see a country which I had not seen before. I therefore entered a ship bound for Surat,[2] having left a letter for my father declaring my intentions."

## CHAPTER IX
### The history of Imlac continued

"WHEN I first entered upon the world of waters, and lost sight of land, I looked round about me with pleasing terrour, and thinking my soul enlarged by the boundless prospect,[3] imagined that I could gaze round for ever without satiety; but, in a short time, I grew weary of looking on barren uniformity, where I could only see again what I had already seen. I then descended into the ship, and doubted for a while whether all my future pleasures would not end like this in disgust and disappointment. 'Yet, surely,' said I, 'the ocean and the land are very different; the only variety of water is rest and motion, but the earth has mountains and vallies, desarts and cities: it is inhabited by men of different

---

1 Any art or species of knowledge. *Dictionary.*

2 A major port city in west-central India where the British established their first Indian trading post in 1612.

3 Compare to Edmund Burke's *Philosophical Enquiry into the Origin of our Ideas of the Sublime and the Beautiful* (1757): "A level plain of a vast extent on land, is certainly no mean idea; the prospect of such a plain may be as extensive as a prospect of the ocean: but can it ever fill the mind with anything so great as the ocean itself? This is owing to several causes; but it is owing to none more than this, that the ocean is an object of no small terror. Indeed, terror is in all cases whatsoever, either more openly or latently, the ruling principle of the sublime" (Oxford: Oxford UP, 1990) 53–54.

customs and contrary opinions; and I may hope to find variety in life, though I should miss it in nature.'

"With this thought I quieted my mind; and amused myself during the voyage, sometimes by learning from the sailors the art of navigation, which I have never practiced, and sometimes by forming schemes for my conduct in different situations, in not one of which I have been ever placed.

"I was almost weary of my naval amusements when we landed safely at Surat. I secured my money, and purchasing some commodities for show, joined myself to a caravan[1] that was passing into the inland country. My companions, for some reason or other, conjecturing that I was rich, and, by my inquiries and admiration, finding that I was ignorant, considered me as a novice whom they had a right to cheat, and who was to learn at the usual expence the art of fraud. They exposed me to the theft of servants, and the exaction[2] of officers, and saw me plundered upon false pretences, without any advantage to themselves, but that of rejoicing in the superiority of their own knowledge."

"Stop a moment," said the prince. "Is there such depravity in man, as that he should injure another without benefit to himself? I can easily conceive that all are pleased with superiority; but your ignorance was merely accidental, which, being neither your crime nor your folly, could afford them no reason to applaud themselves; and the knowledge which they had, and which you wanted, they might as effectually have shewn by warning as betraying you."

"Pride," said Imlac, "is seldom delicate, it will please itself with very mean advantages; and envy feels not its own happiness, but when it may be compared with the misery of others. They were my enemies because they grieved to think me rich, and my oppressors because they delighted to find me weak."

"Proceed," said the prince: "I doubt not of the facts which you relate, but imagine that you impute them to mistaken motives."

"In this company," said Imlac, "I arrived at Agra, the capital of Indostan,[3] the city in which the great Mogul[4] commonly resides.

---

1   A troop or body of merchants or pilgrims, as they travel in the East. *Dictionary*.

2   Extortion; unjust demand. *Dictionary*.

3   Agra is a city seven hundred miles north-east of Surat and sometime capital of the Mughal empire, best known as the site of the Taj Mahal. Indostan (Hindustan) was a European name for northern India.

4   Emperor of the Mughal dynasty, which ruled much of the Indian subcontinent from the sixteenth to nineteenth centuries. *OED*.

I applied myself to the language of the country, and in a few months was able to converse with the learned men; some of whom I found morose and reserved, and others easy and communicative; some were unwilling to teach another what they had with difficulty learned themselves; and some shewed that the end of their studies was to gain the dignity of instructing.

"To the tutor of the young princes I recommended myself so much, that I was presented to the emperour as a man of uncommon knowledge. The emperour asked me many questions concerning my country and my travels; and though I cannot now recollect any thing that he uttered above the power of a common man, he dismissed me astonished at his wisdom, and enamoured of his goodness.

"My credit was now so high, that the merchants, with whom I had travelled, applied to me for recommendations to the ladies of the court. I was surprised at their confidence of solicitation, and gently reproached them with their practices on the road. They heard me with cold indifference, and shewed no tokens of shame or sorrow.

"They then urged their request with the offer of a bribe; but what I would not do for kindness I would not do for money; and refused them, not because they had injured me, but because I would not enable them to injure others; for I knew they would have made use of my credit to cheat those who should buy their wares.

"Having resided at Agra till there was no more to be learned, I travelled into Persia,[1] where I saw many remains of ancient magnificence, and observed many new accommodations[2] of life. The Persians are a nation eminently social, and their assemblies afforded me daily opportunities of remarking characters and manners, and of tracing human nature through all its variations.

"From Persia I passed into Arabia,[3] where I saw a nation at once pastoral and warlike; who live without any settled habitation; whose only wealth is their flocks and herds; and who have yet carried on, through all ages, an hereditary war with all mankind, though they neither covet nor envy their possessions."

---

1  Now Iran. Johnson admired John Chardin's *Travels in Persia 1673–7* (1720). Meloccaro 215 n.6.
2  Conveniences, things requisite for ease or refreshment. *Dictionary*.
3  The Arabian peninsula.

# CHAPTER X
## Imlac's history continued. A dissertation upon poetry

"WHEREVER I went, I found that Poetry was considered as the highest learning, and regarded with a veneration somewhat approaching to that which man would pay to the Angelick Nature. And it yet fills me with wonder, that, in almost all countries, the most ancient poets are considered as the best: whether it be that every other kind of knowledge is an acquisition gradually attained, and poetry is a gift conferred at once; or that the first poetry of every nation surprised them as a novelty, and retained the credit by consent which it received by accident at first: or whether, as the province of poetry is to describe Nature and Passion, which are always the same, the first writers took possession of the most striking objects for description, and the most probable occurrences for fiction, and left nothing to those that followed them, but transcription of the same events, and new combinations of the same images. Whatever be the reason, it is commonly observed that the early writers are in possession of nature, and their followers of art: that the first excel in strength and invention, and the latter in elegance and refinement.

"I was desirous to add my name to this illustrious fraternity. I read all the poets of Persia and Arabia, and was able to repeat by memory the volumes that are suspended in the mosque of Mecca.[1] But I soon found that no man was ever great by imitation. My desire of excellence impelled me to transfer my attention to nature and to life. Nature was to be my subject, and men to be my auditors: I could never describe what I had not seen: I could not hope to move those with delight or terrour, whose interests and opinions I did not understand.

"Being now resolved to be a poet, I saw everything with a new purpose; my sphere of attention was suddenly magnified: no kind of knowledge was to be overlooked. I ranged mountains and deserts for images and resemblances, and pictured upon my mind every tree of the forest and flower of the valley. I observed with equal care the crags of the rock and the pinnacles of the palace. Sometimes I wandered along the mazes of the rivulet, and sometimes watched the changes of the summer clouds. To a poet

---

1  The *Gentleman's Magazine* XXIII (1753): 272 describes the alleged practice of suspending venerated poems in the Ka'bah, the shrine in the Great Mosque, Mecca. Kolb 41 n.9.

nothing can be useless. Whatever is beautiful, and whatever is dreadful, must be familiar to his imagination: he must be conversant with all that is awfully vast or elegantly little.[1] The plants of the garden, the animals of the wood, the minerals of the earth, and meteors of the sky, must all concur to store his mind with inexhaustible variety: for every idea is useful for the inforcement or decoration of moral or religious truth; and he, who knows most, will have most power of diversifying his scenes, and of gratifying his reader with remote allusions and unexpected instruction.

"All the appearances of nature I was therefore careful to study, and every country which I have surveyed has contributed something to my poetical powers."

"In so wide a survey," said the prince, "you must surely have left much unobserved. I have lived, till now, within the circuit of these mountains, and yet cannot walk abroad without the sight of something which I had never beheld before, or never heeded."

"The business of a poet," said Imlac, "is to examine, not the individual, but the species; to remark general properties and large appearances: he does not number the streaks of the tulip, or describe the different shades in the verdure of the forest. He is to exhibit in his portraits of nature such prominent and striking features, as recal the original to every mind; and must neglect the minuter discriminations, which one may have remarked, and another have neglected, for those characteristicks which are alike obvious to vigilance and carelesness.

"But the knowledge of nature is only half the task of a poet; he must be acquainted likewise with all the modes of life. His character requires that he estimate the happiness and misery of every condition; observe the power of all the passions in all their combinations, and trace the changes of the human mind as they are modified by various institutions and accidental influences of climate or custom, from the spriteliness of infancy to the despondence of decrepitude. He must divest himself of the prejudices of his age or country; he must consider right and wrong in their abstracted and invariable state; he must disregard present laws and opinions, and rise to general and transcendental truths, which will always be the same: he must therefore content himself

---

1  "Greatness of dimension is a powerful cause of the sublime.... However, it may not be amiss to add to these remarks upon magnitude, that, as the great extreme of dimension is sublime, so the last extreme of littleness is in some measure sublime likewise ..." Burke 66.

with the slow progress of his name; contemn the applause of his own time, and commit his claims to the justice of posterity. He must write as the interpreter of nature, and the legislator of mankind, and consider himself as presiding over the thoughts and manners of future generations; as a being superiour to time and place.

"His labour is not yet at an end: he must know many languages and many sciences; and, that his stile may be worthy of his thoughts, must by incessant practice, familiarize to himself every delicacy of speech and grace of harmony."

## CHAPTER XI
### Imlac's narrative continued. A hint on pilgrimage

IMLAC now felt the enthusiastic[1] fit, and was proceeding to aggrandize his own profession, when the prince cried out, "Enough! Thou hast convinced me, that no human being can ever be a poet. Proceed with thy narration."

"To be a poet," said Imlac, "is indeed very difficult." "So difficult," returned the prince, "that I will at present hear no more of his labours. Tell me whither you went when you had seen Persia."

"From Persia," said the poet, "I travel'd through Syria, and for three years resided in Palestine, where I conversed with great numbers of the northern and western nations of Europe; the nations which are now in possession of all power and all knowledge; whose armies are irresistible, and whose fleets command the remotest parts of the globe. When I compared these men with the natives of our own kingdom, and those that surround us, they appeared almost another order of beings. In their countries it is difficult to wish for any thing that may not be obtained: a thousand arts, of which we never heard, are continually labouring for their convenience and pleasure; and whatever their own climate has denied them is supplied by their commerce."

"By what means," said the prince, "are the Europeans thus powerful? or why, since they can so easily visit Asia and Africa for trade or conquest, cannot the Asiaticks and Africans invade their coasts, plant colonies in their ports, and give laws to their natural princes? The same wind that carries them back would bring us thither."

---

1 Elevated in fancy; exalted in ideas. Vehemently hot in any cause. *Dictionary.*

"They are more powerful, Sir, than we," answered Imlac, "because they are wiser; knowledge will always predominate over ignorance, as man governs the other animals. But why their knowledge is more than ours, I know not what reason can be given, but the unsearchable will of the Supreme Being."

"When," said the prince with a sigh, "shall I be able to visit Palestine, and mingle with this mighty confluence of nations? Till that happy moment shall arrive, let me fill up the time with such representations as thou canst give me. I am not ignorant of the motive that assembles such numbers in that place, and cannot but consider it as the center of wisdom and piety, to which the best and wisest men of every land must be continually resorting."

"There are some nations," said Imlac, "that send few visitants to Palestine; for many numerous and learned sects in Europe, concur to censure pilgrimage as superstitious, or deride it as ridiculous."

"You know," said the prince, "how little my life has made me acquainted with diversity of opinions: it will be too long to hear the arguments on both sides; you, that have considered them, tell me the result."

"Pilgrimage," said Imlac, "like many other acts of piety, may be reasonable or superstitious, according to the principles upon which it is performed. Long journies in search of truth are not commanded. Truth, such as is necessary to the regulation of life, is always found where it is honestly sought. Change of place is no natural cause of the increase of piety, for it inevitably produces dissipation of mind. Yet, since men go every day to view the fields where great actions have been performed, and return with stronger impressions of the event, curiousity of the same kind may naturally dispose us to view that country whence our religion[1] had its beginning; and I believe no man surveys those awful scenes without some confirmation of holy resolutions. That the Supreme Being may be more easily propitiated in one place than in another, is the dream of idle superstition; but that some places may operate upon our own minds in an uncommon manner, is an opinion which hourly experience will justify. He who supposes that his vices may be more successfully combated in Palestine, will, perhaps, find himself mistaken, yet he may go thither

---

1   Some minority ethnic groups in Abyssinia practiced Islam, but as members of the country's ruling class, Rasselas and Imlac would be Abyssinian Christians (see Introduction, p. 18).

without folly: he who thinks they will be more freely pardoned, dishonours at once his reason and religion."

"These," said the prince, "are European distinctions. I will consider them another time. What have you found to be the effect of knowledge? Are those nations happier than we?"

"There is so much infelicity," said the poet, "in the world, that scarce any man has leisure from his own distresses to estimate the comparative happiness of others. Knowledge is certainly one of the means of pleasure, as is confessed by the natural desire which every mind feels of increasing its ideas. Ignorance is mere privation, by which nothing can be produced: it is a vacuity in which the soul sits motionless and torpid for want of attraction; and, without knowing why, we always rejoice when we learn, and grieve when we forget. I am therefore inclined to conclude, that, if nothing counteracts the natural consequences of learning, we grow more happy as our minds take a wider range.

"In enumerating the particular comforts of life we shall find many advantages on the side of the Europeans. They cure wounds and diseases with which we languish and perish. We suffer inclemencies of weather which they can obviate. They have engines for the dispatch of many laborious works, which we must perform by manual industry. There is such communication between distant places, that one friend can hardly be said to be absent from another. Their policy removes all publick inconveniencies: they have roads cut through their mountains, and bridges laid upon their rivers. And, if we descend to the privacies of life, their habitations are more commodious, and their possessions are more secure."

"They are surely happy," said the prince, "who have all these conveniencies, of which I envy none so much as the facility with which separated friends interchange their thoughts."

"The Europeans," answered Imlac, "are less unhappy than we, but they are not happy. Human life is every where a state in which much is to be endured, and little to be enjoyed."

## CHAPTER XII
### The story of Imlac continued

"I am not yet willing," said the prince, "to suppose that happiness is so parsimoniously distributed to mortals; nor can believe but that, if I had the choice of life, I should be able to fill every day with pleasure. I would injure no man, and should provoke no resentment: I would relieve every distress, and should enjoy the benedictions of gratitude. I would choose my friends among the wise, and my wife among the virtuous; and therefore should be in no danger from treachery, or unkindness. My children should, by my care, be learned and pious, and would repay to my age what their childhood had received. What would dare to molest him who might call on every side to thousands enriched by his bounty, or assisted by his power? And why should not life glide quietly away in the soft reciprocation of protection and reverence? All this may be done without the help of European refinements, which appear by their effects to be rather specious than useful. Let us leave them and persue our journey."

"From Palestine," said Imlac, "I passed through many regions of Asia; in the more civilized kingdoms as a trader, and among the Barbarians of the mountains as a pilgrim. At last I began to long for my native country, that I might repose after my travels, and fatigues, in the places where I had spent my earlier years, and gladden my old companions with the recital of my ádventures. Often did I figure to myself those, with whom I had sported away the gay hours of dawning life, sitting round me in its evening, wondering at my tales, and listening to my counsels.

"When this thought had taken possession of my mind, I considered every moment as wasted which did not bring me nearer to Abissinia. I hastened into Egypt, and, notwithstanding my impatience, was detained ten months in the contemplation of its ancient magnificence, and in enquiries after the remains of its ancient learning. I found in Cairo a mixture of all nations; some brought thither by the love of knowledge, some by the hope of gain, and many by the desire of living after their own manner without observation, and of lying hid in the obscurity of multitudes: for, in a city, populous as Cairo, it is possible to obtain at the same time the gratifications of society, and the secrecy of solitude.

"From Cairo I travelled to Suez,[1] and embarked on the Red sea, passing along the coast till I arrived at the port from which I had departed twenty years before. Here I joined myself to a caravan and re-entered my native country.

"I now expected the caresses of my kinsmen, and the congratulations of my friends, and was not without hope that my father, whatever value he had set upon riches, would own with gladness and pride a son who was able to add to the felicity and honour of

---

1  Egyptian seaport on the Red Sea.

the nation. But I was soon convinced that my thoughts were vain. My father had been dead fourteen years, having divided his wealth among my brothers, who were removed to some other provinces. Of my companions the greater part was in the grave, of the rest some could with difficulty remember me, and some considered me as one corrupted by foreign manners.

"A man used to vicissitudes[1] is not easily dejected. I forgot, after a time, my disappointment, and endeavoured to recommend myself to the nobles of the kingdom: they admitted me to their tables, heard my story, and dismissed me. I opened a school, and was prohibited to teach. I then resolved to sit down in the quiet of domestick life, and addressed a lady that was fond of my conversation, but rejected my suit, because my father was a merchant.

"Wearied at last with solicitation and repulses, I resolved to hide myself for ever from the world, and depend no longer on the opinion or caprice of others. I waited for the time when the gate of the *happy valley* should open that I might bid farewell to hope and fear: the day came; my performance was distinguished with favour, and I resigned myself with joy to perpetual confinement."

"Hast thou here found happiness at last?" said Rasselas. "Tell me without reserve; art thou content with thy condition? or, dost thou wish to be again wandering and inquiring? All the inhabitants of this valley celebrate their lot, and, at the annual visit of the emperour, invite others to partake of their felicity."

"Great prince," said Imlac, "I shall speak the truth: I know not one of all your attendants who does not lament the hour when he entered this retreat. I am less unhappy than the rest, because I have a mind replete with images, which I can vary and combine at my pleasure. I can amuse my solitude by the renovation of the knowledge which begins to fade from my memory, and by recollection of the accidents of my past life. Yet all this ends in the sorrowful consideration, that my acquirements are now useless, and that none of my pleasures can be again enjoyed. The rest, whose minds have no impression but of the present moment, are either corroded by malignant passions, or sit stupid in the gloom of perpetual vacancy."

"What passions can infest those," said the prince, "who have no rivals? We are in a place where impotence precludes malice, and where all envy is repressed by community of enjoyments."

---

1  Revolution; change. *Dictionary*.

"There may be community," said Imlac, "of material possessions, but there can never be community of love or of esteem. It must happen that one will please more than another; he that knows himself despised will always be envious; and still more envious and malevolent, if he is condemned to live in the presence of those who despise him. The invitations, by which they allure others to a state which they feel to be wretched, proceed from the natural malignity of hopeless misery. They are weary of themselves, and of each other, and expect to find relief in new companions. They envy the liberty which their folly has forfeited, and would gladly see all mankind imprisoned like themselves.

"From this crime, however, I am wholly free. No man can say that he is wretched by my persuasion. I look with pity on the crowds who are annually soliciting admission to captivity, and wish that it were lawful for me to warn them of their danger."

"My dear Imlac," said the prince, "I will open to thee my whole heart. I have long meditated an escape from the happy valley. I have examined the mountains on every side, but find myself insuperably barred: teach me the way to break my prison; thou shalt be the companion of my flight, the guide of my rambles, the partner of my fortune, and my sole director in the *choice of life*."

"Sir," answered the poet, "your escape will be difficult, and, perhaps, you may soon repent your curiosity. The world, which you figure to yourself smooth and quiet as the lake in the valley, you will find a sea foaming with tempests, and boiling with whirlpools: you will be sometimes overwhelmed by the waves of violence, and sometimes dashed against the rocks of treachery. Amidst wrongs and frauds, competitions and anxieties, you will wish a thousand times for these seats of quiet, and willingly quit hope to be free from fear."

"Do not seek to deter me from my purpose," said the prince: "I am impatient to see what thou hast seen; and, since thou art thyself weary of the valley, it is evident, that thy former state was better than this. Whatever be the consequence of my experiment, I am resolved to judge with my own eyes of the various conditions of men, and then to make deliberately my *choice of life*."

"I am afraid," said Imlac, "you are hindered by stronger restraints than my persuasions; yet, if your determination is fixed, I do not counsel you to despair. Few things are impossible to diligence and skill."

# CHAPTER XIII
## Rasselas discovers the means of escape

THE prince now dismissed his favourite to rest, but the narrative of wonders and novelties filled his mind with perturbation. He revolved all that he had heard, and prepared innumerable questions for the morning.

Much of his uneasiness was now removed. He had a friend to whom he could impart his thoughts, and whose experience could assist him in his designs. His heart was no longer condemned to swell with silent vexation. He thought that even the *happy valley* might be endured with such a companion, and that, if they could range the world together, he should have nothing further to desire.

In a few days the water was discharged, and the ground dried. The prince and Imlac then walked out together to converse without the notice of the rest. The prince, whose thoughts were always on the wing, as he passed by the gate, said, with a countenance of sorrow, "Why art thou so strong, and why is man so weak?"

"Man is not weak," answered his companion; "knowledge is more than equivalent to force. The master of mechanicks laughs at strength. I can burst the gate, but cannot do it secretly. Some other expedient must be tried."

As they were walking on the side of the mountain, they observed that the conies,[1] which the rain had driven from their burrows, had taken shelter among the bushes, and formed holes behind them, tending upwards in an oblique line. "It has been the opinion of antiquity," said Imlac, "that human reason borrowed many arts from the instinct of animals; let us, therefore, not think ourselves degraded by learning from the coney. We may escape by piercing the mountain in the same direction. We will begin where the summit hangs over the middle part, and labour upward till we shall issue out beyond the prominence."

The eyes of the prince, when he heard this proposal, sparkled with joy. The execution was easy, and the success certain.

No time was now lost. They hastened early in the morning to chuse a place proper for their mine. They clambered with great fatigue among crags and brambles, and returned without having discovered any part that favoured their design. The second and

---

1 A rabbit; an animal that burroughs in the ground. *Dictionary.*

the third day were spent in the same manner, and with the same frustration. But, on the fourth, they found a small cavern, concealed by a thicket, where they resolved to make their experiment.

Imlac procured instruments proper to hew stone and remove earth, and they fell to their work on the next day with more eagerness than vigour. They were presently exhausted by their efforts, and sat down to pant upon the grass. The prince, for a moment, appeared to be discouraged. "Sir," said his companion, "practice will enable us to continue our labour for a longer time; mark, however, how far we have advanced, and you will find that our toil will some time have an end. Great works are performed, not by strength, but perseverance: yonder palace was raised by single stones, yet you see its height and spaciousness. He that shall walk with vigour three hours a day will pass in seven years a space equal to the circumference of the globe."

They returned to their work day after day, and, in a short time, found a fissure in the rock, which enabled them to pass far with very little obstruction. This Rasselas considered as a good omen. "Do not disturb your mind," said Imlac, "with other hopes or fears than reason may suggest: if you are pleased with prognosticks of good, you will be terrified likewise with tokens of evil, and your whole life will be a prey to superstition. Whatever facilitates our work is more than an omen, it is a cause of success. This is one of those pleasing surprises which often happen to active resolution. Many things difficult to design prove easy to performance."

## CHAPTER XIV
### Rasselas and Imlac receive an unexpected visit

THEY had now wrought their way to the middle, and solaced their toil with the approach of liberty, when the prince, coming down to refresh himself with air, found his sister Nekayah standing before the mouth of the cavity. He started and stood confused, afraid to tell his design, and yet hopeless to conceal it. A few moments determined him to repose on her fidelity, and secure her secrecy by a declaration without reserve.

"Do not imagine," said the princess, "that I came hither as a spy: I had long observed from my window, that you and Imlac directed your walk every day towards the same point, but I did not suppose you had any better reason for the preference than a cooler shade, or more fragrant bank; nor followed you with any other design than to partake of your conversation. Since then not suspicion but fondness has detected you, let me not lose the advantage of my discovery. I am equally weary of confinement with yourself, and not less desirous of knowing what is done or suffered in the world. Permit me to fly with you from this tasteless tranquility, which will yet grow more loathsome when you have left me. You may deny me to accompany you, but cannot hinder me from following."

The prince, who loved Nekayah above his other sisters, had no inclination to refuse her request, and grieved that he had lost an opportunity of shewing his confidence by a voluntary communication. It was therefore agreed that she should leave the valley with them; and that, in the mean time, she should watch, lest any other straggler should, by chance or curiosity, follow them to the mountain.

At length their labour was at an end; they saw light beyond the prominence, and, issuing to the top of the mountain, beheld the Nile, yet a narrow current, wandering beneath them.

The prince looked round with rapture, anticipated all the pleasures of travel, and in thought was already transported beyond his father's dominions. Imlac, though very joyful at his escape, had less expectation of pleasure in the world, which he had before tried, and of which he had been weary.

Rasselas was so much delighted with a wider horizon, that he could not soon be persuaded to return into the valley. He informed his sister that the way was open, and that nothing now remained but to prepare for their departure.

## CHAPTER XV
### The prince and princess leave the valley,
### and see many wonders

THE prince and princess had jewels sufficient to make them rich whenever they came into a place of commerce, which, by Imlac's direction, they hid in their cloaths, and, on the night of the next full moon, all left the valley. The princess was followed only by a single favourite, who did not know whither she was going.

They clambered through the cavity, and began to go down on the other side. The princess and her maid turned their eyes towards every part, and, feeling nothing to bound their prospect, considered themselves as in danger of being lost in a dreary vacuity. They stopped and trembled. "I am almost afraid," said the princess, "to begin a journey of which I cannot perceive an end, and to venture into this immense plain where I may be approached on every side by men whom I never saw." The prince felt nearly the same emotions, though he thought it more manly to conceal them.

Imlac smiled at their terrours, and encouraged them to proceed; but the princess continued irresolute till she had been imperceptibly drawn forward too far to return.

In the morning they found some shepherds in the field, who set milk and fruits before them. The princess wondered that she did not see a palace ready for her reception, and a table spread with delicacies; but, being faint and hungry, she drank the milk and eat the fruits, and thought them of a higher flavour than the products of the valley.

They travelled forward by easy journeys, being all unaccustomed to toil or difficulty, and knowing, that though they might be missed, they could not be persued. In a few days they came into a more populous region, where Imlac was diverted[1] with the admiration which his companions expressed at the diversity of manners, stations and employments.

Their dress was such as might not bring upon them the suspicion of having any thing to conceal, yet the prince, wherever he came, expected to be obeyed, and the princess was frighted, because those that came into her presence did not prostrate themselves before her. Imlac was forced to observe them with great vigilance, lest they should betray their rank by their unusual behaviour, and detained them several weeks in the first village to accustom them to the sight of common mortals.

By degrees the royal wanderers were taught to understand that they had for a time laid aside their dignity, and were to expect only such regard as liberality and courtesy could procure. And Imlac, having, by many admonitions, prepared them to endure the tumults of a port, and the ruggedness of the commercial race, brought them down to the sea-coast.

The prince and his sister, to whom every thing was new, were gratified equally at all places, and therefore remained for some months at the port without any inclination to pass further. Imlac was content with their stay, because he did not think it safe to expose them, unpractised in the world, to the hazards of a foreign country.

At last he began to fear lest they should be discovered, and proposed to fix a day for their departure. They had no pretensions to judge for themselves, and referred the whole scheme to

---

1  To please; to exhilarate. *Dictionary*.

his direction. He therefore took passage in a ship to Suez; and, when the time came, with great difficulty prevailed on the princess to enter the vessel. They had a quick and prosperous voyage, and from Suez travelled by land to Cairo.

## CHAPTER XVI
### They enter Cairo, and find every man happy

AS they approached the city, which filled the strangers with astonishment, "This," said Imlac to the prince, "is the place where travellers and merchants assemble from all the corners of the earth. You will here find men of every character, and every occupation. Commerce is here honourable: I will act as a merchant, and you shall live as strangers, who have no other end of travel than curiosity; it will soon be observed that we are rich; our reputation will procure us access to all whom we shall desire to know; you will see all the conditions of humanity, and enable yourself at leisure to make your *choice of life*."

They now entered the town, stunned by the noise, and offended by the crowds. Instruction had not yet so prevailed over habit, but that they wondered to see themselves pass undistinguished along the street, and met by the lowest of the people without reverence or notice. The princess could not at first bear the thought of being leveled with the vulgar, and, for some days, continued in her chamber, where she was served by her favourite Pekuah as in the palace of the valley.

Imlac, who understood traffick,[1] sold part of the jewels the next day, and hired a house, which he adorned with such magnificence, that he was immediately considered as a merchant of great wealth. His politeness[2] attracted many acquaintance, and his generosity made him courted by many dependants. His table was crowded by men of every nation, who all admired his knowledge, and solicited his favour. His companions, not being able to mix in the conversation, could make no discovery[3] of their ignorance or surprise, and were gradually initiated in the world as they gained knowledge of the language.

The prince had, by frequent lectures, been taught the use and nature of money; but the ladies could not, for a long time, com-

---

1   Commerce; merchandising; large trade; exchange of commodities. *Dictionary.*
2   Elegance of manners; gentility; good breeding. *Dictionary.*
3   The act of revealing or disclosing any secret. *Dictionary.*

prehend what the merchants did with small pieces of gold and silver, or why things of so little use should be received as equivalent to the necessaries of life.

They studied the language two years, while Imlac was preparing to set before them the various ranks and conditions of mankind. He grew acquainted with all who had any thing uncommon in their fortune or conduct. He frequented the voluptuous and the frugal, the idle and the busy, the merchants and the men of learning.

The prince, being now able to converse with fluency, and having learned the caution necessary to be observed in his intercourse with strangers, began to accompany Imlac to places of resort, and to enter into all assemblies, that he might make his *choice of life*.

For some time he thought choice needless, because all appeared to him equally happy. Wherever he went he met gayety and kindness, and heard the song of joy, or the laugh of carelessness. He began to believe that the world overflowed with universal plenty, and that nothing was withheld either from want or merit; that every hand showered liberality, and every heart melted with benevolence: "and who then," says he, "will be suffered to be wretched?"

Imlac permitted the pleasing delusion, and was unwilling to crush the hope of inexperience; till one day, having sat a while silent, "I know not," said the prince, "what can be the reason that I am more unhappy than any of our friends. I see them perpetually and unalterably cheerful, but feel my own mind restless and uneasy. I am unsatisfied with those pleasures which I seem most to court; I live in the crowds of jollity, not so much to enjoy company as to shun myself, and am only loud and merry to conceal my sadness."

"Every man," said Imlac, "may, by examining his own mind, guess what passes in the minds of others: when you feel that your own gaiety is counterfeit, it may justly lead you to suspect that of your companions not to be sincere. Envy is commonly reciprocal. We are long before we are convinced that happiness is never to be found, and each believes it possessed by others, to keep alive the hope of obtaining it for himself. In the assembly, where you passed the last night, there appeared such spriteliness of air, and volatility of fancy, as might have suited beings of an higher order, formed to inhabit serener regions inaccessible to care or sorrow: yet, believe me, prince, there was not one who did not dread the moment when solitude should deliver him to the tyranny of reflection."

"This," said the prince, "may be true of others, since it is true of me; yet, whatever be the general infelicity of man, one condition is more happy than another, and wisdom surely directs us to take the least evil in the *choice of life*."

"The causes of good and evil," answered Imlac, "are so various and uncertain, so often entangled with each other, so diversified by various relations, and so much subject to accidents which cannot be foreseen, that he who would fix his condition upon incontestable reasons of preference, must live and die inquiring and deliberating."

"But surely," said Rasselas, "the wise men, to whom we listen with reverence and wonder, chose that mode of life for themselves which they thought most likely to make them happy."

"Very few," said the poet, "live by choice. Every man is placed in his present condition by causes which acted without his foresight, and with which he did not always willingly co-operate; and therefore you will rarely meet one who does not think the lot of his neighbour better than his own."

"I am pleased to think," said the prince, "that my birth has given me at least one advantage over others, by enabling me to determine for myself. I have here the world before me; I will review it at leisure: surely happiness is somewhere to be found."

## CHAPTER XVII
### The prince associates with young men of spirit and gaiety

RASSELAS rose next day, and resolved to begin his experiments upon life. "Youth," cried he, "is the time of gladness: I will join myself to the young men, whose only business is to gratify their desires, and whose time is all spent in a succession of enjoyments."

To such societies he was readily admitted, but a few days brought him back weary and disgusted. Their mirth was without images,[1] their laughter without motive; their pleasures were gross and sensual, in which the mind had no part; their conduct was at once wild and mean; they laughed at order and at law, but the frown of power dejected, and the eye of wisdom abashed them.

The prince soon concluded, that he should never be happy in a course of life of which he was ashamed. He thought it unsuitable to a reasonable being to act without a plan, and to be sad or cheerful only by chance. "Happiness," said he, "must be

---

1 An idea; a representation of any thing to the mind. *Dictionary*.

something solid and permanent, without fear and without uncertainty."

But his young companions had gained so much of his regard by their frankness and courtesy, that he could not leave them without warning and remonstrance. "My friends," said he, "I have seriously considered our manners and our prospects, and find that we have mistaken our own interest. The first years of man must make provision for the last. He that never thinks never can be wise. Perpetual levity must end in ignorance; and intemperance, though it may fire the spirits for an hour, will make life short or miserable. Let us consider that youth is of no long duration, and that in maturer age, when the enchantments of fancy shall cease, and phantoms of delight dance no more about us, we shall have no comforts but the esteem of wise men, and the means of doing good. Let us, therefore, stop, while to stop is in our power: let us live as men who are sometime to grow old, and to whom it will be the most dreadful of all evils not to count their past years but by follies, and to be reminded of their former luxuriance of health only by the maladies which riot has produced."

They stared a while in silence one upon another, and, at last, drove him away by a general chorus of continued laughter.

The consciousness that his sentiments were just, and his intentions kind, was scarcely sufficient to support him against the horrour of derision. But he recovered his tranquility, and persued his search.

## CHAPTER XVIII
### The prince finds a wise and happy man

AS he was one day walking in the street, he saw a spacious building which all were, by the open doors, invited to enter: he followed the stream of people, and found it a hall or school of declamation,[1] in which professors read lectures to their auditory.[2] He fixed his eye upon a sage raised above the rest, who discoursed with great energy on the government of the passions. His look was venerable, his action graceful, his pronunciation clear, and his diction elegant. He shewed, with great strength of

---

1  A discourse addressed to the passions; an harangue; a set speech; a piece of rhetorick. *Dictionary*.
2  An audience; a collection of persons assembled to hear. *Dictionary*.

sentiment,[1] and variety of illustration, that human nature is degraded and debased, when the lower faculties predominate over the higher; that when fancy, the parent of passion, usurps the dominion of the mind, nothing ensues but the natural effect of unlawful government, perturbation and confusion; that she betrays the fortresses of the intellect to rebels, and excites her children to sedition against reason their lawful sovereign. He compared reason to the sun, of which the light is constant, uniform, and lasting; and fancy to a meteor, of bright but transitory luster, irregular in its motion, and delusive in its direction.

He then communicated the various precepts given from time to time for the conquest of passion, and displayed the happiness of those who had obtained the important victory, after which man is no longer the slave of fear, nor the fool of hope; is no more emaciated by envy, inflamed by anger, emasculated by tenderness, or depressed by grief; but walks on calmly through the tumults or the privacies of life, as the sun persues alike his course through the calm or the stormy sky.

He enumerated many examples of heroes immovable by pain or pleasure, who looked with indifference on those modes or accidents to which the vulgar give the names of good and evil. He exhorted his hearers to lay aside their prejudices, and arm themselves against the shafts of malice or misfortune, by invulnerable patience; concluding, that this state only was happiness, and that this happiness was in every one's power.

Rasselas listened to him with the veneration due to the instructions of a superiour being, and, waiting for him at the door, humbly implored the liberty of visiting so great a master of true wisdom. The lecturer hesitated a moment, when Rasselas put a purse of gold into his hand, which he received with a mixture of joy and wonder.

"I have found," said the prince, at his return to Imlac, "a man who can teach all that is necessary to be known, who, from the unshaken throne of rational fortitude, looks down on the scenes of life changing beneath him. He speaks, and attention watches his lips. He reasons, and conviction closes his periods.[2] This man shall be my future guide: I will learn his doctrines, and imitate his life."

"Be not too hasty," said Imlac, "to trust, or to admire, the

---

1 Thought; notion; opinion. *Dictionary*.
2 A complete sentence from one full stop to another. *Dictionary*.

teachers of morality: they discourse like angels, but they live like men."

Rasselas, who could not conceive how any man could reason so forcibly without feeling the cogency of his own arguments, paid his visit in a few days, and was denied admission. He had now learned the power of money, and made his way by a piece of gold to the inner apartment, where he found the philosopher in a room half darkened, with his eyes misty, and his face pale. "Sir," said he, "you are come at a time when all human friendship is useless; what I suffer cannot be remedied, what I have lost cannot be supplied. My daughter, my only daughter, from whose tenderness I expected all the comforts of my age, died last night of a fever. My views, my purposes, my hopes are at an end: I am now a lonely being disunited from society."

"Sir," said the prince, "mortality is an event by which a wise man can never be surprised: we know that death is always near, and it should therefore always be expected." "Young man," answered the philosopher, "you speak like one that has never felt the pangs of separation." "Have you then forgot the precepts," said Rasselas, "which you so powerfully enforced? Has wisdom no strength to arm the heart against calamity? Consider that external things are naturally variable, but truth and reason are always the same." "What comfort," said the mourner, "can truth and reason afford me? of what effect are they now, but to tell me, that my daughter will not be restored?"

The prince, whose humanity would not suffer him to insult misery with reproof, went away convinced of the emptiness of rhetorical sound, and the inefficacy of polished periods and studied sentences.

## CHAPTER XIX
### A Glimpse of pastoral life

HE was still eager upon the same enquiry; and, having heard of a hermit,[1] that lived near the lowest cataract[2] of the Nile, and filled the whole country with the fame of his sanctity, resolved to visit his retreat, and enquire whether that felicity, which publick life could not afford, was to be found in solitude; and whether a

---

1 A solitary; an anchoret; one who retires from society to contemplation and devotion. *Dictionary*.
2 A fall of water from on high; a shoot of water; a cascade. *Dictionary*.

man, whose age and virtue made him venerable, could teach any peculiar art of shunning evils, or enduring them.

Imlac and the princess agreed to accompany him, and, after the necessary preparations, they began their journey. Their way lay through fields, where shepherds tended their flocks, and the lambs were playing upon the pasture. "This," said the poet, "is the life which has been often celebrated for its innocence and quiet: let us pass the heat of the day among the shepherds tents, and know whether all our searches are not to terminate in pastoral[1] simplicity."

The proposal pleased them, and they induced the shepherds, by small presents and familiar questions, to tell their opinion of their own state: they were so rude and ignorant, so little able to compare the good with the evil of the occupation, and so indistinct in their narratives and descriptions, that very little could be learned from them. But it was evident that their hearts were cankered with discontent; that they considered themselves as condemned to labour for the luxury of the rich, and looked up with stupid malevolence toward those that were placed above them.

The princess pronounced with vehemence, that she would never suffer these envious savages to be her companions, and that she should not soon be desirous of seeing any more specimens of rustick happiness; but could not believe that all the accounts of primeval pleasures were fabulous, and was yet in doubt whether life had any thing that could be justly preferred to the placid gratifications of fields and woods. She hoped that the time would come, when with a few virtuous and elegant companions, she should gather flowers planted by her own hand, fondle the lambs of her own ewe, and listen, without care, among brooks and breezes, to one of her maidens reading in the shade.

## CHAPTER XX
### The danger of prosperity

ON the next day they continued their journey, till the heat compelled them to look round for shelter. At a small distance they saw a thick wood, which they no sooner entered than they perceived that they were approaching the habitations of men. The shrubs were diligently cut away to open walks where the shades

---

1 Rural; rustick; beseeming shepherds; imitating shepherds. *Dictionary.*

were darkest; the boughs of opposite trees were artificially inter-woven; seats of flowery turf were raised in vacant spaces, and a rivulet, that wantoned along the side of a winding path, had its banks sometimes opened into small basons, and its stream some-times obstructed by little mounds of stone heaped together to increase its murmurs.

They passed slowly through the wood, delighted with such unexpected accommodations, and entertained each other with conjecturing what, or who he could be, that in those rude and unfrequented regions, had leisure and art for such harmless luxury.

As they advanced, they heard the sound of musick, and saw youths and virgins dancing in the grove; and, going still further, beheld a stately palace built upon a hill surrounded with woods. The laws of eastern hospitality allowed them to enter, and the master welcomed them like a man liberal and wealthy.

He was skillful enough in appearances soon to discern that they were no common guests, and spread his table with magnifi-cence. The eloquence of Imlac caught his attention, and the lofty courtesy of the princess excited his respect. When they offered to depart he entreated their stay, and was the next day still more unwilling to dismiss them than before. They were easily per-suaded to stop, and civility grew up in time to freedom and con-fidence.

The prince now saw all the domesticks[1] cheerful, and all the face of nature smiling round the place, and could not forbear to hope that he should find here what he was seeking; but when he was congratulating the master upon his possessions, he answered with a sigh, "My condition has indeed the appearance of happi-ness, but appearances are delusive. My prosperity puts my life in danger; the Bassa[2] of Egypt is my enemy, incensed only by my wealth and popularity. I have been hitherto protected against him by the princes of the country; but, as the favour of the great is uncertain, I know not how soon my defenders may be persuaded to share the plunder with the Bassa. I have sent my treasures into a distant country, and, upon the first alarm, am prepared to follow them. Then will my enemies riot in my mansion, and enjoy the gardens which I have planted."

---

1 One kept in the same house. *Dictionary*.
2 Bashaw: A title of honour and command among the Turks; the viceroy of a province; the general of an army. *Dictionary*.

They all joined in lamenting his danger, and deprecating his exile; and the princess was so much disturbed with the tumult of grief and indignation, that she retired to her apartment. They continued with their kind inviter a few days longer, and then went forward to find the hermit.

## CHAPTER XXI
### The happiness of solitude. The hermit's history

THEY came on the third day, by the direction of the peasants, to the hermit's cell: it was a cavern in the side of a mountain, over-shadowed with palm-trees; at such a distance from the cataract, that nothing more was heard than a gentle uniform murmur, such as composed the mind to pensive meditation, especially when it was assisted by the wind whistling among the branches. The first rude essay[1] of nature had been so much improved by human labour, that the cave contained several apartments, appropriated to different uses, and often afforded lodging to travellers, whom darkness or tempests happened to overtake.

The hermit sat on a bench at the door, to enjoy the coolness of the evening. On one side lay a book with pens and papers, on the other mechanical instruments of various kinds. As they approached him unregarded, the princess observed that he had not the countenance of a man that had found, or could teach, the way to happiness.

They saluted him with great respect, which he repaid like a man not unaccustomed to the forms of courts. "My children," said he, "if you have lost your way, you shall be willingly supplied with such conveniencies for the night as this cavern will afford. I have all that nature requires, and you will not expect delicacies in a hermit's cell."

They thanked him, and, entering, were pleased with the neatness and regularity of the place. The hermit set flesh and wine before them, though he fed only upon fruits and water. His discourse was cheerful without levity,[2] and pious without enthusiasm.[3] He soon gained the esteem of his guests, and the princess repented of her hasty censure.

---

1   Attempt; endeavour. *Dictionary*.
2   Trifling gaiety; want of seriousness. *Dictionary*.
3   A vain belief of private revelation; a vain confidence of divine favour or communication. *Dictionary*.

At last Imlac began thus: "I do not now wonder that your reputation is so far extended; we have heard at Cairo of your wisdom, and came hither to implore your direction for this young man and maiden in the *choice of life*."

"To him that lives well," answered the hermit, "every form of life is good; nor can I give any other rule for choice, than to remove from all apparent evil."

"He will remove most certainly from evil," said the prince, "who shall devote himself to that solitude which you have recommended by your example."

"I have indeed lived fifteen years in solitude," said the hermit, "but have no desire that my example should gain any imitators. In my youth I professed arms, and was raised by degrees to the highest military rank. I have traversed wide countries at the head of my troops, and seen many battles and sieges. At last, being disgusted by the preferments[1] of a younger officer, and feeling that my vigour was beginning to decay, I resolved to close my life in peace, having found the world full of snares, discord and misery. I had once escaped from the persuit of the enemy by the shelter of this cavern, and therefore chose it for my final residence. I employed artificers to form it into chambers, and stored it with all that I was likely to want.

"For some time after my retreat, I rejoiced like a tempest-beaten sailor at his entrance into the harbour, being delighted with the sudden change of the noise and hurry of war, to stillness and repose. When the pleasure of novelty went away, I employed my hours in examining the plants which grow in the valley, and the minerals which I collected from the rocks. But that enquiry is now grown tasteless and irksome. I have been for some time unsettled and distracted: my mind is disturbed with a thousand perplexities of doubt, and vanities of imagination, which hourly prevail upon me, because I have no opportunities of relaxation or diversion. I am sometimes ashamed to think that I could not secure myself from vice, but by retiring from the exercise of virtue, and begin to suspect that I was rather impelled by resentment, than led by devotion, into solitude. My fancy riots in scenes of folly, and I lament that I have lost so much, and have gained so little. In solitude, if I escape the example of bad men, I want likewise the counsel and conversation of the good. I have been long comparing the evils with the advantages of society, and

---

1 Advancement to a higher station. *Dictionary*.

resolve to return into the world to morrow. The life of a solitary man will be certainly miserable, but not certainly devout."

They heard his resolution with surprise, but, after a short pause, offered to conduct him to Cairo. He dug up a considerable treasure which he had hid among the rocks, and accompanied them to the city, on which, as he approached it, he gazed with rapture.

## CHAPTER XXII
### The happiness of a life led according to nature

RASSELAS went often to an assembly of learned men, who met at stated times to unbend their minds, and compare their opinions. Their manners were somewhat coarse, but their conversation was instructive, and their disputations acute, though sometimes too violent, and often continued till neither controvertist[1] remembered upon what question they began. Some faults were almost general among them: every one was desirous to dictate to the rest, and every one was pleased to hear the genius or knowledge of another depreciated.

In this assembly Rasselas was relating his interview with the hermit, and the wonder with which he heard him censure a course of life which he had so deliberately chosen, and so laudably followed. The sentiments of the hearers were various. Some were of opinion, that the folly of his choice had been justly punished by condemnation to perpetual perseverance. One of the youngest among them, with great vehemence, pronounced him an hypocrite.[2] Some talked of the right of society to the labour of individuals, and considered retirement as a desertion of duty. Others readily allowed, that there was a time when the claims of the publick were satisfied, and when a man might properly sequester himself, to review his life, and purify his heart.

One, who appeared more affected with the narrative than the rest, thought it likely, that the hermit would, in a few years, go back to his retreat, and, perhaps, if shame did not restrain, or death intercept him, return once more from his retreat into the world: "For the hope of happiness," said he, "is so strongly impressed, that the longest experience is not able to efface it. Of the present state, whatever it be, we feel, and are forced to

---

1 Disputant; a man versed or engaged in literary wars or disputations. *Dictionary*.

2 A dissembler in morality or religion. *Dictionary*.

confess, the misery, yet, when the same state is again at a distance, imagination paints it as desirable. But the time will surely come, when desire will be no longer our torment, and no man shall be wretched but by his own fault."

"This," said a philosopher, who had heard him with tokens of great impatience, "is the present condition of a wise man. The time is already come, when none are wretched but by their own fault. Nothing is more idle, than to enquire after happiness, which nature has kindly placed within our reach. The way to be happy is to live according to nature, in obedience to that universal and unalterable law with which every heart is originally impressed; which is not written on it by precept, but engraven by destiny, not instilled by education, but infused at our nativity. He that lives according to nature will suffer nothing from the delusions of hope, or importunities[1] of desire: he will receive and reject with equability of temper; and act or suffer as the reason of things shall alternately prescribe. Other men may amuse themselves with subtle definitions, or intricate raciocination.[2] Let them learn to be wise by easier means: let them observe the hind[3] of the forest, and the linnet[4] of the grove: let them consider the life of animals, whose motions are regulated by instinct; they obey their guide and are happy. Let us therefore, at length, cease to dispute, and learn to live; throw away the incumbrance of precepts, which they who utter them with so much pride and pomp do not understand, and carry with us this simple and intelligible maxim, That deviation from nature is deviation from happiness."

When he had spoken, he looked round him with a placid air, and enjoyed the consciousness of his own beneficence. "Sir," said the prince, with great modesty, "as I, like all the rest of mankind, am desirous of felicity, my closest attention has been fixed upon your discourse: I doubt not the truth of a position which a man so learned has so confidently advanced. Let me only know what it is to live according to nature."

"When I find young men so humble and so docile," said the philosopher, "I can deny them no information which my studies have enabled me to afford. To live according to nature, is to act always with due regard to the fitness arising from the relations

---

1  Incessant solicitations. *Dictionary.*
2  The act of reasoning; the act of deducing consequences from premises. *Dictionary.*
3  The she to a stag; the female of red deer. *Dictionary.*
4  A small singing bird. *Dictionary.*

and qualities of causes and effects; to concur with the great and unchangeable scheme of universal felicity; to co-operate with the general disposition and tendency of the present system of things."

The prince soon found that this was one of the sages whom he should understand less as he heard him longer. He therefore bowed and was silent, and the philosopher, supposing him satisfied, and the rest vanquished, rose up and departed with the air of a man that had co-operated with the present system.

## CHAPTER XXIII
### The prince and his sister divide between them the work of observation

RASSELAS returned home full of reflexions, doubtful how to direct his future steps. Of the way to happiness he found the learned and simple equally ignorant; but, as he was yet young, he flattered himself that he had time remaining for more experiments, and further enquiries. He communicated to Imlac his observations and his doubts, but was answered by him with new doubts, and remarks that gave him no comfort. He therefore discoursed more frequently and freely with his sister, who had yet the same hope with himself, and always assisted him to give some reason why, though he had been hitherto frustrated, he might succeed at last.

"We have hitherto," said she, "known but little of the world: we have never yet been either great or mean. In our own country, though we had royalty, we had no power, and in this we have not yet seen the private recesses of domestick peace. Imlac favours not our search, lest we should in time find him mistaken. We will divide the task between us: you shall try what is to be found in the splendour of courts, and I will range the shades of humbler life. Perhaps command and authority may be the supreme blessings, as they afford most opportunities of doing good: or, perhaps, what this world can give may be found in the modest habitations of middle fortune; too low for great designs, and too high for penury and distress."

## CHAPTER XXIV
### The prince examines the happiness of high stations

RASSELAS applauded the design, and appeared next day with a splendid retinue[1] at the court of the Bassa. He was soon distin-

---

1 A number attending upon a principal person; a train. *Dictionary*.

guished for his magnificence, and admitted, as a prince whose curiosity had brought him from distant countries, to an intimacy with the great officers, and frequent conversation with the Bassa himself.

He was at first inclined to believe, that the man must be pleased with his own condition, whom all approached with reverence, and heard with obedience, and who had the power to extend his edicts to a whole kingdom. "There can be no pleasure," said he, "equal to that of feeling at once the joy of thousands all made happy by wise administration. Yet, since, by the law of subordination,[1] this sublime delight can be in one nation but the lot of one, it is surely reasonable to think that there is some satisfaction more popular and accessible, and that millions can hardly be subjected to the will of a single man, only to fill his particular breast with incommunicable content."

These thoughts were often in his mind, and he found no solution of the difficulty. But as presents and civilities gained him more familiarity, he found that almost every man who stood high in employment hated all the rest, and was hated by them, and that their lives were a continual succession of plots and detections, stratagems and escapes, faction and treachery. Many of those, who surrounded the Bassa, were sent only to watch and report his conduct; every tongue was muttering censure, and every eye was searching for a fault.

At last the letters of revocation[2] arrived, the Bassa was carried in chains to Constantinople, and his name was mentioned no more.

"What are we now to think of the prerogatives of power," said Rasselas to his sister; "is it without any efficacy to good? or, is the subordinate degree only dangerous, and the supreme safe and glorious? Is the Sultan[3] the only happy man in his dominions? or is the Sultan himself subject to the torments of suspicion, and the dread of enemies?"

In a short time the second Bassa was deposed. The Sultan, that had advanced him, was murdered by the Janisaries,[4] and his successor had other views and different favourites.

---

1 The state of being inferior to another. *Dictionary*.
2 Act of recalling. *Dictionary*. In the seventeenth to eighteenth century especially the recall of a representative or ambassador from abroad; also in "letters of revocation." *OED*.
3 The Turkish emperour. *Dictionary*.
4 The guards of the Turkish king. *Dictionary*.

# CHAPTER XXV
## The princess persues her enquiry with more diligence
## than success

THE princess, in the mean time, insinuated herself into many families; for there are few doors, through which liberality, joined with good humour, cannot find its way. The daughters of many houses were airy and cheerful, but Nekayah had been too long accustomed to the conversation of Imlac and her brother to be much pleased with childish levity and prattle which had no meaning. She found their thoughts narrow, their wishes low, and their merriment often artificial. Their pleasures, poor as they were, could not be preserved pure, but were embittered by petty competitions and worthless emulation. They were always jealous of the beauty of each other; of a quality to which solitude can add nothing, and from which detraction can take nothing away. Many were in love with triflers like themselves, and many fancied that they were in love when in truth they were only idle. Their affection was seldom fixed on sense or virtue, and therefore seldom ended but in vexation. Their grief, however, like their joy, was transient; every thing floated in their mind unconnected with the past or future, so that one desire easily gave way to another, as a second stone cast into water effaces and confounds the circles of the first.

With these girls she played as with inoffensive animals, and found them proud of her countenance,[1] and weary of her company.

But her purpose was to examine more deeply, and her affability easily persuaded the hearts that were swelling with sorrow to discharge their secrets in her ear: and those whom hope flattered, or prosperity delighted, often courted her to partake their pleasures.

The princess and her brother commonly met in the evening in a private summer-house on the bank of the Nile, and related to each other the occurrences of the day. As they were sitting together, the princess cast her eyes upon the river that flowed before her. "Answer," said she, "great father of waters, thou that rollest thy floods through eighty nations, to the invocations of the daughter of thy native king. Tell me if thou waterest, through all

---

1 Patronage; appearance of favour. *Dictionary.*

thy course, a single habitation from which thou dost not hear the murmur of complaint?"

"You are then," said Rasselas, "not more successful in private houses than I have been in courts." "I have, since the last partition of our provinces," said the princess, "enabled myself to enter familiarly into many families, where there was the fairest show of prosperity and peace, and know not one house that is not haunted by some fury that destroys its quiet.

"I did not seek ease among the poor, because I concluded that there it could not be found. But I saw many poor whom I had supposed to live in affluence. Poverty has, in large cities, very different appearances: it is often concealed in splendour, and often in extravagance. It is the care of a very great part of mankind to conceal their indigence from the rest: they support themselves by temporary expedients, and every day is lost in contriving for the morrow.

"This, however, was an evil, which, though frequent, I saw with less pain, because I could relieve it. Yet some have refused my bounties; more offended with my quickness to detect their wants, than pleased with my readiness to succour them: and others, whose exigencies compelled them to admit my kindness, have never been able to forgive their benefactress. Many however, have been sincerely grateful without the ostentation of gratitude, or the hope of other favours."

## END OF THE FIRST VOLUME

# CHAPTER XXVI

## The princess continues her remarks upon private life

NEKAYAH perceiving her brother's attention fixed, proceeded in her narrative.

"In families, where there is or is not poverty, there is commonly discord: if a kingdom be, as Imlac tells us, a great family, a family likewise is a little kingdom, torn with factions and exposed to revolutions. An unpractised observer expects the love of parents and children to be constant and equal; but this kindness seldom continues beyond the years of infancy: in a short time the children become rivals to their parents. Benefits are allayed[1] by reproaches, and gratitude debased by envy.

"Parents and children seldom act in concert: each child endeavours to appropriate the esteem or fondness of the parents, and the parents, with yet less temptation, betray each other to their children; thus some place their confidence in the father, and some in the mother, and, by degrees, the house is filled with artifices and feuds.

"The opinions of children and parents, of the young and the old, are naturally opposite, by the contrary effects of hope and despondence, of expectation and experience, without crime or folly on either side. The colours of life in youth and age appear different, as the face of nature in spring and winter. And how can children credit the assertions of parents, which their own eyes show them to be false?

"Few parents act in such a manner as much to enforce their maxims by the credit of their lives. The old man trusts wholly to slow contrivance and gradual progression: the youth expects to force his way by genius, vigour, and precipitance.[2] The old man pays regard to riches, and the youth reverences virtue. The old man deifies prudence: the youth commits himself to magnanimity and chance. The young man, who intends no ill, believes that none is intended, and therefore acts with openness and candour: but his father, having suffered the injuries of fraud, is impelled to suspect, and too often allured to practice it. Age looks with anger on the temerity of youth, and youth with contempt on the scrupulosity of age. Thus parents and children, for the greatest

---

1   To join any thing to another, so as to abate its predominant qualities. *Dictionary*.

2   Rash haste; headlong hurry. *Dictionary*.

part, live on to love less and less: and, if those whom nature has thus closely united are the torments of each other, where shall we look for tenderness and consolation?"

"Surely," said the prince, "you must have been unfortunate in your choice of acquaintance: I am unwilling to believe, that the most tender of all relations is thus impeded in its effects by natural necessity."

"Domestick discord," answered she, "is not inevitably and fatally necessary; but yet is not easily avoided. We seldom see that a whole family is virtuous: the good and evil cannot well agree; and the evil can yet less agree with one another: even the virtuous fall sometimes to variance, when their virtues are of different kinds, and tending to extremes. In general, those parents have most reverence who most deserve it: for he that lives well cannot be despised.

"Many other evils infest private life. Some are the slaves of servants whom they have trusted with their affairs. Some are kept in continual anxiety to the caprice of rich relations, whom they cannot please, and dare not offend. Some husbands are imperious, and some wives perverse: and, as it is always more easy to do evil than good, though the wisdom or virtue of one can very rarely make many happy, the folly or vice of one may often make many miserable."

"If such be the general effect of marriage," said the prince, "I shall, for the future, think it dangerous to connect my interest with that of another, lest I should be unhappy by my partner's fault."

"I have met," said the princess, "with many who live single for that reason; but I never found that their prudence ought to raise envy. They dream away their time without friendship, without fondness, and are driven to rid themselves of the day, for which they have no use, by childish amusements, or vicious delights. They act as beings under the constant sense of some known inferiority, that fills their minds with rancour, and their tongues with censure. They are peevish at home, and malevolent abroad; and, as the out-laws of human nature, make it their business and their pleasure to disturb that society which debars them from its privileges. To live without feeling or exciting sympathy, to be fortunate without adding to the felicity of others, or afflicted without tasting the balm of pity, is a state more gloomy than solitude: it is not retreat but exclusion from mankind. Marriage has many pains, but celibacy has no pleasures."

"What then is to be done?" said Rasselas; "the more we

enquire, the less we can resolve. Surely he is most likely to please himself that has no other inclination to regard."

## CHAPTER XXVII
### Disquisition upon greatness

THE conversation had a short pause. The prince, having considered his sister's observations, told her, that she had surveyed life with prejudice, and supposed misery where she did not find it. "Your narrative," says he, "throws yet a darker gloom upon the prospects of futurity: the predictions of Imlac were but faint sketches of the evils painted by Nekayah. I have been lately convinced that quiet is not the daughter of grandeur, or of power: that her presence is not to be bought by wealth, nor enforced by conquest. It is evident, that as any man acts in a wider compass, he must be more exposed to opposition from enmity or miscarriage from chance; whoever has many to please or to govern, must use the ministry of many agents, some of whom will be wicked, and some ignorant; by some he will be misled, and by others betrayed. If he gratifies one he will offend another: those that are not favoured will think themselves injured; and, since favours can be conferred but upon few, the greater number will be always discontented."

"The discontent," said the princess, "which is thus unreasonable, I hope that I shall always have spirit to despise, and you, power to repress."

"Discontent," answered Rasselas, "will not always be without reason under the most just or vigilant administration of publick affairs. None, however attentive, can always discover that merit which indigence or faction may happen to obscure; and none, however powerful, can always reward it. Yet, he that sees inferiour desert advanced above him, will naturally impute that preference to partiality or caprice; and, indeed, it can scarcely be hoped that any man, however magnanimous by nature, or exalted by condition, will be able to persist for ever in fixed and inexorable justice of distribution: he will sometimes indulge his own affections, and sometimes those of his favourites; he will permit some to please him who can never serve him; he will discover in those whom he loves qualities which in reality they do not possess; and to those, from whom he receives pleasure, he will in his turn endeavour to give it. Thus will recommendations sometimes prevail which were purchased by money, or by the more destructive bribery of flattery and servility.

"He that has much to do will do something wrong, and of that wrong must suffer the consequences; and, if it were possible that he should always act rightly, yet when such numbers are to judge of his conduct the bad will censure and obstruct him by malevolence, and the good sometimes by mistake.

"The highest stations cannot therefore hope to be the abodes of happiness, which I would willingly believe to have fled from thrones and palaces to seats of humble privacy and placid obscurity. For what can hinder the satisfaction, or intercept the expectations, of him whose abilities are adequate to his employments, who sees with his own eyes the whole circuit of his influence, who chooses by his own knowledge all whom he trusts, and whom none are tempted to deceive by hope or fear? Surely he has nothing to do but to love and to be loved, to be virtuous and to be happy."

"Whether perfect happiness would be procured by perfect goodness," said Nekayah, "this world will never afford an opportunity of deciding. But this, at least, may be maintained, that we do not always find visible happiness in proportion to visible virtue. All natural and almost all political evils, are incident[1] alike to the bad and good: they are confounded in the misery of a famine, and not much distinguished in the fury of a faction; they sink together in a tempest, and are driven together from their country by invaders. All that virtue can afford is quietness of conscience, a steady prospect of a happier state; this may enable us to endure calamity with patience; but remember that patience must suppose pain."

## CHAPTER XXVIII
Rasselas and Nekayah continue their conversation

"DEAR princess," said Rasselas, "you fall into the common errours of exaggeratory declamation, by producing, in a familiar disquisition, examples of national calamities, and scenes of extensive misery, which are found in books rather than in the world, and which, as they are horrid, are ordained to be rare. Let us not imagine evils which we do not feel, nor injure life by misrepresentations. I cannot bear that querelous[2] eloquence which threatens every city with a siege like that of Jerusalem, that makes

---

1  Happening; apt to happen. *Dictionary*.
2  *Quarrelous*: Petulant; easily provoked to enmity; quarrelsome. *Dictionary*.

famine attend on every flight of locusts, and suspends pestilence on the wing of every blast that issues from the south.

"On necessary and inevitable evils, which overwhelm kingdoms at once, all disputation is vain: when they happen they must be endured. But it is evident, that these bursts of universal distress are more dreaded than felt: thousands and ten thousands flourish in youth, and wither in age, without the knowledge of any other than domestick evils, and share the same pleasures and vexations whether their kings are mild or cruel, whether the armies of their country persue their enemies, or retreat before them. While courts are disturbed with intestine competitions, and ambassadours are negotiating in foreign countries, the smith still plies his anvil, and the husbandman drives his plow forward; the necessaries of life are required and obtained, and the successive business of the seasons continues to make its wonted revolutions.

"Let us cease to consider what, perhaps, may never happen, and what, when it shall happen, will laugh at human speculation. We will not endeavour to modify the motions of the elements, or to fix the destiny of kingdoms. It is our business to consider what beings like us may perform; each labouring for his own happiness, by promoting within his circle, however narrow, the happiness of others.

"Marriage is evidently the dictate of nature; men and women were made to be companions of each other, and therefore I cannot be persuaded but that marriage is one of the means of happiness."

"I know not," said the princess, "whether marriage be more than one of the innumerable modes of human misery. When I see and reckon the various forms of connubial infelicity, the unexpected causes of lasting discord, the diversities of temper, the oppositions of opinion, the rude collisions of contrary desire where both are urged by violent impulses, the obstinate contests of disagreeing virtues, where both are supported by consciousness of good intention, I am sometimes disposed to think with the severer casuists[1] of most nations, that marriage is rather permitted than approved, and that none, but by the instigation of a passion too much indulged, entangle themselves with indissoluble compacts."

"You seem to forget," replied Rasselas "that you have, even now, represented celibacy as less happy than marriage. Both con-

---

1   One that studies and settles cases of conscience. *Dictionary.*

ditions may be bad, but they cannot both be worst. Thus it happens when wrong opinions are entertained, that they mutually destroy each other, and leave the mind open to truth."

"I did not expect," answered the princess, "to hear that imputed to falsehood which is the consequence only of frailty. To the mind, as to the eye, it is difficult to compare with exactness objects vast in their extent, and various in their parts. Where we see or conceive the whole at once we readily note the discriminations and decide the preference: but of two systems, of which neither can be surveyed by any human being in its full compass of magnitude and multiplicity of complication, where is the wonder, that judging of the whole by parts, I am alternately affected by one and the other as either presses on my memory or fancy? We differ from ourselves just as we differ from each other, when we see only part of the question, as in the multifarious relations of politicks and morality: but when we perceive the whole at once, as in numerical computations, all agree in one judgment, and none ever varies his opinion."

"Let us not add," said the prince, "to the other evils of life, the bitterness of controversy, nor endeavour to vie with each other in subtilties of argument. We are employed in a search, of which both are equally to enjoy the success, or suffer by the miscarriage. It is therefore fit that we assist each other. You surely conclude too hastily from the infelicity of marriage against its institution; will not the misery of life prove equally that life cannot be the gift of heaven? The world must be peopled by marriage, or peopled without it."

"How the world is to be peopled," returned Nekayah, "is not my care, and needs not be yours. I see no danger that the present generation should omit to leave successors behind them: we are not now enquiring for the world, but for ourselves."

## CHAPTER XXIX
### The debate on marriage continued

"THE good of the whole," says Rasselas, "is the same with the good of all its parts. If marriage be best for mankind it must be evidently best for individuals, or a permanent and necessary duty must be the cause of evil, and some must be inevitably sacrificed to the convenience of others. In the estimate which you have made of the two states, it appears that the incommodities of a single life are, in a great measure, necessary and certain, but those of the conjugal state accidental and avoidable.

"I cannot forbear to flatter myself that prudence and benevolence will make marriage happy. The general folly of mankind is the cause of general complaint. What can be expected but disappointment and repentance from a choice made in the immaturity of youth, in the ardour of desire, without judgment, without foresight, without enquiry after conformity of opinions, similarity of manners, rectitude of judgment, or purity of sentiment.

"Such is the common process of marriage. A youth and maiden meeting by chance, or brought together by artifice, exchange glances, reciprocate civilities, go home, and dream of one another. Having little to divert attention, or diversify thought, they find themselves uneasy when they are apart, and therefore conclude that they shall be happy together. They marry, and discover what nothing but voluntary blindness had before concealed; they wear out life in altercations, and charge nature with cruelty.

"From those early marriages proceeds likewise the rivalry of parents and children: the son is eager to enjoy the world before the father is willing to forsake it, and there is hardly room at once for two generations. The daughter begins to bloom before the mother can be content to fade, and neither can forbear to wish for the absence of the other.

"Surely all these evils may be avoided by that deliberation and delay which prudence prescribes to irrevocable choice. In the variety and jollity of youthful pleasures life may be well enough supported without the help of a partner. Longer time will increase experience, and wider views will allow better opportunities of enquiry and selection: one advantage, at least, will be certain; the parents will be visibly older than their children."

"What reason cannot collect," said Nekayah, "and what experiment has not yet taught, can be known only from the report of others. I have been told that late marriages are not eminently happy. This is a question too important to be neglected, and I have often proposed it to those, whose accuracy of remark, and comprehensiveness of knowledge, made their suffrages[1] worthy of regard. They have generally determined, that it is dangerous for a man and woman to suspend their fate upon each other, at a time when opinions are fixed, and habits are established; when friendships have been contracted on both sides, when life has been planned into method, and the mind has long enjoyed the contemplation of its own prospects.

---

1 Vote; voice given in a controverted point. *Dictionary*.

"It is scarcely possible that two travelling through the world under the conduct of chance, should have been both directed to the same path, and it will not often happen that either will quit the track which custom has made pleasing. When the desultory levity of youth has settled into regularity, it is soon succeeded by pride ashamed to yield, or obstinacy delighting to contend. And even though mutual esteem produces mutual desire to please, time itself, as it modifies unchangeably the external mien, determines likewise the direction of the passions, and gives an inflexible rigidity to the manners. Long customs are not easily broken: he that attempts to change the course of his own life, very often labours in vain; and how shall we do that for others which we are seldom able to do for ourselves?"

"But surely," interposed the prince, "you suppose the chief motive of choice forgotten or neglected. Whenever I shall seek a wife, it shall be my first question, whether she be willing to be led by reason?"

"Thus it is," said Nekayah, "that philosophers are deceived. There are a thousand familiar disputes which reason never can decide; questions that elude investigation, and make logick ridiculous; cases where something must be done, and where little can be said. Consider the state of mankind, and enquire how few can be supposed to act upon any occasions, whether small or great, with all the reasons of action present to their minds. Wretched would be the pair above all names of wretchedness, who should be doomed to adjust by reason every morning all the minute detail of a domestick day.

"Those who marry at an advanced age, will probably escape the encroachments of their children; but, in diminution of this advantage, they will be likely to leave them, ignorant and helpless, to a guardian's mercy: or, if that should not happen, they must at least go out of the world before they see those whom they love best either wise or great.

"From their children, if they have less to fear, they have less also to hope, and they lose, without equivalent, the joys of early love, and the convenience of uniting with manners pliant, and minds susceptible of new impressions, which might wear away their dissimilitudes by long cohabitation, as soft bodies by continual attention, conform their surfaces to each other.

"I believe it will be found that those who marry late are best pleased with their children, and those who marry early with their partners."

"The union of these two affections," said Rasselas, "would

produce all that could be wished. Perhaps there is a time when marriage might unite them, a time neither too early for the father, nor too late for the husband."

"Every hour," answered the princess, "confirms my prejudice in favour of the position so often uttered by the mouth of Imlac, 'That nature sets her gifts on the right hand and on the left.' Those conditions, which flatter hope and attract desire, are so constituted, that, as we approach one, we recede from another. There are goods so opposed that we cannot seize both, but by too much prudence, may pass between them at too great a distance to reach either. This is often the fate of long consideration; he does nothing who endeavours to do more than is allowed to humanity. Flatter not yourself with contrarieties of pleasure. Of the blessings set before you make your choice, and be content. No man can taste the fruits of autumn while he is delighting his scent with the flowers of the spring: no man can, at the same time, fill his cup from the source and from the mouth of the Nile."

## CHAPTER XXX
### Imlac enters, and changes the conversation

HERE Imlac entered, and interrupted them. "Imlac," said Rasselas, "I have been taking from the princess the dismal history of private life, and am almost discouraged from further search."

"It seems to me," said Imlac, "that while you are making the choice of life, you neglect to live. You wander about a single city, which, however large and diversified, can now afford few novelties, and forget that you are in a country, famous among the earliest monarchies for the power and wisdom of its inhabitants; a country where the sciences first dawned that illuminate the world, and beyond which the arts cannot be traced of civil society or domestick life.

"The old Egyptians have left behind them monuments of industry and power before which all European magnificence is confessed to fade away. The ruins of their architecture are the schools of modern builders, and from the wonders which time has spared we may conjecture, though uncertainly, what it has destroyed."

"My curiosity," said Rasselas, "does not very strongly lead me to survey piles of stone, or mounds of earth; my business is with man. I came hither not to measure fragments of temples, or trace choaked aqueducts, but to look upon the various scenes of the present world."

"The things that are now before us," said the princess, "require attention, and deserve it. What have I to do with the heroes or the monuments of ancient times? with times which never can return, and heroes, whose form of life was different from all that the present condition of mankind requires or allows."

"To know any thing," returned the poet, "we must know its effects; to see men we must see their works, that we may learn what reason has dictated, or passion has incited, and find what are the most powerful motives of action. To judge rightly of the present we must oppose it to the past; for all judgment is comparative, and of the future nothing can be known. The truth is, that no mind is much employed upon the present: recollection and anticipation fill up almost all our moments. Our passions are joy and grief, love and hatred, hope and fear. Of joy and grief the past is the object, and the future of hope and fear; even love and hatred respect the past, for the cause must have been before the effect.

"The present state of things is the consequence of the former, and it is natural to inquire what were the sources of the good that we enjoy, or of the evil that we suffer. If we act only for ourselves, to neglect the study of history is not prudent: if we are entrusted with the care of others, it is not just. Ignorance, when it is voluntary, is criminal; and he may properly be charged with evil who refused to learn how he might prevent it.

"There is no part of history so generally useful as that which relates the progress of the human mind, the gradual improvement of reason, the successive advances of science, the vicissitudes of learning and ignorance which are the light and darkness of thinking beings, the extinction and resuscitation of arts, and the revolutions of the intellectual world. If accounts of battles and invasions are peculiarly the business of princes, the useful or elegant arts are not to be neglected; those who have kingdoms to govern, have understandings to cultivate.

"Example is always more efficacious than precept. A soldier is formed in war, and a painter must copy pictures. In this, contemplative life has the advantage: great actions are seldom seen, but the labours of art are always at hand for those who desire to know what art has been able to perform.

"When the eye or the imagination is struck with any uncommon work the next transition of an active mind is to the means by which it was performed. Here begins the true use of such contemplation; we enlarge our comprehension by new ideas, and perhaps recover some art lost to mankind, or learn what is less perfectly known in our own country. At least we compare our own with former times, and either rejoice at our improvements, or, what is the first motion towards good, discover our defects."

"I am willing," said the prince, "to see all that can deserve my search." "And I," said the princess, "shall rejoice to learn something of the manners of antiquity."

"The most pompous monument of Egyptian greatness, and one of the most bulky works of manual industry," said Imlac, "are the pyramids; fabricks raised before the time of history, and of which the earliest narratives afford us only uncertain traditions. Of these the greatest is still standing very little injured by time."

"Let us visit them to morrow," said Nekayah. "I have often heard of the Pyramids, and shall not rest, till I have seen them within and without with my own eyes."

## CHAPTER XXXI
### They visit the Pyramids

THE resolution being thus taken, they set out the next day. They laid tents upon their camels, being resolved to stay among the pyramids till their curiosity was finally satisfied. They travelled gently, turned aside to every thing remarkable, stopped from time to time and conversed with the inhabitants, and observed the various appearances of towns ruined and inhabited, of wild and cultivated nature.

When they came to the great pyramid they were astonished at the extent of the base, and the height of the top. Imlac explained to them the principles upon which the pyramidal form was chosen for a fabrick intended to co-extend its duration with that of the world: he showed that its gradual diminution gave it such stability, as defeated all the common attacks of the elements, and could scarcely be overthrown by earthquakes themselves, the least resistible of natural violence. A concussion that should shatter the pyramid would threaten the dissolution of the continent.

They measured all its dimensions, and pitched their tents at its foot. Next day they prepared to enter its interiour apartments, and having hired the common guides climbed up to the first passage, when the favourite of the princess, looking into the cavity, stepped back and trembled. "Pekuah," said the princess, "of what art thou afraid?" "Of the narrow entrance," answered the lady, "and of the dreadful gloom. I dare not enter a place which must surely be inhabited by unquiet souls. The original possessors of these dreadful vaults will start up before us, and, perhaps, shut us in for ever." She spoke, and threw her arms round the neck of her mistress.

"If all your fear be of apparitions," said the prince, "I will promise you safety: there is no danger from the dead; he that is once buried will be seen no more."

"That the dead are seen no more," said Imlac, "I will not undertake to maintain against the concurrent and unvaried testimony of all ages, and of all nations. There is no people, rude or learned, among whom apparitions of the dead are not related and believed. This opinion, which, perhaps, prevails as far as human nature is diffused, could become universal only by its truth: those, that never heard of one another, would not have agreed in a tale which nothing but experience can make credible. That it is doubted by single cavillers[1] can very little weaken the general evidence, and some who deny it with their tongues confess it by their fears.

"Yet I do not mean to add new terrours to those which have already seized upon Pekuah. There can be no reason why specters should haunt the pyramid more than other places, or why they should have power or will to hurt innocence and purity. Our entrance is no violation of their priviledges; we can take nothing from them, how then can we offend them?"

"My dear Pekuah," said the princess, "I will always go before you, and Imlac shall follow you. Remember that you are the companion of the princess of Abissinia."

"If the princess is pleased that her servant should die," returned the lady, "let her command some death less dreadful than enclosure in this horrid cavern. You know I dare not disobey you: I must go if you command me; but, if I once enter, I never shall come back."

The princess saw that her fear was too strong for expostulation or reproof, and embracing her, told her that she should stay in the tent till their return. Pekuah was yet not satisfied, but entreated the princess not to persue so dreadful a purpose as that of entering the recesses of the pyramid. "Though I cannot teach courage," said Nekayah, "I must not learn cowardice; nor leave at last undone what I came hither only to do."

---

1   A man fond of making objections; an unfair adversary; a captious disputant. *Dictionary.*

# CHAPTER XXXII
## They enter the Pyramid

PEKUAH descended to the tents, and the rest entered the pyramid: they passed through the galleries, surveyed the vaults of marble, and examined the chest in which the body of the founder is supposed to have been reposited. They then sat down in one of the most spacious chambers to rest a while before they attempted to return.

"We have now," said Imlac, "gratified our minds with an exact view of the greatest work of man, except the wall of China.

"Of the wall it is very easy to assign the motives. It secured a wealthy and timorous nation from the incursions of Barbarians, whose unskillfulness in arts made it easier for them to supply their wants by rapine than by industry, and who from time to time poured in upon the habitations of peaceful commerce, as vultures descend upon domestick fowl. Their celerity[1] and fierceness made the wall necessary, and their ignorance made it efficacious.

"But for the pyramids no reason has ever been given adequate to the cost and labour of the work. The narrowness of the chambers proves that it could afford no retreat from enemies, and treasures might have been reposited at far less expence with equal security. It seems to have been erected only in compliance with that hunger of imagination which preys incessantly upon life, and must be always appeased by some employment. Those who have already all that they can enjoy, must enlarge their desires. He that has built for use, till use is supplied, must begin to build for vanity, and extend his plan to the utmost power of human performance, that he may not be soon reduced to form another wish.

"I consider this mighty structure as a monument of the insufficiency of human enjoyments. A king, whose power is unlimited, and whose treasures surmount all real and imaginary wants, is compelled to solace, by the erection of a pyramid, the satiety of dominion and tastelesness of pleasures, and to amuse the tediousness of declining life, by seeing thousands labouring without end, and one stone, for no purpose, laid upon another. Whoever thou art, that, not content with a moderate condition, imaginest happiness in royal magnificence, and dreamest that

---

1  Swiftness; speed; velocity. *Dictionary.*

command or riches can feed the appetite of novelty with perpetual gratifications, survey the pyramids, and confess thy folly!"

## CHAPTER XXXIII
### The princess meets with an unexpected misfortune

THEY rose up, and returned through the cavity at which they had entered, and the princess prepared for her favourite a long narrative of dark labyrinths, and costly rooms, and of the different impressions which the varieties of the way had made upon her. But, when they came to their train, they found every one silent and dejected: the men discovered shame and fear in their countenances, and the women were weeping in the tents.

What had happened they did not try to conjecture, but immediately enquired. "You had scarcely entered into the pyramid," said one of the attendants, "when a troop of Arabs rushed upon us: we were too few to resist them, and too slow to escape. They were about to search the tents, set us on our camels, and drive us along before them, when the approach of some Turkish horsemen put them to flight; but they seized the lady Pekuah with her two maids, and carried them away: the Turks are now persuing them by our instigation, but I fear they will not be able to overtake them."

The princess was overpowered with surprise and grief. Rasselas, in the first heat of his resentment, ordered his servants to follow him, and prepared to persue the robbers with his saber in his hand. "Sir," said Imlac, "what can you hope from violence or valour? the Arabs are mounted on horses trained to battle and retreat; we have only beasts of burden. By leaving our present station we may lose the princess, but cannot hope to regain Pekuah."

In a short time the Turks returned, having not been able to reach the enemy. The princess burst out into new lamentations, and Rasselas could scarcely forbear to reproach them with cowardice; but Imlac was of opinion, that the escape of the Arabs was no addition to their misfortune, for, perhaps, they would have killed their captives rather than have resigned them.

## CHAPTER XXIV
### They return to Cairo without Pekuah

THERE was nothing to be hoped from longer stay. They returned to Cairo repenting of their curiosity, censuring the negligence of the government, lamenting their own rashness which had neglected to procure a guard, imagining many expedients by which the loss of Pekuah might have been prevented, and resolving to do something for her recovery, though none could find any thing proper to be done.

Nekayah retired to her chamber, where her women attempted to comfort her, by telling her that all had their troubles, and that lady Pekuah had enjoyed much happiness in the world for a long time, and might reasonably expect a change of fortune. They hoped that some good would befal her wheresoever she was, and that their mistress would find another friend who might supply her place.

The princess made them no answer, and they continued the form of condolence, not much grieved in their hearts that the favourite was lost.

Next day the prince presented to the Bassa a memorial[1] of the wrong which he had suffered, and a petition for redress. The Bassa threatened to punish the robbers, but did not attempt to catch them, nor, indeed, could any account or description be given by which he might direct the persuit.

It soon appeared that nothing would be done by authority. Governors, being accustomed to hear of more crimes than they can punish, and more wrongs than they can redress, set themselves at ease by indiscriminate negligence, and presently forget the request when they lose sight of the petitioner.

Imlac then endeavoured to gain some intelligence by private agents. He found many who pretended to an exact knowledge of all the haunts of the Arabs, and to regular correspondence with their chiefs, and who readily undertook the recovery of Pekuah. Of these, some were furnished with money for their journey, and came back no more; some were liberally paid for accounts which a few days discovered to be false. But the princess would not suffer any means, however improbable, to be left untried. While she was doing something she kept her hope alive. As one expedient failed, another was suggested; when one messenger returned unsuccessful, another was dispatched to a different quarter.

Two months had now passed, and of Pekuah nothing had been heard; the hopes which they had endeavoured to raise in each

---

1   A statement of facts forming the basis of or expressed in the form of a
    petition or remonstrance to a person in authority, a government, etc.
    *OED.*

other grew more languid, and the princess, when she saw nothing more to be tried, sunk down inconsolable in hopeless dejection. A thousand times she reproached herself with the easy compliance by which she permitted her favourite to stay behind her. "Had not my fondness," said she, "lessened my authority, Pekuah had not dared to talk of her terrours. She ought to have feared me more than specters. A severe look would have overpowered her; a peremptory command would have compelled obedience. Why did foolish indulgence prevail upon me? Why did I not speak and refuse to hear?"

"Great princess," said Imlac, "do not reproach yourself for your virtue, or consider that as blameable by which evil has accidentally been caused. Your tenderness for the timidity of Pekuah was generous and kind. When we act according to our duty, we commit the event to him by whose laws our actions are governed, and who will suffer none to be finally punished for obedience. When, in prospect of some good, whether natural or moral, we break the rules prescribed us, we withdraw from the direction of superiour wisdom, and take all consequences upon ourselves. Man cannot so far know the connexion of causes and events, as that he may venture to do wrong in order to do right. When we persue our end by lawful means, we may always console our miscarriage by the hope of future recompense. When we consult only our own policy, and attempt to find a nearer way to good, by overleaping the settled boundaries of right and wrong, we cannot be happy even by success, because we cannot escape the consciousness of our fault; but, if we miscarry, the disappointment is irremediably embittered. How comfortless is the sorrow of him, who feels at once the pangs of guilt, and the vexation of calamity which guilt has brought upon him?

"Consider, princess, what would have been your condition, if the lady Pekuah had entreated to accompany you, and, being compelled to stay in the tents, had been carried away; or how would you have born the thought, if you had forced her into the pyramid, and she died before you in agonies of terrour."

"Had either happened," said Nekayah, "I could not have endured life till now: I should have been tortured to madness by the remembrance of such cruelty, or must have pined away in abhorrence of myself."

"This at least," said Imlac, "is the present reward of virtuous conduct, that no unlucky consequence can oblige us to repent it."

# CHAPTER XXXV
## The princess languishes for want of Pekuah

NEKAYAH, being thus reconciled to herself, found that no evil is insupportable but that which is accompanied with consciousness of wrong. She was from that time, delivered from the violence of tempestuous sorrow, and sunk into silent pensiveness and gloomy tranquility. She sat from morning to evening recollecting all that had been done or said by her Pekuah, treasured up with care every trifle on which Pekuah had set an accidental value, and which might recal to mind any little incident or careless conversation. The sentiments of her, whom she now expected to see no more, were treasured in her memory as rules of life, and she deliberated to no other end than to conjecture on any occasion what would have been the opinion of Pekuah.

The women, by whom she was attended, knew nothing of her real condition,[1] and therefore she could not talk to them but with caution and reserve. She began to remit her curiosity, having no great care to collect notions which she had no convenience[2] of uttering.[3] Rasselas endeavoured first to comfort and afterwards to divert her; he hired musicians, to whom she seemed to listen, but did not hear them, and procured masters to instruct her in various arts, whose lectures, when they visited her again, were again to be repeated. She had lost her taste of pleasure and her ambition of excellence. And her mind, though forced into short excursions,[4] always recurred to the image of her friend.

Imlac was every morning earnestly enjoined to renew his enquiries, and was asked every night whether he had yet heard of Pekuah, till not being able to return the princess the answer that she desired, he was less and less willing to come into her presence. She observed his backwardness, and commanded him to attend her. "You are not," said she, "to confound impatience with resentment, or to suppose that I charge you with negligence, because I repine at your unsuccessfulness. I do not much wonder at your absence; I know that the unhappy are never pleasing, and that all naturally avoid the contagion of misery. To hear complaints is wearisome alike to the wretched and the happy; for who

---

1 Rank. *Dictionary.*
2 Fitness of time or place. *Dictionary.*
3 Without Pekuah to talk to, Nekayah is less interested in the choice-of-life inquiry.
4 Digression; ramble from a subject. *Dictionary.*

would cloud by adventitious grief the short gleams of gaiety which life allows us? or who, that is struggling under his own evils, will add to them the miseries of another?

"The time is at hand, when none shall be disturbed any longer by the sighs of Nekayah: my search after happiness is now at an end. I am resolved to retire from the world with all its flatteries and deceits, and will hide myself in solitude, without any other care than to compose my thoughts, and regulate my hours by a constant succession of innocent occupations, till, with a mind purified from all earthly desires, I shall enter into that state, to which all are hastening, and in which I hope again to enjoy the friendship of Pekuah."

"Do not entangle your mind," said Imlac, "by irrevocable determinations, nor increase the burthen of life by a voluntary accumulation of misery: the weariness of retirement will continue or increase when the loss of Pekuah is forgotten. That you have been deprived of one pleasure is no very good reason for rejection of the rest."

"Since Pekuah was taken from me," said the princess, "I have no pleasure to reject or to retain. She that has no one to love or trust has little to hope. She wants the radical[1] principle of happiness. We may, perhaps, allow that what satisfaction this world can afford, must arise from the conjunction of wealth, knowledge and goodness: wealth is nothing but as it is bestowed, and knowledge nothing but as it is communicated: they must therefore be imparted to others, and to whom could I now delight to impart them? Goodness affords the only comfort which can be enjoyed without a partner, and goodness may be practiced in retirement."

"How far solitude may admit goodness, or advance it, I shall not," replied Imlac, "dispute at present. Remember the confession of the pious hermit. You will wish to return into the world, when the image of your companion has left your thoughts." "That time," said Nekayah, "will never come. The generous frankness, the modest obsequiousness,[2] and the faithful secrecy of my dear Pekuah, will always be more missed, as I shall live longer to see vice and folly."

"The state of a mind oppressed with a sudden calamity," said Imlac, "is like that of the fabulous inhabitants of the new created

---

1 Primitive; original. *Dictionary*. Forming the root, basis, or foundation; original, primary. *OED*.
2 Obedience; compliance. *Dictionary*.

earth, who, when the first night came upon them, supposed that day would never return. When the clouds of sorrow gather over us, we see nothing beyond them, nor can imagine how they will be dispelled: yet a new day succeeded to the night, and sorrow is never long without a dawn of ease. But they who restrain themselves from receiving comfort, do as the savages would have done, had they put out their eyes when it was dark. Our minds, like our bodies, are in continual flux; something is hourly lost, and something acquired. To lose much at once is inconvenient to either, but while the vital powers remain uninjured, nature will find the means of reparation. Distance has the same effect on the mind as on the eye, and while we glide along the stream of time, whatever we leave behind us is always lessening, and that which we approach increasing in magnitude. Do not suffer life to stagnate; it will grow muddy for want of motion: commit yourself again to the current of the world; Pekuah will vanish by degrees; you will meet in your way some other favourite, or learn to diffuse[1] yourself in general conversation."

"At least," said the prince, "do not despair before all remedies have been tried: the enquiry after the unfortunate lady is still continued, and shall be carried on with yet greater diligence, on condition that you will promise to wait a year for the event, without any unalterable resolution."

Nekayah thought this a reasonable demand, and made the promise to her brother, who had been advised by Imlac to require it. Imlac had, indeed, no great hope of regaining Pekuah, but he supposed, that if he could secure the interval of a year, the princess would be then in no danger of a cloister.[2]

## CHAPTER XXXVI
Pekuah is still remembered. The progress of sorrow

NEKAYAH, seeing that nothing was omitted for the recovery of her favourite, and having, by her promise, set her intention of retirement at a distance, began imperceptibly to return to common cares and common pleasures. She rejoiced without her own consent at the suspension of her sorrows, and sometimes caught herself with indignation in the act of turning away her

---

1  To spread; to scatter; to disperse. *Dictionary*.
2  A religious retirement; a monastery; a nunnery. *Dictionary*.

mind from the remembrance of her, whom yet she resolved never to forget.

She then appointed a certain hour of the day for meditation on the merits and fondness of Pekuah, and for some weeks retired constantly at the time fixed, and returned with her eyes swollen and her countenance clouded. By degrees she grew less scrupulous, and suffered any important and pressing avocation[1] to delay the tribute of daily tears. She then yielded to less occasions; sometimes forgot what she was indeed afraid to remember, and, at last, wholly released herself from the duty of periodical affliction.

Her real love of Pekuah was yet not diminished. A thousand occurrences brought her back to memory, and a thousand wants, which nothing but the confidence of friendship can supply, made her frequently regretted. She, therefore, solicited Imlac never to desist from enquiry, and to leave no art of intelligence untried, that, at least, she might have the comfort of knowing that she did not suffer by negligence or sluggishness. "Yet what," said she, "is to be expected from our persuit of happiness, when we find the state of life to be such, that happiness itself is the cause of misery? Why should we endeavour to attain that, of which the possession cannot be secured? I shall henceforward fear to yield my heart to excellence, however bright, or to fondness, however tender, lest I should lose again what I have lost in Pekuah."

## CHAPTER XXXVII
### The princess hears news of Pekuah

IN seven months, one of the messengers, who had been sent away upon the day when the promise was drawn from the princess, returned, after many unsuccessful rambles, from the borders of Nubia,[2] with an account that Pekuah was in the hands of an Arab chief, who possessed a castle or fortress on the extremity of Egypt. The Arab, whose revenue was plunder, was willing to restore her, with her two attendants, for two hundred ounces of gold.

The price was no subject of debate. The princess was in extasies when she heard that her favourite was alive, and might so

---

1  The business that calls, or the call that summons away. *Dictionary.*
2  Ancient kingdom in the Nile valley, encompassing parts of modern-day Egypt, Sudan, and Ethiopia.

cheaply be ransomed. She could not think of delaying for a moment Pekuah's happiness or her own, but entreated her brother to send back the messenger with the sum required. Imlac, being consulted, was not very confident of the veracity of the relator, and was still more doubtful of the Arab's faith, who might, if he were too liberally trusted, detain at once the money and the captives. He thought it dangerous to put themselves in the power of the Arab, by going into his district, and could not expect that the Rover[1] would so much expose himself as to come into the lower country, where he might be seized by the forces of the Bassa.

It is difficult to negotiate where neither will trust. But Imlac, after some deliberation, directed the messenger to propose that Pekuah should be conducted by ten horsemen to the monastry of St. Anthony,[2] which is situated in the deserts of Upper-Egypt, where she should be met by the same number, and her ransome should be paid.

That no time might be lost, as they expected that the proposal would not be refused, they immediately began their journey to the monastry; and, when they arrived, Imlac went forward with the former messenger to the Arab's fortress. Rasselas was desirous to go with them, but neither his sister nor Imlac would consent. The Arab, according to the custom of his nation, observed the laws of hospitality with great exactness to those who put themselves into his power, and, in a few days, brought Pekuah with her maids, by easy journeys, to their place appointed, where receiving the stipulated price, he restored her with great respect to liberty and her friends, and undertook to conduct them back towards Cairo beyond all danger of robbery or violence.

The princess and her favourite embraced each other with transport too violent to be expressed, and went out together to pour the tears of tenderness in secret, and exchange professions of kindness and gratitude. After a few hours they returned into the refectory of the convent,[3] where, in the presence of the prior and his brethren, the prince required of Pekuah the history of her adventures.

---

1  A robber; a pirate. *Dictionary*.
2  St. Anthony is considered one of the founders of Christian monasticism. In the early fourth century, after living in solitary ascetic retreat in the desert, he instructed followers in monastic life. A monastery that bears his name was founded just after his death on a mountain between the Nile and the Red Sea; today it houses Coptic Christian monks.
3  A religious house; an abbey; a monastery; a nunnery. *Dictionary*.

# CHAPTER XXXVIII
## The adventures of the lady Pekuah

"AT what time, and in what manner, I was forced away," said Pekuah, "your servants have told you. The suddenness of the event struck me with surprise, and I was at first rather stupefied than agitated with any passion of either fear or sorrow. My confusion was encreased by the speed and tumult of our flight while we were followed by Turks, who, as it seemed, soon despaired to overtake us, or were afraid of those whom they made a shew of menacing.

"When the Arabs saw themselves out of danger they slackened their course, and as I was less harassed by external violence, I began to feel more uneasiness in my mind. After some time we stopped near a spring shaded with trees in a pleasant meadow, where we were set upon the ground, and offered such refreshments as our masters were partaking. I was suffered to sit with my maids apart from the rest, and none attempted to comfort or insult us. Here I first began to feel the full weight of my misery. The girls sat weeping in silence, and from time to time looked on me for succour. I knew not to what condition we were doomed, nor could conjecture where would be the place of our captivity, or whence to draw any hope of deliverance. I was in the hands of robbers and savages, and had no reason to suppose that their pity was more than their justice, or that they would forbear the gratification of any ardour of desire, or caprice of cruelty. I, however, kissed my maids, and endeavoured to pacify them by remarking, that we were yet treated with decency, and that, since we were now carried beyond persuit, there was no danger of violence to our lives.

"When we were to be set again on horseback, my maids clung round me, and refused to be parted, but I commanded them not to irritate those who had us in their power. We travelled the remaining part of the day through an unfrequented and pathless country, and came by moonlight to the side of a hill, where the rest of the troop was stationed. Their tents were pitched, and their fires kindled, and our chief was welcomed as a man much beloved by his dependants.

"We were received into a large tent, where we found women who had attended their husbands in the expedition. They set before us the supper which they had provided, and I eat it rather to encourage my maids than to comply with any appetite of my own. When the meat was taken away they spread the carpets for repose. I was weary, and hoped to find in sleep that remission of distress which nature seldom denies. Ordering myself therefore to be undrest, I observed that the women looked very earnestly upon me, not expecting, I suppose, to see me so submissively attended. When my upper vest was taken off, they were apparently struck with the splendour of my cloaths, and one of them timorously laid her hand upon the embroidery. She then went out, and, in a short time, came back with another woman, who seemed to be of higher rank, and greater authority. She did, at her entrance, the usual act of reverence, and, taking me by the hand, placed me in a smaller tent, spread with finer carpets, where I spent the night quietly with my maids.

"In the morning, as I was sitting on the grass, the chief of the troop came towards me. I rose up to receive him, and he bowed with great respect. 'Illustrious lady,' said he, 'my fortune is better than I had presumed to hope; I am told by my women, that I have a princess in my camp.' 'Sir,' answered I, 'your women have deceived themselves and you; I am not a princess, but an unhappy stranger who intended soon to have left this country, in which I am now to be imprisoned for ever.' 'Whoever, or whencesoever, you are,' returned the Arab, 'your dress, and that of your servants, show your rank to be high, and your wealth to be great. Why should you, who can so easily procure your ransome, think yourself in danger of perpetual captivity? The purpose of my incursions is to encrease my riches, or more properly to gather tribute. The sons of Ishmael[1] are the natural and hereditary lords of this part of the continent, which is usurped by late invaders,[2] and low-born tyrants, from whom we are compelled to take by the sword what is denied to justice. The violence of war admits no distinction; the lance that is lifted at guilt and power will sometimes fall on innocence and gentleness.'

"'How little,' said I, 'did I expect that yesterday it should haven fallen upon me.'

"'Misfortunes,' answered the Arab, 'should always be expected. If the eye of hostility could learn reverence or pity, excellence like yours had been exempt from injury. But the angels of affliction spread their toils alike for the virtuous and the wicked, for the mighty and the mean. Do not be disconsolate; I am not one of the

---

1 Outcast son of Abraham and Hagar (Genesis xvi. 11–15), traditionally said to be the ancestor of the Arab peoples.
2 Ottoman Turks.

lawless and cruel rovers of the desert; I know the rules of civil life: I will fix your ransome, give a pasport to your messenger, and perform my stipulation with nice punctuality.'[1]

"You will easily believe that I was pleased with his courtesy; and finding that his predominant passion was desire of money, I began now to think my danger less, for I knew that no sum would be thought too great for the release of Pekuah. I told him that he should have no reason to charge me with ingratitude, if I was used with kindness, and that any ransome, which could be expected for a maid of common rank, would be paid, but that he must not persist to rate me as a princess. He said, he would consider what he should demand, and then, smiling, bowed and retired.

"Soon after the women came about me, each contending to be more officious[2] than the other, and my maids themselves were served with reverence. We travelled onwards by short journeys. On the fourth day the chief told me, that my ransome must be two hundred ounces of gold, which I not only promised him, but told him, that I would add fifty more, if I and my maids were honourably treated.

"I never knew the power of gold before. From that time I was the leader of the troop. The march of every day was longer or shorter as I commanded, and the tents were pitched where I chose to rest. We now had camels and other conveniences for travel, my own women were always at my side, and I amused myself with observing the manners of the vagrant[3] nations, and with viewing remains of ancient edifices with which these deserted countries appear to have been, in some distant age, lavishly embellished.

"The chief of the band was a man far from illiterate: he was able to travel by the stars or the compass, and had marked in his erratick expeditions such places as are most worthy the notice of a passenger.[4] He observed to me, that buildings are always best preserved in places little frequented, and difficult of access: for, when once a country declines from its primitive splendour, the more inhabitants are left, the quicker ruin will be made. Walls supply stones more easily than quarries, and palaces and temples

---

1 Nicety; scrupulous exactness. *Dictionary*.
2 Kind; doing good offices. *Dictionary*.
3 Wandering; unfixed; unsettled. *Dictionary*.
4 A traveller; one who is upon the road; a wayfarer. *Dictionary*.

will be demolished to make stables of granate, and cottages of porphyry.[1]

## CHAPTER XXXIX
### The adventures of Pekuah continued

"WE wandered about in this manner for some weeks, whether, as our chief pretended, for my gratification, or, as I rather suspected, for some convenience of his own. I endeavoured to appear contented where sullenness and resentment would have been of no use, and that endeavour conduced much to the calmness of my mind; but my heart was always with Nekayah, and the troubles of the night much overbalanced the amusements of the day. My women, who threw all their cares upon their mistress, set their minds at ease from the time when they saw me treated with respect, and gave themselves up to the incidental alleviations of our fatigue without solicitude or sorrow. I was pleased with their pleasure, and animated with their confidence. My condition had lost much of its terrour, since I found that the Arab ranged the country merely to get riches. Avarice is an uniform and tractable[2] vice: other intellectual distempers are different in different constitutions of the mind; that which sooths the pride of one will offend the pride of another; but to the favour of the covetous there is a ready way, bring money and nothing is denied.

"At last we came to the dwelling of our chief, a strong and spacious house built with stone in an island of the Nile, which lies, as I was told, under the tropick. 'Lady,' said the Arab, 'you shall rest after your journey a few weeks in this place, where you are to consider yourself as sovereign. My occupation is war: I have therefore chosen this obscure residence, from which I can issue unexpected, and to which I can retire unpersued. You may now repose in security: here are few pleasures, but here is no danger.' He then led me into the inner apartments, and seating me on the richest couch, bowed to the ground. His women, who considered me as a rival, looked on me with malignity; but being soon informed that I was a great lady detained only for my ransome, they began to vie with each other in obsequiousness and reverence.

---

1  Marble of a particular kind. *Dictionary.*
2  Manageable; docile; compliant; obsequious; practicable; governable. *Dictionary.*

"Being again comforted with new assurances of speedy liberty, I was for some days diverted from impatience by the novelty of the place. The turrets overlooked the country to a great distance, and afforded a view of many windings of the stream. In the day I wandered from one place to another as the course of the sun varied the splendour of the prospect, and saw many things which I had never seen before. The crocodiles and river-horses[1] are common in this unpeopled region, and I often looked upon them with terrour, though I knew that they could not hurt me. For some time I expected to see mermaids and tritons, which, as Imlac has told me, the European travellers have stationed in the Nile, but no such beings ever appeared, and the Arab, when I enquired after them, laughed at my credulity.

"At night the Arab always attended me to a tower set apart for celestial observations, where he endeavoured to teach me the names and courses of the stars. I had no great inclination to this study, but an appearance of attention was necessary to please my instructor, who valued himself for his skill, and, in a little while, I found some employment requisite to beguile the tediousness of time, which was to be passed always amidst the same objects. I was weary of looking in the morning on things from which I had turned away weary in the evening: I therefore was at last willing to observe the stars rather than do nothing, but could not always compose my thoughts, and was very often thinking on Nekayah when others imagined me contemplating the sky. Soon after the Arab went upon another expedition, and then my only pleasure was to talk with my maids about the accident by which we were carried away, and the happiness that we should all enjoy at the end of our captivity."

"There were women in your Arab's fortress," said the princess, "why did you not make them your companions, enjoy their conversation, and partake their diversions? In a place where they found business or amusement, why should you alone sit corroded with idle melancholy? or why could not you bear for a few months that condition to which they were condemned for life?"

"The diversions of the women," answered Pekuah, "were only childish play, by which the mind accustomed to stronger operations could not be kept busy. I could do all which they delighted in doing by powers merely sensitive,[2] while my intellectual facul-

---

1 Hippopotamus. *Dictionary.*
2 Having sense or perception, but not reason. *Dictionary.*

ties were flown to Cairo. They ran from room to room as a bird hops from wire to wire in his cage. They danced for the sake of motion, as lambs frisk in a meadow. One sometimes pretended to be hurt that the rest might be alarmed, or hid herself that another might seek her. Part of their time passed in watching the progress of light bodies that floated on the river, and part in marking the various forms into which clouds broke in the sky.

"Their business was only needlework, in which I and my maids sometimes helped them; but you know that the mind will easily straggle from the fingers, nor will you suspect that captivity and absence from Nekayah could receive solace from silken flowers.

"Nor was much satisfaction to be hoped from their conversation: for of what could they be expected to talk? They had seen nothing; for they had lived from early youth in that narrow spot: of what they had not seen they could have no knowledge, for they could not read. They had no ideas but of the few things that were within their view, and had hardly names for any thing but their cloaths and their food. As I bore a superiour character, I was often called to terminate their quarrels, which I decided as equitably as I could. If it could have amused me to hear the complaints of each against the rest, I might have been often detained by long stories, but the motives of their animosity were so small that I could not listen without intercepting[1] the tale."

"How," said Rasselas "can the Arab, whom you represented as a man of more than common accomplishments, take any pleasure in his seraglio[2] when it is filled only with women like these. Are they exquisitely beautiful?"

"They do not," said Pekuah, "want that unaffecting and ignoble beauty which may subsist without spriteliness or sublimity, without energy of thought or dignity of virtue. But to a man like the Arab such beauty was only a flower casually plucked and carelesly thrown away. Whatever pleasures he might find among them, they were not those of friendship or society. When they were playing about him he looked on them with inattentive superiority: when they vied for his regard he sometimes turned away disgusted. As they had no knowledge, their talk could take

---

1 To obstruct; to cut off; to stop from being communicated. *Dictionary.*
2 A house of women kept for debauchery. *Dictionary.* The part of a Muslim dwelling-house (esp. of the palace of a sovereign or great noble) in which the women are secluded; the apartments reserved for wives and concubines; a harem. *OED.*

nothing from the tediousness of life: as they had no choice, their fondness, or appearance of fondness, excited in him neither pride nor gratitude; he was not exalted in his own esteem by the smiles of a woman who saw no other man, nor was much obliged by that regard, of which he could never know the sincerity, and which he might often perceive to be exerted not so much to delight him as to pain a rival. That which he gave, and they received, as love, was only a careless distribution of superfluous time, such love as man can bestow upon that which he despises, such as has neither hope nor fear, neither joy nor sorrow."

"You have reason, lady, to think yourself happy," said Imlac, "that you have been thus easily dismissed. How could a mind, hungry for knowledge, be willing, in an intellectual famine, to lose such a banquet as Pekuah's conversation?"

"I am inclined to believe," answered Pekuah, "that he was for some time in suspense; for, notwithstanding his promise, whenever I proposed to dispatch a messenger to Cairo, he found some excuse for delay. While I was detained in his house he made many incursions into the neighboring countries, and, perhaps, he would have refused to discharge me, had his plunder been equal to his wishes. He returned always courteous, related his adventures, delighted to hear my observations, and endeavoured to advance my acquaintance with the stars. When I had importuned him to send away my letters, he soothed me with professions of honour and sincerity; and, when I could be no longer decently denied, put his troop again in motion, and left me to govern in his absence. I was much afflicted by this studied procrastination, and was sometimes afraid that I should be forgotten; that you would leave Cairo, and I must end my days in an island of the Nile.

"I grew at last hopeless and dejected, and cared so little to entertain him, that he for a while more frequently talked with my maids. That he should fall in love with them, or with me, might have been equally fatal, and I was not much pleased with the growing friendship. My anxiety was not long; for, as I recovered some degree of chearfulness, he returned to me, and I could not forbear to despise my former uneasiness.

"He still delayed to send for my ransome, and would, perhaps, never have determined, had not your agent found his way to him. The gold, which he would not fetch, he could not reject when it was offered. He hastened to prepare for our journey hither, like a man delivered from the pain of an intestine conflict. I took leave of my companions in the house, who dismissed me with cold indifference."

Nekayah, having heard her favourite's relation, rose and embraced her, and Rasselas gave her an hundred ounces of gold, which she presented to the Arab for the fifty that were promised.

## CHAPTER XL
### The history of a man of learning

THEY returned to Cairo, and were so well pleased at finding themselves together, that none of them went much abroad. The prince began to love learning, and one day declared to Imlac, that he intended to devote himself to science, and pass the rest of his days in literary solitude.

"Before you make your final choice," answered Imlac, "you ought to examine its hazards, and converse with some of those who are grown old in the company of themselves. I have just left the observatory of one of the most learned astronomers in the world, who has spent forty years in unwearied attention to the motions and appearances of the celestial bodies, and has drawn out his soul in endless calculations. He admits a few friends once a month to hear his deductions and enjoy his discoveries. I was introduced as a man of knowledge worthy of his notice. Men of various ideas and fluent conversation are commonly welcome to those whose thoughts have been long fixed upon a single point, and who find the images of other things stealing away. I delighted him with my remarks, he smiled at the narrative of my travels, and was glad to forget the constellations, and descend for a moment into the lower world.

"On the next day of vacation I renewed my visit, and was so fortunate as to please him again. He relaxed from that time the severity of his rule, and permitted me to enter at my own choice. I found him always busy, and always glad to be relieved. As each knew much which the other was desirous of learning, we exchanged our notions with great delight. I perceived that I had every day more of his confidence, and always found new cause of admiration in the profundity of his mind. His comprehension is vast, his memory capacious and retentive, his discourse is methodical, and his expression clear.

"His integrity and benevolence are equal to his learning. His deepest researches and most favourite studies are willingly interrupted for any opportunity of doing good by his counsel or his riches. To his closest retreat, at his most busy moments, all are admitted that want his assistance: 'For though I exclude idleness and pleasure, I will never,' says he, 'bar my doors against charity.

To man is permitted the contemplation of the skies, but the practice of virtue is commanded.'"

"Surely," said the princess, "this man is happy."

"I visited him," said Imlac, "with more and more frequency, and was every time more enamoured of his conversation: he was sublime without haughtiness, courteous without formality, and communicative without ostentation. I was at first, great princess, of your opinion, thought him the happiest of mankind, and often congratulated him on the blessing that he enjoyed. He seemed to hear nothing with indifference but the praises of his condition, to which he always returned a general answer, and diverted the conversation to some other topick.

"Amidst this willingness to be pleased, and labour to please, I had quickly reason to imagine that some painful sentiment pressed upon his mind. He often looked up earnestly towards the sun, and let his voice fall in the midst of his discourse. He would sometimes, when we were alone, gaze upon me in silence with the air of a man who longed to speak what he was yet resolved to suppress. He would often send for me with vehement injunctions of haste, though, when I came to him, he had nothing extraordinary to say. And sometimes, when I was leaving him, would call me back, pause a few moments and then dismiss me.

## CHAPTER XLI
The astronomer discovers[1] the cause of his uneasiness

"AT last the time came when the secret burst his reserve. We were sitting together last night in the turret of his house, watching the emersion[2] of a satellite of Jupiter. A sudden tempest clouded the sky, and disappointed our observation. We sat a while silent in the dark, and then he addressed himself to me in these words: 'Imlac, I have long considered thy friendship as the greatest blessing of my life. Integrity without knowledge is weak and useless, and knowledge without integrity is dangerous and dreadful. I have found in thee all the qualities requisite for trust, benevolence, experience, and fortitude. I have long discharged[3] an office which I must soon quit at the call of nature, and shall rejoice in the hour of imbecility and pain to devolve it upon thee.'

---

1  To make known; not to disguise; to reveal. *Dictionary.*
2  The time when a star, having been obscured by its too near approach to the sun, appears again. *Dictionary.*
3  To perform; to execute. *Dictionary.*

"I thought myself honoured by this testimony, and protested that whatever could conduce to his happiness would add likewise to mine.

"'Hear, Imlac, what thou wilt not without difficulty credit. I have possessed for five years the regulation of weather, and the distribution of the seasons: the sun has listened to my dictates, and passed from tropick to tropick by my direction; the clouds, at my call, have poured their waters, and the Nile has overflowed at my command; I have restrained the rage of the dogstar,[1] and mitigated the fervours of the crab.[2] The winds alone, of all the elemental powers, have hitherto refused my authority, and multitudes have perished by equinoctial tempests which I found myself unable to prohibit or restrain. I have administered this great office with exact justice, and made to the different nations of the earth an impartial dividend of rain and sunshine. What must have been the misery of half the globe, if I had limited the clouds to particular regions, or confined the sun to either side of the equator?'"

## CHAPTER XLII
### The opinion of the astronomer is explained and justified

"I suppose he discovered in me, through the obscurity of the room, some tokens of amazement and doubt, for, after a short pause, he proceeded thus:

"'Not to be easily credited will neither surprise nor offend me; for I am, probably, the first of human beings to whom this trust has been imparted. Nor do I know whether to deem this distinction a reward or punishment; since I have possessed it I have been far less happy than before, and nothing but the consciousness of good intention could have enabled me to support the weariness of unremitted vigilance.'

"'How long, Sir,' said I, 'has this great office been in your hands?'

---

1 The star which gives the name to the dogdays. *Dictionary*. Sirius, or *Alpha Canis Majoris*, is the brightest star in the night sky. The ancient Egyptians were aware that it rose just before sunrise at the same time of year that the Nile began its annual floods and long believed that the star caused the floods. In European culture it was "traditionally associated with frenzy and madness." Meloccaro 227 n.4.

2 The sign in the zodiack. *Dictionary*. "The constellation Cancer, another astronomical formation associated with madness." Meloccaro 227 n.5.

"'About ten years ago,' said he, 'my daily observations of the changes of the sky led me to consider, whether, if I had the power of the seasons, I could confer greater plenty upon the inhabitants of the earth. This contemplation fastened on my mind, and I sat days and nights in imaginary dominion, pouring upon this country and that the showers of fertility, and seconding every fall of rain with a due proportion of sunshine. I had yet only the will to do good, and did not imagine that I should ever have the power.

"'One day as I was looking on the fields withering with heat, I felt in my mind a sudden wish that I could send rain on the southern mountains, and raise the Nile to an inundation. In the hurry of my imagination I commanded rain to fall, and, by comparing the time of my command, with that of the inundation, I found that the clouds had listned to my lips.'

"'Might not some other cause,' said I, 'produce this concurrence? the Nile does not always rise on the same day.'

"'Do not believe,' said he with impatience, 'that such objections could escape me: I have reasoned long against my own conviction, and laboured against truth with the utmost obstinacy. I sometimes suspected myself of madness, and should not have dared to impart this secret but to a man like you, capable of distinguishing the wonderful from the impossible, and the incredible from the false.'

"'Why, Sir,' said I, 'do you call that incredible, which you know, or think you know, to be true?'

"'Because,' said he, 'I cannot prove it by any external evidence; and I know too well the laws of demonstration to think that my conviction ought to influence another, who cannot, like me, be conscious of its force. I, therefore, shall not attempt to gain credit by disputation. It is sufficient that I feel this power, that I have long possessed, and every day exerted it. But the life of man is short, the infirmities of age increase upon me, and the time will soon come when the regulator of the year must mingle with the dust. The care of appointing a successor has long disturbed me; the night and the day have been spent in comparisons of all the characters which have come to my knowledge, and I have yet found none so worthy as thyself.

CHAPTER XLIII
The astronomer leaves Imlac his directions

"HEAR, therefore, what I shall impart, with attention, such as the welfare of a world requires. If the task of a king be considered as difficult, who has the care only of a few millions, to whom he cannot do much good or harm, what must be the anxiety of him, on whom depends the action of the elements, and the great gifts of light and heat!—Hear me therefore with attention.

"'I have diligently considered the position of the earth and sun, and formed innumerable schemes in which I changed their situation. I have sometimes turned aside the axis of the earth, and sometimes varied the ecliptick of the sun: but I have found it impossible to make a disposition by which the world may be advantaged; what one region gains, another loses by any imaginable alteration, even without considering the distant parts of the solar system with which we are unacquainted. Do not, therefore, in thy administration of the year, indulge thy pride by innovation; do not please thyself with thinking that thou canst make thyself renowned to all future ages, by disordering the seasons. The memory of mischief is no desirable fame. Much less will it become thee to let kindness or interest prevail. Never rob other countries of rain to pour it on thine own. For us the Nile is sufficient.'

"I promised that when I possessed the power, I would use it with inflexible integrity, and he dismissed me, pressing my hand. 'My heart,' said he, 'will be now at rest, and my benevolence will no more destroy my quiet: I have found a man of wisdom and virtue, to whom I can chearfully bequeath the inheritance of the sun.'"

The prince heard this narration with very serious regard, but the princess smiled, and Pekuah convulsed herself with laughter. "Ladies," said Imlac, "to mock the heaviest of human afflictions is neither charitable nor wise. Few can attain this man's knowledge, and few practise his virtues; but all may suffer his calamity. Of the uncertainties of our present state, the most dreadful and alarming is the uncertain continuance of reason."

The princess was recollected,[1] and the favourite was abashed. Rasselas, more deeply affected, enquired of Imlac, whether he thought such maladies of the mind frequent, and how they were contracted.

## CHAPTER XLIV
### The dangerous prevalence of imagination

"DISORDERS of intellect," answered Imlac, "happen much more often than superficial observers will easily believe. Perhaps,

---

1  To recover reason or resolution. *Dictionary*.

if we speak with rigorous exactness, no human mind is in its right state. There is no man whose imagination does not sometimes predominate over his reason, who can regulate his attention wholly by his will, and whose ideas will come and go at his command. No man will be found in whose mind airy notions do not sometimes tyrannise, and force him to hope or fear beyond the limits of sober probability. All power of fancy over reason is a degree of insanity; but while this power is such as we can controul and repress, it is not visible to others, nor considered as any depravation of the mental faculties: it is not pronounced madness but when it comes ungovernable, and apparently influences speech or action.

"To indulge the power of fiction, and send imagination out upon the wing, is often the sport of those who delight too much in silent speculation. When we are alone we are not always busy; the labour of excogitation[1] is too violent to last long; the ardour of enquiry will sometimes give way to idleness or satiety. He who has nothing external that can divert him, must find pleasure in his own thoughts, and must conceive himself what he is not; for who is pleased with what he is? He then expatiates in boundless futurity, and culls from all imaginable conditions that which for the present moment he should most desire, amuses his desires with impossible enjoyments, and confers upon his pride unattainable dominion. The mind dances from scene to scene, unites all pleasures in all combinations, and riots in delights which nature and fortune, with all their bounty cannot bestow.

"In time some particular train of ideas fixes the attention, all other intellectual gratifications are rejected, the mind, in weariness or leisure, recurs constantly to the favourite conception, and feasts on the luscious falsehood whenever she is offended with the bitterness of truth. By degrees the reign of fancy is confirmed; she grows first imperious, and in time despotick. Then fictions begin to operate as realities, false opinions fasten upon the mind, and life passes in dreams of rapture or of anguish.

"This, Sir, is one of the dangers of solitude, which the hermit has confessed not always to promote goodness, and the astronomer's misery has proved to be not always propitious to wisdom."

"I will no more," said the favourite, "imagine myself the queen of Abissinia. I have often spent the hours, which the princess gave

---

1   To invent; to strike out by thinking. *Dictionary.*

to my own disposal, in adjusting ceremonies and regulating the court; I have repressed the pride of the powerful, and granted the petitions of the poor; I have built new palaces in more happy situations, planted groves upon the tops of mountains, and have exulted in the beneficence of royalty, till, when the princess entered, I had almost forgotten to bow down before her."

"And I," said the princess, "will not allow myself any more to play the shepherdess in my waking dreams. I have often soothed my thoughts with the quiet and innocence of pastoral employments, till I have in my chamber heard the winds whistle, and the sheep bleat; sometimes freed the lamb entangled in the thicket, and sometimes with my crook encountered the wolf. I have a dress like that of the village maids, which I put on to help my imagination, and a pipe on which I play softly, and suppose myself followed by my flocks."

"I will confess," said the prince, "an indulgence of fantastick[1] delight more dangerous than yours. I have frequently endeavoured to image the possibility of a perfect government, by which all wrong should be restrained, all vice reformed, and all the subjects preserved in tranquility and innocence. This thought produced innumerable schemes of reformation, and dictated many useful regulations and salutary edicts. This has been the sport and sometimes the labour of my solitude; and I start, when I think with how little anguish I once supposed the death of my father and my brothers."

"Such," says Imlac, "are the effects of visionary schemes: when we first form them we know them to be absurd, but familiarise them by degrees, and in time lose sight of their folly."

## CHAPTER XLV
### They discourse with an old man

THE evening was now far past, and they rose to return home. As they walked along the bank of the Nile, delighted with the beams of the moon quivering on the water, they saw at a small distance an old man, whom the prince had often heard in the assembly of the sages. "Yonder," said he, "is one whose years have calmed his passions, but not clouded his reason: let us close the disquisitions of the night, by enquiring what are his sentiments of his own state, that we may know whether youth alone is to struggle with

---

1   Subsisting only in the fancy; imaginary. *Dictionary.*

vexation, and whether any better hope remains for the latter part of life."

Here the sage approached and saluted[1] them. They invited him to join their walk, and prattled a while as acquaintance that had unexpectedly met one another. The old man was chearful and talkative, and the way seemed short in his company. He was pleased to find himself not disregarded, accompanied them to their house, and, at the prince's request, entered with them. They placed him in the seat of honour, and set wine and conserves before him.

"Sir," said the princess, "an evening walk must give to a man of learning, like you, pleasures which ignorance and youth can hardly conceive. You know the qualities and the causes of all that you behold, the laws by which the river flows, the periods in which the planets perform their revolutions. Every thing must supply you with contemplation, and renew the consciousness of your own dignity."

"Lady," answered he, "let the gay and the vigorous expect pleasure in their excursions, it is enough that age can obtain ease. To me the world has lost its novelty: I look round, and see what I remember to have seen in happier days. I rest against a tree, and consider, that in the same shade I once disputed upon the annual overflow of the Nile with a friend who is now silent in the grave. I cast my eyes upwards, fix them on the changing moon, and think with pain on the vicissitudes of life. I have ceased to take much delight in physical[2] truth; for what have I to do with those things which I am soon to leave?"

"You may at least recreate[3] yourself," said Imlac, "with the recollection of an honourable and useful life, and enjoy the praise which all agree to give you."

"Praise," said the sage, with a sigh, "is to an old man an empty sound. I have neither mother to be delighted with the reputation of her son, nor wife to partake the honours of her husband. I have outlived my friends and my rivals. Nothing is now of much importance; for I cannot extend my interest beyond myself. Youth is delighted with applause, because it is considered as the earnest of some future good, and because the prospect of life is far

---

1 To greet; to hail. To kiss. *Dictionary.*
2 Relating to nature or to natural philosophy; not moral. *Dictionary.*
3 To refresh after toil; to amuse or divert in weariness. To delight; to gratify. *Dictionary.*

extended: but to me, who am now declining to decrepitude, there is little to be feared from the malevolence of men, and yet less to be hoped from their affections or esteem. Something they may yet take away, but they can give me nothing. Riches would now be useless, and high employment would be pain. My retrospect of life recalls to my view many opportunities of good neglected, much time squandered upon trifles, and more lost in idleness and vacancy. I leave many great designs unattempted, and many great attempts unfinished. My mind is burthened with no heavy crime, and therefore I compose myself to tranquility; endeavour to abstract my thoughts from hopes and cares, which, though reason knows them to be vain, still try to keep their old possession of the heart; expect, with serene humility, that hour which nature cannot long delay; and hope to possess in a better state that happiness which here I could not find, and that virtue which here I have not attained."

He rose and went away, leaving his audience not much elated with the hope of long life. The prince consoled himself with remarking, that it was not reasonable to be disappointed by this account; for age had never been considered as the season of felicity, and, if it was possible to be easy in decline and weakness, it was likely that the days of vigour and alacrity might be happy: that the noon of life might be bright, if the evening could be calm.

The princess suspected that age was querulous and malignant, and delighted to repress the expectations of those who had newly entered the world. She had seen the possessors of estates look with envy on their heirs, and known many who enjoy pleasure no longer than they can confine it to themselves.

Pekuah conjectured, that the man was older than he appeared, and was willing to impute his complaints to delirious dejection; or else supposed that he had been unfortunate, and was therefore discontented: "For nothing," said she, "is more common than to call our own condition, the condition of life."

Imlac, who had no desire to see them depressed, smiled at the comforts which they could so readily procure to themselves, and remembered, that at the same age, he was equally confident of unmingled prosperity, and equally fertile of consolatory expedients. He forbore to force upon them unwelcome knowledge, which time itself would too soon impress. The princess and her lady retired; the madness of the astronomer hung upon their minds, and they desired Imlac to enter upon his office, and delay next morning the rising of the sun.

# CHAPTER XLVI
## The princess and Pekuah visit the astronomer

THE princess and Pekuah having talked in private of Imlac's astronomer, thought his character at once so amiable and so strange, that they could not be satisfied without a nearer knowledge, and Imlac was requested to find the means of bringing them together.

This was somewhat difficult; the philosopher had never received any visits from women, though he lived in a city that had in it many Europeans who followed the manners of their own countries, and many from other parts of the world that lived there with European liberty. The ladies would not be refused, and several schemes were proposed for the accomplishment of their design. It was proposed to introduce them as strangers in distress, to whom the sage was always accessible; but, after some deliberation, it appeared, that by this artifice, no acquaintance could be formed, for their conversation would be short, and they could not decently importune him often. "This," said Rasselas, "is true; but I have yet a stronger objection against the misrepresentation of your state. I have always considered it as treason against the great republick of human nature, to make any man's virtues the means of deceiving him, whether on great or little occasions. All imposture weakens confidence and chills benevolence. When the sage finds that you are not what you seemed, he will feel the resentment natural to a man who, conscious of great abilities, discovers that he has been tricked by understandings meaner than his own, and, perhaps, the distrust, which he can never afterwards wholly lay aside, may stop the voice of counsel, and close the hand of charity; and where will you find the power of restoring his benefactions to mankind, or his peace to himself?"

To this no reply was attempted, and Imlac began to hope that their curiosity would subside; but, next day, Pekuah told him, she had now found an honest pretence for a visit to the astronomer, for she would solicite permission to continue under him the studies in which she had been initiated by the Arab, and the princess might go with her either as a fellow-student, or because a woman could not decently come alone. "I am afraid," said Imlac, "that he will be soon weary of your company: men advanced far in knowledge do not love to repeat the elements of their art, and I am not certain that even of the elements, as he will deliver them connected with inferences, and mingled with reflections, you are a very capable auditress." "That," said Pekuah, "must be my care: I ask of you only to take me thither. My knowledge is, perhaps, more than you imagine it, and by concurring always with his opinions I shall make him think it greater than it is."

The astronomer, in pursuance of this resolution, was told, that a foreign lady, travelling in search of knowledge, had heard of his reputation, and was desirous to become his scholar. The uncommonness of the proposal raised at once his surprize and curiosity, and when, after a short deliberation, he consented to admit her, he could not stay without impatience till the next day.

The ladies dressed themselves magnificently, and were attended by Imlac to the astronomer, who was pleased to see himself approached with respect by persons of so splendid an appearance. In the exchange of the first civilities he was timorous and bashful; but when the talk became regular, he recollected[1] his powers, and justified the character which Imlac had given. Enquiring of Pekuah what could have turned her inclination towards astronomy, he received from her a history of her adventure at the pyramid, and of the time passed in the Arab's island. She told her tale with ease and elegance, and her conversation took possession of his heart. The discourse was then turned to astronomy: Pekuah displayed what she knew: he looked upon her as a prodigy of genius, and intreated her not to desist from a study which she had so happily begun.

They came again and again, and were every time more welcome than before. The sage endeavoured to amuse them, that they might prolong their visits, for he found his thoughts grow brighter in their company; the clouds of solicitude vanished by degrees, as he forced himself to entertain, and he grieved when he was left at their departure to his old employment of regulating the seasons.

The princess and her favourite had now watched his lips for several months, and could not catch a single word from which they could judge whether he continued, or not, in the opinion of his preternatural[2] commission. They often contrived to bring him to an open declaration, but he easily eluded all their attacks, and on which side soever they pressed him escaped from them to some other topick.

---

1 To gather what is scattered; to gather again. *Dictionary*.
2 Different from what is natural; irregular. *Dictionary*.

As their familiarity increased they invited him often to the house of Imlac, where they distinguished him by extraordinary respect. He began gradually to delight in sublunary pleasures. He came early and departed late; laboured to recommend himself by assiduity and compliance; excited their curiosity after new arts, that they might still want his assistance; and when they made any excursion of pleasure or enquiry, entreated to attend them.

By long experience of his integrity and wisdom, the prince and his sister were convinced that he might be trusted without danger; and lest he should draw any false hopes from the civilities which he received, discovered to him their condition, with the motives of their journey, and required his opinion on the choice of life.

"Of the various conditions which the world spreads before you, which you shall prefer," said the sage, "I am not able to instruct you. I can only tell that I have chosen wrong. I have passed my time in study without experience; in the attainment of sciences which can, for the most part, be but remotely useful to mankind. I have purchased knowledge at the expence of all the common comforts of life: I have missed the endearing elegance of female friendship, and the happy commerce of domestick tenderness. If I have obtained any prerogatives above other students, they have been accompanied with fear, disquiet, and scrupulosity; but even of these prerogatives, whatever they were, I have, since my thoughts have been diversified by more intercourse with the world, begun to question the reality. When I have been for a few days lost in pleasing dissipation,[1] I am always tempted to think that my enquiries have ended in errour, and that I have suffered much, and suffered it in vain."

Imlac was delighted to find that the sage's understanding was breaking through its mists, and resolved to detain him from the planets till he should forget his talk of ruling them, and reason should recover its original influence.

From this time the astronomer was received into familiar friendship, and partook of all their projects and pleasures: his respect kept him attentive, and the activity of Rasselas did not leave much time unengaged. Something was always to be done; the day was spent in making observations which furnished talk for the evening, and the evening was closed with a scheme for the morrow.

---

1 Distraction of the mental faculties or energies from concentration on serious subjects ... a diversion; a frivolous amusement. *OED.*

The sage confessed to Imlac, that since he had mingled in the gay tumults of life, and divided his hours by a succession of amusements, he found the conviction of his authority over the skies fade gradually from his mind, and began to trust less to an opinion which he never could prove to others, and which he now found subject to variation from causes in which reason had no part. "If I am accidentally left alone for a few hours," said he, "my inveterate persuasion rushes upon my soul, and my thoughts are chained down by some irresistible violence, but they are soon disentangled by the prince's conversation, and instantaneously released at the entrance of Pekuah. I am like a man habitually afraid of spectres, who is set at ease by a lamp, and wonders at the dread which harrassed him in the dark, yet, if his lamp be extinguished, feels again the terrours which he knows that when it is light he shall feel no more. But I am sometimes afraid lest I indulge my quiet by criminal negligence, and voluntarily forget the great charge with which I am intrusted. If I favour myself in a known errour, or am determined by my own ease in a doubtful question of this importance, how dreadful is my crime!"

"No disease of the imagination," answered Imlac, "is so difficult of cure, as that which is complicated with the dread of guilt: fancy and conscience then act interchangeably upon us, and so often shift their places, that the illusions of one are not distinguished from the dictates of the other. If fancy presents images not moral or religious, the mind drives them away when they give it pain, but when the melancholick notions take the form of duty, they lay hold on the faculties without opposition, because we are afraid to exclude or banish them. For this reason the superstitious are often melancholy, and the melancholy almost always superstitious.

"But do not let the suggestions of timidity overpower your better reason: the danger of neglect can be but as the probability of the obligation, which when you consider it with freedom, you find very little, and that little growing every day less. Open your heart to the influence of the light, which, from time to time, breaks in upon you: when scruples importune you, which you in your lucid moments know to be vain, do not stand to parley,[1] but fly to business or to Pekuah, and keep this thought always prevalent, that you are only one atom of the mass of humanity, and have neither such virtue nor vice, as that you should be singled out for supernatural favours or afflictions."

---

1  Oral treaty; talk; conference; discussion by word of mouth. *Dictionary*.

# CHAPTER LXVII
## The prince enters and brings a new topick

"ALL this," said the astronomer, "I have often thought, but my reason has been so long subjugated by an uncontrolable and overwhelming idea, that it durst not confide in its own decisions. I now see how fatally I betrayed my quiet, by suffering chimeras[1] to prey upon me in secret; but melancholy shrinks from communication, and I never found a man before, to whom I could impart my troubles, though I had been certain of relief. I rejoice to find my own sentiments confirmed by yours, who are not easily deceived, and can have no motive or purpose to deceive. I hope that time and variety will dissipate the gloom that has so long surrounded me, and the latter part of my days will be spent in peace."

"Your learning and virtue," said Imlac, "may justly give you hopes."

Rasselas then entered with the princess and Pekuah, and enquired whether they had contrived any new diversion for the next day. "Such," said Nekayah, "is the state of life, that none are happy but by the anticipation of change: the change itself is nothing; when we have made it, the next wish is to change again. The world is not yet exhausted; let me see something to morrow which I never saw before."

"Variety," said Rasselas, "is so necessary to content, that even the happy valley disgusted me by the recurrence of its luxuries; yet I could not forbear to reproach myself with impatience, when I saw the monks of St. Anthony support without complaint, a life, not of uniform delight, but uniform hardship."

"Those men," answered Imlac, "are less wretched in their silent convent than the Abissinian princes in their prison of pleasure. Whatever is done by the monks is incited by an adequate and reasonable motive. Their labour supplies them with necessaries; it therefore cannot be omitted, and is certainly rewarded. Their devotion prepares them for another state, and reminds them of its approach, while it fits them for it. Their time is regularly distributed; one duty succeeds another, so that they are not left open to the distractions of unguided choice, nor lost in the shades of list-

---

1   A vain and wild fancy, as remote from reality as the existence of the poetical chimera, a monster feigned to have the head of a lion, the belly of a goat, and the tail of a dragon. *Dictionary*.

less inactivity. There is a certain task to be performed at an appropriated hour; and their toils are cheerful, because they consider them as acts of piety, by which they are always advancing towards endless felicity."

"Do you think," said Nekayah, "that the monastick rule is a more holy and less imperfect state than any other? May not he equally hope for future happiness who converses openly with mankind, who succours the distressed by his charity, instructs the ignorant by his learning, and contributes by his industry to the general system of life; even though he should omit some of the mortifications which are practised in the cloister, and allow himself such harmless delights as his condition may place within his reach?"

"This," said Imlac, "is a question which has long divided the wise, and perplexed the good. I am afraid to decide on either part. He that lives well in the world is better than he that lives well in a monastery. But, perhaps, every one is not able to stem the temptations of publick life; and, if he cannot conquer, he may properly retreat. Some have little power to do good, and have likewise little strength to resist evil. Many are weary of their conflicts with adversity, and are willing to eject those passions which have long busied them in vain. And many are dismissed by age and diseases from the more laborious duties of society. In monasteries the weak and timorous may be happily sheltered, the weary may repose, and the penitent may meditate. Those retreats of prayer and contemplation have something so congenial to the mind of man, that, perhaps, there is scarcely one that does not purpose to close his life in pious abstraction with a few associates serious as himself."

"Such," said Pekuah, "has often been my wish, and I have heard the princess declare, that she should not willingly die in a croud."

"The liberty of using harmless pleasures," proceeded Imlac, "will not be disputed; but it is still to be examined what pleasures are harmless. The evil of any pleasure that Nekayah can image is not in the act itself, but in its consequences. Pleasure, in itself harmless, may become mischievous, by endearing to us a state which we know to be transient and probatory,[1] and withdrawing our thoughts from that, of which every hour brings us nearer to

---

1 Serving for trial. *Dictionary*.

the beginning, and of which no length of time will bring us to the end. Mortification is not virtuous in itself, nor has any other use, but that it disengages us from the allurements of sense. In the state of future perfection to which we all aspire, there will be pleasure without danger, and security without restraint."

The princess was silent, and Rasselas, turning to the astronomer, asked him, whether he could not delay her retreat, by shewing her something which she had not seen before.

"Your curiosity," said the sage, "has been so general, and your pursuit of knowledge so vigorous, that novelties are not now very easily to be found: but what you can no longer procure from the living may be given by the dead. Among the wonders of this country are the catacombs,[1] or the ancient repositories, in which the bodies of the earliest generations were lodged, and where, by the virtue of the gums which embalmed them, they yet remain without corruption."

"I know not," said Rasselas, "what pleasure the sight of the catacombs can afford, but, since nothing else is offered, I am resolved to view them, and shall place this with many other things which I have done, because I would do something."

They hired a guard of horsemen, and the next day visited the catacombs.[2] When they were about to descend into the sepulchral caves, "Pekuah," said the princess, "we are now again invading the habitations of the dead; I know that you will stay behind; let me find you safe when I return." "No, I will not be left," answered Pekuah; "I will go down between you and the prince."

They then all descended, and roved with wonder through the labyrinth of subterraneous passages, where the bodies were laid in rows on either side.

---

1 Subterraneous cavities for the burial of the dead. *Dictionary*. See Arthur J. Weitzman, "More Light on *Rasselas*: The Background of the Egyptian Episodes" (*Philological Quarterly* 48.1 [January 1969]): 42–58.

2 As O.F. Emerson points out, there are no catacombs in Cairo, but there are catacomb-like structures at Saqqârah, part of the necropolis of the ancient city of Memphis, about 15 miles southwest of Cairo. Emerson, ed., *History of Rasselas, Prince of Abyssinia* (New York: Henry Holt, 1895), 176–77.

# CHAPTER XLVIII
## Imlac discourses on the nature of the soul[1]

"WHAT reason, "said the prince, "can be given, why the Egyptians should thus expensively preserve those carcasses which some nations consume with fire, others lay to mingle with the earth, and all agree to remove from their sight, as soon as decent rites can be performed?"

"The original[2] of ancient customs," said Imlac, "is commonly unknown; the practice often continues when the cause has ceased; and concerning superstitious ceremonies it is vain to conjecture; for what reason did not dictate reason cannot explain. I have long believed that the practice of embalming arose only from tenderness to the remains of relations or friends, and to this opinion I am more inclined, because it seems impossible that this care should have been general: had all the dead been embalmed, their repositories must in time have been more spacious than the dwellings of the living. I suppose only the rich or honourable were secured from corruption, and the rest left to the course of nature.

"But it is commonly supposed that the Egyptians believed the soul to live as long as the body continued undissolved, and therefore tried this method of eluding death."

"Could the wise Egyptians," said Nekayah, "think so grosly of the soul? If the soul could once survive its separation, what could it afterwards receive or suffer from the body?"

"The Egyptians would doubtless think erroneously," said the astronomer, "in the darkness of heathenism, and the first dawn of philosophy. The nature of the soul is still disputed amidst all our opportunities of clearer knowledge: some yet say, that it may be material,[3] who, nevertheless, believe it to be immortal."

"Some," answered Imlac, "have indeed said that the soul is material, but I can scarcely believe that any man has thought it, who knew how to think; for all the conclusions of reason enforce the immateriality of mind, and all the notices of sense and investigations of science concur to prove the unconsciousness of matter.

---

1  See Gwin J. Kolb. "The Intellectual Background to the Discourse on the Soul in *Rasselas*" (*Philological Quarterly* 54 [1975]): 357–69.
2  Fountain; source; that which gives beginning or existence. *Dictionary.*
3  Consisting of matter; corporeal; not spiritual. *Dictionary.*

"It was never supposed that cogitation is inherent in matter, or that every particle is a thinking being. Yet, if any part of matter be devoid of thought, what part can we suppose to think? Matter can differ from matter only in form, density, bulk, motion, and direction of motion: to which of these, however varied or combined, can consciousness be annexed? To be round or square, to be solid or fluid, to be great or little, to be moved slowly or swiftly one way or another, are modes of material existence, all equally alien from the nature of cogitation. If matter be once without thought, it can only be made to think by some new modification, but all the modifications which it can admit are equally unconnected with cogitative powers."

"But the materialists,"[1] said the astronomer, "urge that matter may have qualities with which we are unacquainted."

"He who will determine," returned Imlac, "against that which he knows, because there may be something which he knows not; he that can set hypothetical possibility against acknowledged certainty, is not to be admitted among reasonable beings. All that we know of matter is, that matter is inert, senseless and lifeless; and if this conviction cannot be opposed but by referring us to something that we know not, we have all the evidence that human intellect can admit. If that which is known may be over ruled by that which is unknown, no being, not omniscient, can arrive at certainty."

"Yet let us not," said the astronomer, "too arrogantly limit the Creator's power."

"It is no limitation of omnipotence," replied the poet, "to suppose that one thing is not consistent with another, that the same proposition cannot be at once true and false, that the same number cannot be even and odd, that cogitation cannot be conferred on that which is created incapable of cogitation."

"I know not," said Nekayah, "any great use of this question. Does that immateriality, which, in my opinion, you have sufficiently proved, necessarily include eternal duration?"

"Of immateriality," said Imlac, "our ideas are negative, and therefore obscure. Immateriality seems to imply a natural power of perpetual duration as a consequence of exemption from all causes of decay: whatever perishes is destroyed by the solution[2]

---

1  One who denies spiritual substances. *Dictionary*.
2  Disruption; breach; disjunction; separation. *Dictionary*.

of its contexture,[1] and separation of its parts; nor can we conceive how that which has no parts, and therefore admits no solution, can be naturally corrupted or impaired."

"I know not," said Rasselas, "how to conceive any thing without extension:[2] what is extended must have parts, and you allow, that whatever has parts may be destroyed."

"Consider your own conceptions," replied Imlac, "and the difficulty will be less. You will find substance without extension. An ideal[3] form is no less real than material bulk: yet an ideal form has no extension. It is no less certain, when you think on a pyramid, that your mind possesses the idea of a pyramid, than that the pyramid itself is standing. What space does the idea of a pyramid occupy more than the idea of a grain of corn? or how can either idea suffer laceration? As is the effect such is the cause; as thought is, such is the power that thinks; a power impassive[4] and indiscerpible."[5]

"But the Being," said Nekayah, "whom I fear to name, the Being which made the soul, can destroy it."

"He, surely, can destroy it," answered Imlac, "since, however imperishable, it receives from a superiour nature its power of duration. That it will not perish by any inherent cause of decay, or principle of corruption, may be shown by philosophy; but philosophy can tell no more. That it will not be annihilated by him that made it, we must humbly learn from higher authority."

The whole assembly stood a while silent and collected. "Let us return," said Rasselas, "from this scene of mortality. How gloomy would be these mansions of the dead to him who did not know that he shall never die; that what now acts shall continue its agency, and what now thinks shall think on for ever. Those that lie here stretched before us, the wise and the powerful of ancient times, warn us to remember the shortness of our present state: they were, perhaps, snatched away while they were busy, like us, in the choice of life."

---

1 The disposition of parts one amongst others; the composition of any thing out of separate parts; the system; the constitution; the manner in which any thing is woven or formed. *Dictionary*.
2 The state of being extended. *Dictionary*. The property of being extended or of occupying space; spatial magnitude. *OED*.
3 Mental; intellectual; not perceived by the senses. *Dictionary*.
4 Exempt from the agency of external causes. *Dictionary*.
5 Indiscerptible: Not to be separated; incapable of being broken or destroyed by dissolution of parts. *Dictionary*.

"To me," said the princess, "the choice of life is become less important; I hope hereafter to think only on the choice of eternity."

They then hastened out of the caverns, and, under the protection of their guard, returned to Cairo.

## CHAPTER XLIX
### The conclusion, in which nothing is concluded

IT was now the time of the inundation of the Nile: a few days after their visit to the catacombs, the river began to rise.

They were confined to their house. The whole region being under water gave them no invitation to any excursions, and, being well supplied with materials for talk, they diverted themselves with comparisons of the different forms of life which they had observed, and with various schemes of happiness which each of them had formed.

Pekuah was never so much charmed with any place as the convent of St. Anthony, where the Arab restored her to the princess, and wished only to fill it with pious maidens, and to be made prioress of the order: she was weary of expectation and disgust, and would gladly be fixed in some unvariable state.

The princess thought, that of all sublunary things, knowledge was the best: She desired first to learn all sciences, and then purposed to found a college of learned women, in which she would preside, that, by conversing with the old, and educating the young, she might divide her time between the acquisition and communication of wisdom, and raise up for the next age models of prudence, and patterns of piety.

The prince desired a little kingdom, in which he might administer justice in his own person, and see all the parts of government with his own eyes; but he could never fix the limits of his dominion, and was always adding to the number of his subjects.

Imlac and the astronomer were contented to be driven along the stream of life without directing their course to any particular port.

Of these wishes that they had formed they well knew that none could be obtained. They deliberated a while what was to be done, and resolved, when the inundation should cease, to return to Abissinia.

## FINIS

# Appendix A: Other Writing by Samuel Johnson

## 1. From Father Jerome Lobo, *A Voyage to Abyssinia* (1735)

[Johnson's first book-length publication was a translation from the French of a travel book by a Jesuit missionary, Father Jerome Lobo's *Voyage to Abyssinia* (1735). The selected passages show Johnson praising Lobo's realistic descriptions and give an example of Lobo's description of the Abyssinian landscape, which Johnson may have recalled when he wrote *Rasselas*.]

### The Preface

The following relation is so curious and entertaining, and the dissertations that accompany it so judicious and instructive, that the translator is confident his attempt stands in need of no apology, whatever censures may fall on the performance.

The Portuguese traveller, contrary to the general vein of his countrymen, has amused his reader with no romantick absurdities or incredible fictions; whatever he relates, whether true or not, is at least probable, and he who tells nothing exceeding the bounds of probability, has a right to demand, that they should believe him, who cannot contradict him.

He appears by his modest and unaffected narration to have described things as he saw them, to have copied nature from the life, and to have consulted his senses not his imagination; he meets with no basilisks[1] that destroy with their eyes, his crocodiles devour their prey without tears, and his cataracts fall from the rock without deafening the neighbouring inhabitants.

The reader will here find no regions cursed with irremediable barrenness, or bless'd with spontaneous fecundity, no perpetual gloom or unceasing sunshine; nor are the nations here described either devoid of all sense of humanity, or consummate in all private and social virtues, here are no Hottentots[2] without

---

1 A kind of serpent, called also a cockatrice, which is said to drive away all others by his hissing, and to kill by looking. *Dictionary*.
2 Pejorative name for the Khoekhoe, people of southern Africa. A person of inferior intellect or culture; one degraded in the scale of civilization, or ignorant of the usages of civilized society. *OED*.

religion, polity, or articulate language, no Chinese perfectly polite, and completely skill'd in all sciences: he will discover, what will always be discover'd by a diligent and impartial enquirer, that wherever human nature is to be found, there is a mixture of vice and virtue, a contest of passion and reason, and that the Creator doth not appear partial in his distributions, but has balanced in most countries their particular inconveniences by particular favours. [...]

## Chapter VII

[...] After a march of some days, we came to an opening between the mountains, the only passage out of Dancali[1] into Abyssinia. Heaven seems to have made this place on purpose for the repose of weary travelers, who here exchange the tortures of parching thirst, burning sands, and a sultry climate, for the pleasures of shady trees, the refreshment of a clear stream, and the luxury of a cooling breeze. We arrived at this happy place about noon, and the next day at evening left those fanning winds, and woods flourishing with unfading verdure, for the dismal barrenness of the vast uninhabitable plains, from which Abyssinia is supply'd with salt. These plains are surrounded with high mountains, continually covered with thick clouds which the sun draws from the lakes that are here, from which the water runs down into the plain, and is there congealed into salt. Nothing can be more curious, than to see the channels and aquaducts that nature has formed in this hard rock, so exact and of such admirable contrivance, that they seem to be the work of men. To this place caravans of Abyssinia are continually resorting, to carry salt into all parts of the empire, which they set a great value upon, and which in their country is of the same use as money. The superstitious Abyssins imagine, that the cavities of the mountains are inhabited by evil spirits which appear in different shapes, calling those that pass, by their names as in a familiar acquaintance, who, if they go to them, are never seen afterwards. This relation was confirm'd by the Moorish officer who came with us, who, as he said, had lost a servant in that manner, the man certainly fell into the hands of the Galles,[2] who lurk in those dark retreats, cut the throats of the merchants, and carry off their effects.

---

1  Denakil, a region in the north of modern Ethiopia.
2  A pejorative name for the Oromo, one the major ethnic groups in Ethiopia.

# Chapter X

The Nile, which the natives call *Abavi*, that is, the Father of Waters, rises first in Sacala a province of the kingdom of Goiama,[1] which is one of the most fruitful and agreeable of all the Abyssinian dominions. This province is inhabited by a nation of the Agaus,[2] who call themselves Christians, but by daily intermarriages they have allied themselves to the pagan Agaus, and adopted all their customs and ceremonies. These two nations are very numerous, fierce, and unconquerable, inhabiting a country full of mountains, which are covered with woods, and hollow'd by nature into vast caverns, many of which are capable of containing several numerous families, and hundreds of cows; to these recesses the Agaus betake themselves when they are driven out of the plain, where it is almost impossible to find them, and certain ruin to pursue them. This people encreases extremely, every man being allowed so many wives as he hath hundreds of cows, and it is seldom that the hundreds are required to be compleat.

In the eastern part of this kingdom on the declivity of a mountain, whose descent is so easy that it seems a beautiful plain, is that source of the Nile, which has been sought after at so much expence of labour, and about which such variety of conjectures hath been form'd without success. This spring, or rather these two springs, are two holes each about two feet diameter, a stone's cast distant from each other, the one is but about five feet and an half in depth; at least we could not get our plummet[3] farther, perhaps because it was stopped by roots, for the whole place is full of trees; of the other which is somewhat less, with a line of ten feet we could find no bottom, and were assured by the inhabitants, that none ever had been found. 'Tis believed here, that these springs are the vents of a great subterraneous lake, and they have this circumstance to favour their opinion; that the ground is always moist, and so soft, that the water boils up under foot as one walks upon it; this is more visible after rains, for then the ground yields and sinks so much, that I believe it is chiefly supported by the roots of trees, that are interwoven one with another: such is the ground round about these fountains. At a

---

1 A region of Abyssinia, now the province Gojam.
2 An ancient people who lived in northern and central Ethiopia.
3 A weight of lead hung at a string, by which depths are sounded, and perpendicularity is discerned. *Dictionary*.

little distance to the south, is a village named Guix, through which the way lies to the top of the mountain, from whence the traveller discovers a vast extent of land, which appears like a deep valley, though the mountain rises so imperceptibly, that those who go up or down it, are scarce sensible of any declivity. [...]

## 2. *The Vanity of Human Wishes* (1749)

The Tenth Satire of Juvenal[1] Imitated

Let Observation, with extensive view,
Survey mankind, from China to Peru;
Remark each anxious toil, each eager strife,
And watch the busy scenes of crowded life;
Then say how hope and fear, desire and hate,　　　　　5
O'erspread with snares the clouded maze of fate,
Where wav'ring man, betrayed by vent'rous pride,
To tread the dreary paths without a guide,
As treach'rous phantoms in the mist delude,
Shuns fancied ills, or chases airy good;　　　　　10
How rarely reason guides the stubborn choice,
Rules the bold hand, or prompts the suppliant voice;
How nations sink, by darling schemes oppress'd,
When vengeance listens to the fool's request.
Fate wings with ev'ry wish th' afflictive dart,　　　　　15
Each gift of nature, and each grace of art,
With fatal heat impetuous courage glows,
With fatal sweetness elocution flows,
Impeachment stops the speaker's pow'rful breath,
And restless fire precipitates on death.　　　　　20
　　　But scarce observ'd, the knowing and the bold
Fall in the gen'ral massacre of gold;
Wide-wasting pest! that rages unconfin'd,
And crouds with crimes the records of mankind;
For gold his sword the hireling ruffian draws,　　　　　25
For gold the hireling judge distorts the laws;
Wealth heap'd on wealth, nor truth nor safety buys,
The dangers gather as the treasures rise.
　　　Let hist'ry tell where rival kings command,
And dubious title shakes the madded land,　　　　　30

---

1　Decimus Junius Juvenalis (c. 55?–127), Roman satiric poet.

When statues glean the refuse of the sword,
How much more safe the vassal than the lord;
Low skulks the hind[1] beneath the rage of pow'r,
And leaves the wealthy traitor in the Tow'r,
Untouch'd his cottage, and his slumbers sound,                35
Tho' confiscation's vultures hover round.

    The needy traveller, secure and gay,
Walks the wild heath, and sings his toil away.
Does envy seize thee? crush th' upbraiding joy,
Increase his riches and his peace destroy;                    40
Now fears in dire vicissitude invade,
The rustling brake alarms, and quiv'ring shade,
Nor light nor darkness bring his pain relief,
One shews the plunder, and one hides the thief.

    Yet still one gen'ral cry the skies assails,          45
And gain and grandeur load the tainted gales;
Few know the toiling statesman's fear or care,
Th' insidious rival and the gaping heir.

    Once more, Democritus,[2] arise on earth,
With chearful wisdom and instructive mirth,                   50
See motly life in modern trappings dress'd,
And feed with varied fools th' eternal jest:
Thou who couldst laugh where want enchain'd caprice,
Toil crush'd conceit, and man was of a piece;
Where wealth unlov'd without a mourner dy'd,                  55
And scarce a sycophant was fed by pride;
Where ne'er was known the form of mock debate,
Or see a new-made mayor's unwieldy state;
Where change of fav'rites made no change of laws,
And senates heard before they judg'd a cause;                60
How wouldst thou shake at Britain's modish[3] tribe,
Dart the quick taunt, and edge the piercing gibe?
Attentive truth and nature to descry,
And pierce each scene with philosophic eye.
To thee were solemn toys or empty shew,                      65
The robes of pleasure and the veils of woe:
All aid the farce, and all thy mirth maintain,

---

1  A servant. *Dictionary*.
2  Greek philosopher of the late fifth century BCE, known as the laughing philosopher for his response to human folly.
3  Fashionable; formed according to the reigning custom. *Dictionary*.

Whose joys are causeless, or whose griefs are vain.

Such was the scorn that fill'd the sage's mind,
Renew'd at ev'ry glance on humankind;        70
How just that scorn ere yet thy voice declare,
Search every state, and canvass ev'ry pray'r.

Unnumbered suppliants crowd Preferment's gate,
Athirst for wealth, and burning to be great;
Delusive Fortune hears th' incessant call,       75
They mount, they shine, evaporate, and fall.
On ev'ry stage the foes of peace attend,
Hate dogs their flight, and insult mocks their end.
Love ends with hope, the sinking statesman's door
Pours in the morning worshiper no more;      80
For growing names the weekly scribbler lies,
To growing wealth the dedicator flies,
From every room descends the painted face,
That hung the bright Palladium of the place,
And smoak'd in kitchens, or in auctions sold,      85
To better features yields the frame of gold;
For now no more we trace in ev'ry line
Heroic worth, benevolence divine:
The form distorted justifies the fall,
And detestation rids th'indignant wall.      90

But will not Britain hear the last appeal,
Sign her foes' doom, or guard her fav'rites' zeal?
Through Freedom's sons no more remonstrance rings,
Degrading nobles and controuling kings;
Our supple tribes repress their patriot throats,      95
And ask no questions but the price of votes;
With weekly libels and septennial ale,[1]
Their wish is full to riot and to rail.

In full-blown dignity, see Wolsey[2] stand,
Law in his voice, and fortune in his hand:      100
To him the church, the realm, their pow'rs consign,
Thro' him the rays of regal bounty shine,
Turn'd by his nod the stream of honour flows,
His smile alone security bestows:

---

1  The Septennial Act of 1716 required parliamentary elections to be held
    at least every seven years, thus ale given to potential voters by candi-
    dates for election.
2  Thomas Cardinal Wolsey (c. 1475–1530), Archbishop of York, Lord
    Chancellor, who rose to and dramatically fell from great heights of
    power during Henry VIII's reign.

Still to new heights his restless wishes tow'r,                105
Claim leads to claim, and pow'r advances pow'r;
Till conquest unresisted ceas'd to please,
And rights submitted, left him none to seize.
At length his sov'reign frowns—the train of state
Mark the keen glance, and watch the sign to hate.              110
Where-e'er he turns he meets a stranger's eye,
His suppliants scorn him, and his followers fly;
At once is lost the pride of aweful state,
The golden canopy, the glitt'ring plate,
The regal palace, the luxurious board,                         115
The liv'ried army, and the menial lord.
With age, with cares, with maladies oppress'd,
He seeks the refuge of monastic rest.
Grief aids disease, remember'd folly stings,
And his last sighs reproach the faith of kings.                120
    Speak thou, whose thoughts at humble peace repine,
Shall Wolsey's wealth, with Wolsey's end be thine?
Or liv'st thou now, with safer pride content,
The wisest justice on the banks of Trent?
For why did Wolsey near the steeps of fate,                    125
On weak foundations raise th' enormous weight?
Why but to sink beneath misfortune's blow,
With louder ruin to the gulphs below?
    What gave great Villiers[1] to th'assassin's knife,
And fixed disease on Harley's[2] closing life?                 130
What murder'd Wentworth,[3] and what exil'd Hyde,[4]

---

1   George Villiers (1592–1628), first duke of Buckingham, favorite of
    James I and Charles I who was assassinated during controversy over his
    political and financial dealings.
2   Robert Harley (1661–1724), first earl of Oxford and Mortimer, Tory
    politician, Chancellor of the Exchequer, Lord Treasurer. He was sus-
    pected of Jabobitism; articles of impeachment were brought against him
    and he was imprisoned in 1715. He was released when the charges were
    dropped in 1717. He amassed a great library, part of which Johnson cat-
    alogued (1744–46).
3   Thomas Wentworth (1593–1641), first earl of Strafford, lord lieutenant
    of Ireland, chief councillor of Charles I, was accused of treason by the
    House of Commons, impeached, and executed despite the king's efforts
    to protect him.
4   Edward Hyde (1609–74), first earl of Clarendon, lord chancellor to
    Charles II. His daughter married James, duke of York (later James II).
    Facing impeachment, he went into exile in 1667 and died abroad.

By kings protected, and to kings ally'd?
What but their wish indulg'd in courts to shine,
And pow'r too great to keep, or to resign?
    When first the college rolls receive his name, 135
The young enthusiast quits his ease for fame;
Through all his veins the fever of renown
Burns from the strong contagion of the gown;
O'er Bodley's dome[1] his future labours spread,
And Bacon's mansion* trembles o'er his head. 140
Are these thy views? proceed, illustrious youth,
And virtue guard thee to the throne of Truth!
Yet should thy soul indulge the gen'rous heat,
Till captive Science yields her last retreat;
Should Reason guide thee with her brightest ray, 145
And pour on misty Doubt resistless day;
Should no false Kindness lure to loose delight,
Nor Praise relax, nor Difficulty fright;
Should tempting Novelty thy cell refrain,
And Sloth effuse[2] her opiate fumes in vain; 150
Should Beauty blunt on fops her fatal dart,
Nor claim the triumph of a letter'd heart;
Should no disease thy torpid[3] veins invade,
Nor Melancholy's phantoms haunt thy shade;
Yet hope not life from grief or danger free, 155
Nor think the doom of man revers'd for thee:
Deign on the passing world to turn thine eyes,
And pause awhile from letters, to be wise;
There mark what ills the scholar's life assail,

---

\*   There is a tradition, that the study of friar Bacon, built on an arch over
the bridge, will fall, when a man greater than Bacon shall pass under it.
[Johnson's note. Roger Bacon (c. 1214–92?), philosopher and Franciscan
friar who taught at Oxford. "The reputed 'mansion' of Roger Bacon was
a gatehouse at the north end of Folly Bridge at Oxford. It was demolished in 1779." E.L. McAdam, Jr. with George Milne, eds., *Poems, Yale
Edition of the Works of Samuel Johnson*, Vol. VI (New Haven: Yale UP,
1964) 98.]

---

1   The Bodleian Library, Oxford University.
2   To pour out; to spill; to shed. *Dictionary.*
3   Numbed; motionless; sluggish; not active. *Dictionary.*

Toil, envy, want, the patron,[1] and the jail.                    160
See nations slowly wise, and meanly just,
To buried merit raise the tardy bust.
If dreams yet flatter, once again attend,
Hear Lydiat's[2] life, and Galileo's[3] end.

    Nor deem, when learning her last prize bestows,          165
The glitt'ring eminence exempt from foes;
See when the vulgar 'scape, despis'd or aw'd,
Rebellion's vengeful talons seize on Laud.[4]
From meaner minds, tho' smaller fines content,
The plunder'd palace or sequester'd rent;                         170
Marked out by dangerous parts he meets the shock,
And fatal Learning leads him to the block:
Around his tomb let Art and Genius weep,
But hear his death, ye blockheads, hear and sleep.

    The festal[5] blazes, the triumphal show,                175
The ravish'd standard, and the captive foe,
The senate's thanks, the gazette's pompous tale,
With force resistless o'er the brave prevail.
Such bribes the rapid Greek[6] o'er Asia whirled,

---

1  Replaces "garret" in the first edition. Johnson had been encouraged to
   dedicate his *Plan of an English Dictionary* (1747) to Philip Dormer, Lord
   Chesterfield, in return for financial support of the project, which
   Chesterfield never delivered. Shortly before the *Dictionary* appeared,
   Chesterfield published essays praising the work; Johnson wrote Chesterfield a letter castigating him for suddenly playing the public role of
   patron after rudely neglecting Johnson when his patronage would have
   been welcome. See Boswell 181–89. In the *Dictionary*, Johnson defines
   "patron" as "commonly a wretch who supports with insolence and is
   paid with flattery."
2  Thomas Lydiat (1572–1646), fellow of New College, Oxford, accomplished mathematician, chronologist, astronomer, and Protestant thinker
   who was persecuted for his Royalist sympathies and repeatedly imprisoned for debt.
3  Galileo Galilei (1564–1642), natural philosopher, astronomer, mathematician, who was imprisoned for heresy by the Inquisition in 1633 and
   then spent the rest of his life under house arrest.
4  William Laud (1573–1645), chancellor of Oxford University, archbishop
   of Canterbury under Charles I who was impeached for high treason and
   advancement of popery by the House of Commons in 1640, imprisoned
   in the Tower, and eventually executed.
5  Of or pertaining to a feast or festivity. *OED*.
6  Alexander the Great.

For such the steady Romans shook the world;                              180
For such in distant lands the Britons shine,
And stain with blood the Danube or the Rhine;
This pow'r has praise, that virtue scarce can warm,
Till fame supplies the universal charm.
Yet Reason frowns on War's unequal game,                                 185
Where wasted nations raise a single name,
And mortgag'd states their grandsires' wreaths regret,
From age to age in everlasting debt;
Wreaths which at last the dear-bought right convey
To rust on medals, or on stones decay.                                   190
      On what foundation stands the warrior's pride,
How just his hopes let Swedish Charles[1] decide;
A frame of adamant, a soul of fire,
No dangers fright him, and no labours tire;
O'er love, o'er fear, extends his wide domain,                           195
Unconquer'd lord of pleasure and of pain;
No joys to him pacific scepters yield,
War sounds the trump, he rushes to the field;
Behold surrounding kings their pow'r combine,
And one capitulate,[2] and one resign;[3]                                200
Peace courts his hand, but spreads her charms in vain;
"Think nothing gained," he cries, "till nought remain,
On Moscow's walls till Gothic standards fly,
And all be mine beneath the polar sky."
The march begins in military state,                                       205
And nations on his eye suspended wait;
Stern Famine guards the solitary coast,
And Winter barricades the realms of Frost;
He comes, not want and cold his course delay;—
Hide, blushing Glory, hide Pultowa's[4] day:                             210
The vanquish'd hero leaves his broken bands,
And shews his miseries in distant lands;
Condemn'd a needy suppliant to wait,

---

1  Charles XII of Sweden (1682–1717) won major battles from a young
   age and relied heavily on warfare to solve disputes, to the eventual dis-
   advantage of Sweden. He died in battle. Johnson considered Charles as
   a subject for a play. McAdam 101.
2  Frederick IV of Denmark capitulated to Charles in 1700.
3  Augustus II of Poland resigned his throne to Charles in 1704.
4  Site of the Russian Peter the Great's victory over Charles in 1709.

While ladies interpose,[1] and slaves debate.
But did not Chance at length her error mend? 215
Did no subverted empire mark his end?
Did rival monarchs give the fatal wound?
Or hostile millions press him to the ground?
His fall was destin'd to a barren strand,
A petty fortress, and a dubious hand; 220
He left the name, at which the world grew pale,
To point a moral, or adorn a tale.
     All times their scenes of pompous woes afford,
From Persia's tyrant[2] to Bavaria's lord.[3]
In gay hostility, and barb'rous pride, 225
With half mankind embattled at his side,
Great Xerxes comes to seize the certain prey,
And starves exhausted regions in his way;
Attendant Flatt'ry counts his myriads o'er,
Till counted myriads soothe his pride no more; 230
Fresh praise is tried till madness fires his mind,
The waves he lashes, and enchains the wind;
New pow'rs are claim'd, new pow'rs are still bestow'd,
Till rude resistance lops the spreading god;
The daring Greeks deride the martial show, 235
And heap their valleys with the gaudy foe;
Th' insulted sea with humbler thoughts he gains,
A single skiff to speed his flight remains;
Th' incumber'd oar scarce leaves the dreaded coast
Through purple billows and a floating host. 240
     The bold Bavarian, in a luckless hour,
Tries the dread summits of Cesarean pow'r,
With unexpected legions bursts away,
And sees defenseless realms[4] receive his sway;
Short sway! fair Austria[5] spreads her mournful charms, 245

---

1  Probably a reference to Peter's empress Catherine.
2  Xerxes (519–465 BCE), Persian king, mounted a major invasion of
   Greece across the Hellespont and was defeated in 480 BCE, signalling
   the end of his empire.
3  Charles Albert (1697–1745), Elector of Bavaria, started the War of the
   Austrian Succession (1740–48). He was briefly named Charles VII,
   Holy Roman Emperor in 1742.
4  He invaded Upper Austria and Bohemia.
5  Maria Theresa (1717–80), daughter of Emperor Charles VI, who also
   claimed the right of succession. Most European powers participated in
   this war.

The queen, the beauty, sets the world in arms;
From hill to hill the beacon's rousing blaze
Spreads wide the hope of plunder and of praise;
The fierce Croatian, and the wild Hussar,[1]
And all the sons of ravage croud the war;                    250
The baffled prince in honour's flatt'ring bloom
Of hasty greatness finds the fatal doom,
His foes' derision, and his subjects' blame,
And steals to death from anguish and from shame.

    Enlarge my life with multitude of days,                    255
In health, in sickness, thus the suppliant prays;
Hides from himself his state, and shuns to know,
That life protracted is protracted woe.
Time hovers o'er, impatient to destroy,
And shuts up all the passages of joy:                        260
In vain their gifts the bounteous seasons pour,
The fruit autumnal, and the vernal flow'r,
With listless eyes the dotard views the store,
He views, and wonders that they please no more;
Now pall the tasteless meats, and joyless wines,             265
And Luxury with sighs her slave resigns.
Approach, ye minstrels, try the soothing strain,
Diffuse the tuneful lenitives[2] of pain:
No sounds alas would touch th' impervious ear,
Though dancing mountains witness'd Orpheus[3] near;          270
Nor lute nor lyre his feeble pow'rs attend,
Nor sweeter music of a virtuous friend,
But everlasting dictates croud his tongue,
Perversely grave, or positively wrong.
The still returning tale, and ling'ring jest,               275
Perplex the fawning niece and pamper'd guest,
While growing hopes scarce awe the gath'ring sneer,
And scarce a legacy can bribe to hear;
The watchful guests still hint the last offense,
The daughter's petulance, the son's expense,                280
Improve his heady rage with treach'rous skill,
And mould his passions till they make his will.

    Unnumber'd maladies his joints invade,
Lay siege to life and press the dire blockade;

---

1  Hungarian light cavalry.
2  Any thing applied to ease pain. *Dictionary*.
3  Superb musician in Greek mythology, son of a Muse.

But unextinguish'd Avarice still remains, 285
And dreaded losses aggravate his pains;
He turns, with anxious heart and cripled hands,
His bonds of debt, and mortgages of lands;
Or views his coffers with suspicious eyes,
Unlocks his gold, and counts it till he dies. 290
    But grant, the virtues of a temp'rate prime
Bless with an age exempt from scorn or crime;
An age that melts with unperceiv'd decay,
And glides in modest innocence away;
Whose peaceful day Benevolence endears, 295
Whose night congratulating Conscience cheers;
The gen'ral fav'rite as the gen'ral friend:
Such age there is, and who shall wish its end?
    Yet ev'n on this her load Misfortune flings,
To press the weary minutes' flagging wings: 300
New sorrow rises as the day returns,
A sister sickens, or a daughter mourns.
Now kindred Merit fills the sable bier,
Now lacerated Friendship claims a tear.
Year chases year, decay pursues decay, 305
Still drops some joy from with'ring life away;
New forms arise, and diff'rent views engage,
Superfluous lags the vet'ran on the stage,
Till pitying Nature signs the last release,
And bids afflicted worth retire to peace. 310
    But few there are whom hours like these await,
Who set unclouded in the gulphs of fate.
From Lydia's monarch[1] should the search descend,
By Solon cautioned to regard his end,
In life's last scene what prodigies surprise, 315
Fears of the brave, and follies of the wise?
From Marlb'rough's[2] eyes the streams of dotage flow,

---

1  In Herodotus' fictitious account of a meeting between the wealthy
    Croesus (reigned 560–546 BCE), last king of Lydia, and Solon
    (630–560 BCE), Athenian lawgiver, Solon warns Croesus that riches do
    not constitute happiness and that he cannot judge a man's happiness
    until he sees how his life ends.
2  John Churchill (1650–1722), first duke of Marlborough, brilliant
    general during the War of the Spanish Succession (1702–13), known
    especially for his victory of the battle at Blenheim, was impaired in his
    last years by the effects of two paralytic strokes.

And Swift[1] expires a driv'ler and a show.

The teeming[2] mother, anxious for her race,
Begs for each birth the fortune of a face:       320
Yet Vane[3] could tell what ills from beauty spring;
And Sedley[4] cursed the form that pleas'd a king.
Ye nymphs of rosy lips and radiant eyes,
Whom Pleasure keeps too busy to be wise,
Whom Joys with soft varieties invite,       325
By day the frolick, and the dance by night,
Who frown with vanity, who smile with art,
And ask the latest fashion of the heart,
What care, what rules your heedless charms shall save,
Each nymph your rival, and each youth your slave?       330
Against your fame with fondness hates combines,
The rival batters, and the lover mines.
With distant voice neglected Virtue calls,
Less heard and less, the faint remonstrance falls;
Tir'd with contempt, she quits the slipp'ry reign,       335
And Pride and Prudence take her seat in vain.
In croud at once, where none the pass defend,
The harmless Freedom, and the private Friend.
The guardians yield, by force superior ply'd;
By Int'rest, Prudence; and by Flatt'ry, Pride.       340
Now beauty falls betray'd, despis'd, distress'd,
And hissing Infamy proclaims the rest.

Where then shall Hope and Fear their objects find?
Must dull Suspense corrupt the stagnant mind?
Must helpless man, in ignorance sedate,       345
Roll darkling down the torrent of his fate?
Must no dislike alarm, no wishes rise,

---

1   Jonathan Swift (1667–1745), writer and dean of St. Patrick's Cathedral,
    Dublin, whose final five years of life were marked by bouts of insanity
    and illness. "Servants are said to have shown him to tourists for a fee."
    McAdam 106.

2   To be pregnant; to engender young. *Dictionary*.

3   Anne Vane (1705?–36), mistress of Frederick Lewis, Prince of Wales,
    was the subject of scandal during her life but a sentimental tragedy,
    *Vanella*, published after her death depicted her dying from the Prince's
    neglect.

4   Catharine Sedley (1657–1717), mistress of James, Duke of York (later
    James II), who broke off his affair with her when he ascended to the
    throne.

No cries attempt the mercies of the skies?
Enquirer, cease, petitions yet remain,
Which heav'n may hear, nor deem religion vain.                  350
Still raise for good the supplicating voice,
But leave to heav'n the measure and the choice,
Safe in his pow'r, whose eyes discern afar
The secret ambush of a specious pray'r.
Implore his aid, in his decisions rest,                        355
Secure whate'er he gives, he gives the best.
Yet when the sense of sacred presence fires,
And strong devotion to the skies aspires,
Pour forth thy fervours for a healthful mind,
Obedient passions, and a will resign'd;                        360
For love, which scarce collective man can fill;
For patience sov'reign o'er transmuted ill;
For faith, that panting for a happier seat,
Counts death kind Nature's signal of retreat:
These goods for man the laws of heav'n ordain,                 365
These goods he grants, who grants the pow'r to gain;
With these celestial wisdom calms the mind,
And makes the happiness she does not find.

## 3. *Rambler* No. 4, Saturday, 31 March 1750: "The Modern Form of Romances"

*Simul et jucunda et idonea dicere vitae.*
Horace, *Ars Poetica*, l.334.

And join both profit and delight in one.
Creech.[1]

The works of fiction, with which the present generation seems
more particularly delighted, are such as exhibit life in its true
state, diversified only by accidents that daily happen in the world,
and influenced by passions and qualities which are really to be
found in conversing with mankind.

This kind of writing may be termed not improperly the
comedy of romance, and is to be conducted nearly by the rules
of comic poetry. Its province is to bring about natural events by
easy means, and to keep up curiosity without the help of wonder:
it is therefore precluded from the machines and expedients of the

---

1   Thomas Creech (1659–1700), translator and classical scholar.

heroic romance, and can neither employ giants to snatch away a lady from the nuptial rites, nor knights to bring her back from captivity; it can neither bewilder its personages in desarts, nor lodge them in imaginary castles.

I remember a remark made by Scaliger upon Pontanus,[1] that all his writings are filled with the same images; and that if you take from him his lillies and his roses, his satyrs and his dryads, he will have nothing left that can be called poetry. In like manner, almost all the fictions of the last age will vanish, if you deprive them of a hermit and a wood, a battle and a shipwreck.

Why this wild strain of imagination found reception so long, in polite and learned ages, it is not easy to conceive; but we cannot wonder that, while readers could be procured, the authors were willing to continue it: for when a man had by practice gained some fluency of language, he had no further care than to retire to his closet, let loose his invention, and heat his mind with incredibilities; a book was thus produced without fear of criticism, without the toil of study, without knowledge of nature, or acquaintance with life.

The task of our present writers is very different; it requires together with that learning which is to be gained from books, that experience which can never be attained by solitary diligence, but must arise from general converse, and accurate observation of the living world. Their performances have, as Horace expresses it, *plus oneris quantum veniae minus*, little indulgence, and therefore more difficulty.[2] They are engaged in portraits of which every one knows the original, and can detect any deviation from exactness of resemblance. Other writings are safe, except from the malice of learning, but these are in danger from every common reader; as the slipper ill executed was censured by a shoemaker who happened to stop in his way at Venus of Apelles.[3]

But the fear of not being approved as just copyers of human manners, is not the most important concern that an author of this sort ought to have before him. These books are written chiefly to the young, the ignorant, and the idle, to whom they serve as lectures of conduct, and introductions into life. They are the enter-

---

1  Julius Caesar Scaliger (1484–1558), French classical scholar (born in Italy). Johnson may be referring to his *Poetics*, VI.4. Giovanni Pontano (1426–1503), celebrated writer of Renaissance Italy.

2  Horace, *Epistles II and Epistle to the Pisones (Ars Poetica)*, Niall Rudd, ed. (Cambridge: Cambridge UP, 1989) II.I.170 [p. 48].

3  Pliny *Natural History*, Vol. IX, H. Rackham, ed., *Loeb Classical Library* (Cambridge: Harvard UP, 1961) Book XXXV.36.85 [p. 324-25].

tainment of minds unfurnished with ideas, and therefore easily susceptible of impressions; not fixed by principles, and therefore easily following the current of fancy; not informed by experience, and consequently open to every false suggestion and partial account.

That the highest degree of reverence should be paid to youth, and that nothing indecent should be suffered to approach their eyes or ears; are precepts extorted by sense and virtue from an ancient writer, by no means eminent for chastity of thought.[1] The same kind, tho' not the same degree of caution, is required in every thing which is laid before them, to secure them from unjust prejudices, perverse opinions, and incongruous combinations of images.

In the romances formerly written, every transaction and sentiment was so remote from all that passes among men, that the reader was in very little danger of making any applications to himself; the virtues and crimes were equally beyond his sphere of activity; and he amused himself with heroes and with traitors, deliverers and persecutors, as with beings of another species, whose actions were regulated upon motives of their own, and who had neither faults nor excellencies in common with himself.

But when an adventurer is levelled with the rest of the world, and acts in such scenes of the universal drama, as may be the lot of any other man; young spectators fix their eyes upon him with closer attention, and hope by observing his behaviour and success to regulate their own practices, when they shall be engaged in the like part.

For this reason these familiar histories may perhaps be made of greater use than the solemnities of professed morality, and convey the knowledge of vice and virtue with more efficacy than axioms and definitions. But if the power of example is so great, as to take possession of the memory by a kind of violence, and produce effects almost without the intervention of the will, care ought to be taken that, when the choice is unrestrained, the best examples only should be exhibited; and that which is likely to operate so strongly, should not be mischievous or uncertain in its effects.

The chief advantage which these fictions have over real life is, that their authors are at liberty, tho' not to invent, yet to select objects, and to cull from the mass of mankind, those individuals

---

1 Juvenal's Satire XIV discusses the impressionableness of children and warns parents not to set bad examples through their own behavior. See Susanna Morton Brand, ed., *Juvenal and Persius*, *Loeb Classical Library*, Vol. 91 (Cambridge: Harvard UP, 2004) 456-85.

upon which the attention ought most to be employ'd; as a diamond, though it cannot be made, may be polished by art, and placed in such a situation, as to display that lustre which before was buried among common stones.

It is justly considered as the greatest excellency of art, to imitate nature; but it is necessary to distinguish those parts of nature, which are most proper for imitation: greater care is still required in representing life, which is so often discoloured by passion, or deformed by wickedness. If the world be promiscuously described, I cannot see of what use it can be to read the account; or why it may not be as safe to turn the eye immediately upon mankind, as upon a mirror which shows all that presents itself without discrimination.

It is therefore not a sufficient vindication of a character, that it is drawn as it appears, for many characters ought never to be drawn; nor of a narrative, that the train of events is agreeable to observation and experience, for that observation which is called knowledge of the world, will be found much more frequently to make men cunning than good. The purpose of these writings is surely not only to show mankind, but to provide that they may be seen hereafter with less hazard; to teach the means of avoiding the snares which are laid by Treachery for Innocence, without infusing any wish for that superiority with which the betrayer flatters his vanity; to give the power of counteracting fraud, without the temptation to practise it; to initiate youth by mock encounters in the art of necessary defence, and to increase prudence without impairing virtue.

Many writers, for the sake of following nature, so mingle good and bad qualities in their principal personages, that they are both equally conspicuous; and as we accompany them through their adventures with delight, and are led by degrees to interest ourselves in their favour, we lose the abhorrence of their faults, because they do not hinder our pleasure, or, perhaps, regard them with some kindness for being united with so much merit.

There have been men indeed splendidly wicked, whose endowments threw a brightness on their crimes, and whom scarce any villainy made perfectly detestable, because they never could be wholly divested of their excellencies; but such have been in all ages the great corrupters of the world, and their resemblance ought no more to be preserved, than the art of murdering without pain.

Some have advanced, without due attention to the consequences of this notion, that certain virtues have their correspondent faults, and therefore that to exhibit either apart is to deviate from probability. Thus men are observed by Swift to be "grateful in the same degree as they are resentful."[1] This principle, with others of the same kind, supposes man to act from a brute impulse, and persue a certain degree of inclination, without any choice of the object; for, otherwise, though it should be allowed that gratitude and resentment arise from the same constitution of the passions, it follows not that they will be equally indulged when the reason is consulted; yet unless that consequence be admitted, this sagacious maxim becomes an empty sound, without any relation to practice or to life.

Nor is it evident, that even the first motions to these effects are always in the same proportion. For pride, which produces quickness of resentment, will obstruct gratitude, by unwillingness to admit that inferiority which obligation implies; and it is very unlikely, that he who cannot think he receives a favour will acknowledge or repay it.

It is of the utmost importance to mankind, that positions of this tendency should be laid open and confuted; for while men consider good and evil as springing from the same root, they will spare the one for the sake of the other, and in judging, if not of others at least of themselves, will be apt to estimate their virtues by their vices. To this fatal error all those will contribute, who confound the colours of right and wrong, and instead of helping to settle their boundaries, mix them with so much art, that no common mind is able to disunite them.

In narratives, where historical veracity has no place, I cannot discover why there should be not be exhibited the most perfect idea of virtue; of virtue not angelical, nor above probability, for what we cannot credit we shall never imitate, but the highest and purest that humanity can reach, which, exercised in such trials as the various revolutions of things shall bring upon it, may, by conquering some calamities, and enduring others, teach us what we may hope, and what we can perform. Vice, for vice is necessary to be shewn, should always disgust; nor should the graces of gaiety, or the dignity of courage, be so united with it, as to reconcile it to the mind. Wherever it appears, it should raise hatred by the

---

1   Swift–Pope *Miscellanies* II (1727): 354. "The statement is actually by Pope." W.J. Bate and Albrecht B. Strauss, eds., *The Rambler, Yale Edition of the Works of Samuel Johnson* Vol. III (New Haven: Yale UP, 1969) 23 n.9.

malignity of its practices, and contempt by the meanness of its stratagems; for while it is supported by either parts or spirit, it will be seldom heartily abhorred. The Roman tyrant was content to be hated, if he was but feared;[1] and there are thousands of the readers of romances willing to be thought wicked, if they may be allowed to be wits. It is therefore to be steadily inculcated, that virtue is the highest proof of understanding, and the only solid basis of greatness; and that vice is the natural consequence of narrow thoughts, that it begins in mistake, and ends in ignominy.

## 4. *Rambler* No. 204, Saturday, 29 February 1752: "the History of Ten Days of Seged, Emperor of Ethiopia"

*Nemo tam divos habuit faventes,*
*Crastinum ut possit sibi polliceri.*
Seneca, *Thyestes*, 1.619–20.

Of heav'n's protection who can be
So confident to utter this—?
To-morrow I will spend in bliss.
F. Lewis[2]

Seged, lord of Ethiopia, to the inhabitants of the world: To the sons of presumption, humility, and fear; and to the daughters of sorrow, content and acquiescence.

Thus in the twenty-seventh year of his reign, spoke Seged the monarch of forty nations, the distributer of the waters of the Nile. "At length, Seged, thy toils are at an end, thou hast reconciled disaffection, thou hast suppressed rebellion, thou hast pacified the jealousies of thy courtiers, thou hast chased war from thy confines, and erected fortresses in the lands of thy enemies. All who have offended thee, tremble in thy presence, and wherever thy voice is heard, it is obeyed. Thy throne is surrounded by armies, numerous as the locusts of the summer, and resistless as the blasts of pestilence. Thy magazines are stored with ammunition, thy treasuries overflow with the tribute of conquered kingdoms. Plenty waves upon thy fields, and opulence glitters in thy cities. Thy nod is as the earthquake that shakes the mountains, and thy

---

1 J.C. Rolfe, trans., *Suetonius* vol. 1, "Lives of the Caesars, Book IV: Gaius Caligula," *Loeb Classical Library* vol. 31 (Cambridge: Harvard UP, 1998) 418-507.

2 F. Lewis is unidentified.

smile as the dawn of the vernal day. In thy hand is the strength of thousands, and thy health is the health of millions. Thy palace is gladdened by the song of praise, and thy path perfumed by the breath of benediction. Thy subjects gaze upon thy greatness and think of danger or misery no more. Why, Seged, wilt not thou partake the blessings thou bestowest? Why shouldst thou only forbear to rejoice in this general felicity? Why should thy face be clouded with anxiety, when the meanest of those who call thee sovereign, gives the day to festivity, and the night to peace? At length, Seged, reflect and be wise. What is the gift of conquest but safety, why are riches collected but to purchase happiness?"

Seged then ordered the house of pleasure, built in an island of the lake Dambea,[1] to be prepared for his reception. "I will retire," says he, "for ten days from tumult and care, from counsels and decrees. Long quiet is not the lot of the governors of nations, but a cessation of ten days cannot be denied me. This short interval of happiness may surely be secured from the interruption of fear or perplexity, sorrow or disappointment. I will exclude all trouble from my abode, and remove from my thoughts whatever may confuse the harmony of the concert, or abate the sweetness of the banquet. I will fill the whole capacity of my soul with enjoyment, and try what it is to live without a wish unsatisfied."

In a few days the orders were performed, and Seged hasted to the palace of Dambea, which stood in an island cultivated only for pleasure, planted with every flower that spreads its colours to the sun, and every shrub that sheds fragrance in the air. In one part of this extensive garden, were open walks for excursions in the morning; in another, thick groves, and silent arbours, and bubbling fountains for repose at noon. All that could solace the sense, or flatter the fancy, all that industry could extort from nature, or wealth furnish to art, all that conquest could seize, or beneficence attract, was collected together, and every perception of delight was excited and gratified.

Into this delicious region Seged summoned all the persons in his court, who seemed eminently qualified to receive, or communicate pleasure. His call was readily obeyed; the young, the fair, the vivacious, and the witty, were all in haste to be sated with felicity. They sailed jocund[2] over the lake, which seemed to

---

1 Lobo's *Voyage to Abyssinia* describes Lake Dambia as one of the sources of the Nile.
2 Merry; gay; airy; lively. *Dictionary.*

smooth its surface before them: Their passage was cheered with musick, and their hearts dilated with expectation.

Seged landing here with his band of pleasure, determined from that hour to break off all acquaintance with discontent, to give his heart for ten days to ease and jollity, and then fall back to the common state of man, and suffer his life to be diversified, as before, with joy and sorrow.

He immediately entered his chamber, to consider where he should begin his circle of happiness. He had all the artists of delight before him, but knew not whom to call, since he could not enjoy one, but by delaying the performance of another. He chose and rejected, he resolved and changed his resolution till his faculties were harrassed, and his thoughts confused, then returned to the apartment where his presence was expected, with languid eyes and clouded countenance, and spread the infection of uneasiness over the whole assembly. He observed their depression, and was offended, for he found his vexation encreased by those whom he expected to dissipate and relieve it. He retired again to his private chamber, and sought for consolation in his own mind; one thought flowed in upon another; a long succession of images seized his attention; the moments crept imperceptibly away through the gloom of pensiveness, till having recovered his tranquillity, he lifted up his head, and saw the lake brightened by the setting sun. "Such," said Seged, sighing, "is the longer day of human existence: Before we have learned to use it, we find it at an end."

The regret which he felt for the loss of so great a part of his first day, took from him all disposition to enjoy the evening; and, after having endeavoured, for the sake of his attendants, to force an air of gaiety, and excite the mirth which he could not share, he resolved to refer his hopes to the next morning, and lay down to partake with the slaves of labour and poverty the blessing of sleep.

He rose early the second morning, and resolved now to be happy. He therefore fixed upon the gate of the palace an edict, importing, that whoever, during nine days, should appear in the presence of the king with dejected countenance, or utter any expression of discontent or sorrow, should be driven forever from the palace of Dambea.

This edict was immediately made known in every chamber of the court, and bower of the gardens. Mirth was frighted away, and they who were before dancing in the lawns, or singing in the shades, were at once engaged in the care of regulating their looks, that Seged might find his will punctually obeyed, and see none among them liable to banishment.

Seged now met every face settled in a smile; but a smile that betrayed solicitude,[1] timidity, and constraint. He accosted his favourites with familiarity and softness; but they durst not speak without premeditation, lest they should be convicted of discontent or sorrow. He proposed diversions, to which no objection was made, because objection would have implied uneasiness; but they were regarded with indifference by the courtiers, who had no other desire than to signalize[2] themselves by clamorous exultation. He offered various topics of conversation, but obtained only forced jests, and laborious laughter, and after many attempts to animate his train[3] to confidence and alacrity, was obliged to confess to himself the impotence of command, and resign another day to grief and disappointment.

He at last relieved his companions from their terrors, and shut himself up in his chamber to ascertain, by different measures, the felicity of the succeeding days. At length, he threw himself on the bed and closed his eyes, but imagined, in his sleep, that his palace and gardens were overwhelmed by an inundation, and waked with all the terrors of a man struggling in the water. He composed himself again to rest, but was affrighted by an imaginary irruption[4] into his kingdom, and striving, as is usual in dreams, without ability to move, fancied himself betrayed to his enemies, and again started up with horror and indignation.

It was now day, and fear was so strongly impressed on his mind, that he could sleep no more. He rose, but his thoughts were filled with the deluge and invasion, nor was he able to disengage his attention, or mingle with vacancy and ease in any amusement. At length his perturbation gave way to reason, and he resolved no longer to be harrassed by visionary miseries; but before this resolution could be completed half the day had elapsed: He felt a new conviction of the uncertainty of human schemes, and could not forbear to bewail the weakness of that being, whose quiet was to be interrupted by vapours of the fancy. Having been first disturbed by a dream, he afterwards grieved that a dream could disturb him. He at last discovered, that his

---

1  Anxiety; carefulness. *Dictionary.*
2  To make eminent; to make remarkable. *Dictionary.*
3  A retinue; a number of followers or attendants. *Dictionary.*
4  Inroad; burst of invaders into any place. *Dictionary.*

terrors and grief were equally vain, and, that to lose the present in lamenting the past, was voluntarily to protract a melancholy vision. The third day was now declining, and Seged again resolved to be happy on the morrow.

## 5. *Rambler* no. 205, Tuesday, 3 March 1752

—*Volat ambiguis*
*Mobilis alis hora, nec ulli*
*Praestat velox Fortuna fidem.*
Seneca, *Hippolytus*, 1. 1141–43.

On fickle wings the minutes haste,
And fortune's favours never last.
F. Lewis.

On the fourth morning Seged rose early, refreshed with sleep, vigorous with health, and eager with expectation. He entered the garden, attended by the princes and ladies of his court, and seeing nothing about him but airy cheerfulness, began to say to his heart, "This day shall be a day of pleasure." The sun played upon the water, the birds warbled in the groves, and the gales quivered among the branches. He roved from walk to walk as chance directed him, and sometimes listened to the songs, sometimes mingled with the dancers, sometimes let loose his imagination in flights of merriment; and sometimes uttered grave reflections, and sententious[1] maxims, and feasted on the admiration with which they were received.

Thus the day rolled on, without any accident of vexation, or intrusion of melancholy thoughts. All that beheld him caught gladness from his looks, and the sight of happiness conferred by himself filled his heart with satisfaction: But having passed three hours in this harmless luxury, he was alarmed on a sudden by an universal scream among the women, and turning back, saw the whole assembly flying in confusion. A young crocodile had risen out of the lake, and was ranging the garden in wantonness or hunger. Seged beheld him with indignation, as a disturber of his felicity, and chased him back into the lake, but could not per-

---

1 Abounding with short sentences, axioms, and maxims, short and energetick. *Dictionary*.

suade his retinue to stay, or free their hearts from the terror which had seized upon them. The princesses inclosed themselves in the palace, and could yet scarcely believe themselves in safety. Every attention was fixed upon the late danger and escape, and no mind was any longer at leisure for gay sallies or careless prattle.

Seged had now no other employment than to contemplate the innumerable casualties which lie in ambush on every side to intercept the happiness of man, and break in upon the hour of delight and tranquillity. He had, however, the consolation of thinking, that he had not been now disappointed by his own fault, and that the accident which had blasted the hopes of the day, might easily be prevented by future caution.

That he might provide for the pleasure of the next morning, he resolved to repeal his penal edict, since he had already found that discontent and melancholy were not to be frighted away by the threats of authority, and that pleasure would only reside where she was exempted from controul. He therefore invited all the companions of his retreat to unbounded pleasantry, by proposing prizes for those who should on the following day, distinguish themselves by any festive performances; the tables of the antechamber were covered with gold and pearls, and robes and garlands, decreed the rewards of those who could refine elegance or heighten pleasure.

At this display of riches every eye immediately sparkled, and every tongue was busied in celebrating the bounty and magnificence of the emperor. But when Seged entered in hopes of uncommon entertainment from universal emulation, he found that any passion too strongly agitated, puts an end to that tranquillity which is necessary to mirth, and that the mind, that is to be moved by the gentle ventilations of gaiety, must first be smoothed by a total calm. Whatever we ardently wish to gain, we must in the same degree be afraid to lose, and fear and pleasure cannot dwell together.

All was now care and solicitude. Nothing was done or spoken, but with so visible an endeavour at perfection, as always failed to delight, though it sometimes forced admiration. And Seged could not but observe with sorrow, that his prizes had more influence than himself. As the evening approached, the contest grew more earnest, and those who were forced to allow themselves excelled, began to discover[1] the malignity of defeat, first by angry glances,

---

1  To exhibit to the view. *Dictionary*.

and at last by contemptuous murmurs. Seged likewise shared the anxiety of the day, for considering himself as obliged to distribute with exact justice the prizes which had been so zealously sought, he durst never remit his attention, but passed his time upon the rack of doubt in balancing different kinds of merit, and adjusting[1] the claims of all the competitors.

At last knowing, that no exactness could satisfy those whose hopes he should disappoint, and thinking that on a day set apart for happiness, it would be cruel to oppress any heart with sorrow, he declared that all had pleased him alike, and dismissed all with presents of equal value.

Seged soon saw that his caution had not been able to avoid offence. They who had believed themselves secure of the highest prizes, were not pleased to be levelled with the crowd; and though by the liberality of the king, they received more than his promise had intitled them to expect, they departed unsatisfied, because they were honoured with no distinction, and wanted an opportunity to triumph in the mortification of their opponents. "Behold here," said Seged, "the condition of him who places his happiness in the happiness of others." He then retired to meditate, and, while the courtiers were repining at his distributions, saw the fifth sun go down in discontent.

The next dawn renewed his resolution to be happy. But having learned how little he could effect by settled schemes or preparatory measures, he thought it best to give up one day entirely to chance, and left every one to please and be pleased his own way.

This relaxation of regularity diffused a general complacence through the whole court, and the emperor imagined, that he had at last found the secret of obtaining an interval of felicity. But as he was roving in this careless assembly with equal carelessness, he overheard one of his courtiers in a close arbour murmuring alone: "What merit has Seged above us, that we should thus fear and obey him, a man, whom, whatever he may have formerly performed, his luxury now shews to have the same weakness with ourselves." This charge affected him the more, as it was uttered by one whom he had always observed among the most abject of his flatterers. At first his indignation prompted him to severity; but reflecting, that what was spoken, without intention to be heard, was to be considered as only thought, and was perhaps but

---

1  To regulate; to put in order; to settle in the right form. *Dictionary*. To determine; [...] to assess. *OED*.

the sudden burst of casual and temporary vexation, he invented some decent pretence to send him away, that his retreat might not be tainted with the breath of envy, and after the struggle of deliberation was past, and all desire of revenge utterly suppressed, passed the evening not only with tranquillity, but triumph, though none but himself was conscious of the victory.

The remembrance of this clemency cheered the beginning of the seventh day, and nothing happened to disturb the pleasure of Seged, till looking on the tree that shaded him, he recollected, that under a tree of the same kind he had passed the night after his defeat in the kingdom of Goiama. The reflection on his loss, his dishonour, and the miseries which his subjects suffered from the invader, filled him with sadness. At last he shook off the weight of sorrow, and began to solace himself with his usual pleasures, when his tranquillity was again disturbed by jealousies which the late contest for the prizes had produced, and which, having in vain tried to pacify them by persuasion, he was forced to silence by command.

On the eighth morning Seged was awakened early by an unusual hurry in the apartments, and enquiring the cause, was told, that the Princess Balkis was seized with sickness. He rose and calling the physicians, found that they had little hope of her recovery. Here was an end of jollity: All his thoughts were now upon his daughter, whose eyes he closed on the tenth day.

Such were the days which Seged of Ethiopia had appropriated to a short respiration[1] from the fatigues of war and the cares of government. This narrative he has bequeathed to future generations, that no man hereafter may presume to say, "This day shall be a day of happiness."

---

1   Relief from toil. *Dictionary*.

# Appendix B: Contemporary Responses to Rasselas

## 1. From the *Monthly Review* (May 1759)

[This review, published anonymously, was written by Owen Ruffhead (c.1723–69), a legal and political writer.]

The method of conveying instruction under the mask of fiction or romance, has been justly considered as the most effectual way of rendering the grave dictates of morality agreeable to mankind in general. The diversity of characters, and variety of incidents, in a romance, keeps attention alive; and moral sentiments find access to the mind imperceptibly, when led by amusement: whereas dry, didactic precepts, delivered under a sameness of character, soon grow tiresome to the generality of readers.

But to succeed in the romantic way of writing, requires a sprightliness of imagination, with a natural ease and variety of expression, which, perhaps, oftener falls to the lot of middling writers, than to those of more exalted genius: and therefore, we observe, with less regret, of the learned writer of these volumes, that *tale-telling* evidently is not his talent. He wants the graceful ease, which is the ornament of romance; and he stalks in the solemn buskin,[1] when he ought to tread in the light sock. His stile is so tumid[2] and pompous, that he sometimes deals in *sesquipedalia*,[3] such as excogitation, exaggeratory, &c. with other hard compounds, which it is difficult to pronounce with composed features—as *multifarious, transcendental, indiscerpible*, &c. [...]

This swelling language may shew the writer's learning, but it is certainly no proof of his elegance. If indeed he had put it into the mouth of a pedant only, nothing could be more apt: but unhappily he has so little conception of the propriety of character, that he makes the princess speak in the same lofty strain with the philosopher; and the waiting woman harangue[4] with as much sublimity as her royal mistress.

---

1 A kind of high shoe wore by the ancient actors of tragedy, to raise their stature. *Dictionary.*
2 Pompous; boastful; puffy; falsely sublime. *Dictionary.*
3 Containing a foot and a half. *Dictionary.*
4 To make a speech; to pronounce an oration. *Dictionary.*

With regard to the matter of these little volumes, we are concerned to say, that we cannot discover much invention in the plan, or utility in the design. The topics which the writer has chosen have been so often handled, they are grown threadbare: and with all his efforts to be original, his sentiments are most of them to be found in the Persian and Turkish tales, and other books of the like sort; wherein they are delivered to better purpose, and cloathed in a more agreeable garb. Neither has the end of this work any great tendency to the good of society. It is calculated to prove that discontent prevails among men of all ranks and conditions—the knowledge of which, we may acquire without going to Ethiopia to learn it.

But the inferences which the writer draws from this general discontent are by no means just. He seems to conclude from thence, that felicity is a thing ever in prospect, but never attainable. This conclusion, instead of exciting men to laudable pursuits, which should be the aim of every moral publication, tends to discourage them from all pursuits whatever; and to confirm them in that supine[1] indolence, which is the parent of vice and folly: and which, we dare say, it is not the worthy author's design to encourage.

It does not follow, that because there are discontented mortals in every station of life, that therefore every individual, in those several stations, is discontented. Whatever men may conclude in the gloom of a closet, yet if we look abroad, we shall find Beings who, upon the whole, afford us a moral certainty of their enjoying happiness. A *continued* or constant series of felicity is not the lot of human nature: but there are many who experience frequent returns of pleasure and content, which more than counterbalance the occasional interruptions of pain and inquietude. Such may be deemed really happy, who, in general, feel themselves so; and that there are many such, we see no reasonable cause to doubt.

We are apt to conclude too much from the restless disposition of mankind, and to consider the desire which men express of changing their condition, as a constant mark of discontent and infelicity. But though this is often the case, it is not always so. On the contrary, our eagerness to shift the scene frequently makes a part of present enjoyment. The earnestness with which we pursue some probable, though distant, attainment, keeps the mind in a state of agreeable agitation, which improves its vigour. Be our condition what it will, the mind will soon grow torpid,[2] and a

---

1  Negligent; careless; indolent; drousy; thoughtless; inattentive. *Dictionary.*
2  Numbed; motionless; sluggish; not active. *Dictionary.*

*tedium* will ensue, unless we substitute some pursuit seemingly unconnected with our present state. Our fondness for change, however, does not *always* proceed from discontent merely on account of our present station, or from an expectation of greater and more permanent happiness in prospect. A wise man follows some distant pursuit, not as an *ultimate*, which is to ensure him felicity; but as a *medium* to keep the mind in action, and counter-work the inconveniences with which every state is attended. He is sensible that, when he attains his wishes, he shall still want some-thing to diversify attention, and that further pursuits will be nec-essary to favour the active progress of the mind: such distant pur-suits therefore, as they often engage the mind agreeably, are so far present enjoyments. [...]

[Quotes from *Rasselas*, Chapter XXVII: "Disquisition upon Greatness"]

How unnaturally is this debate supported? The prince, with all the simplicity of a credulous virgin, fondly imagines that people in humble station "have nothing to do but to love and be loved, to be virtuous and to be happy;" while the princess opposes his delusion with bold, manly, and masterly sentiments, enforced with all the energy of declamation. Rasselas, like an innocent and tender pupil, is documented[1] by his philosophic sister, who shews him the folly of his visionary expectations. One would imagine that they had changed sexes: for surely that fond hope and pleas-ing delusion had been more natural to her side: and those deep sentiments and spirited remonstrances had been more becoming in the prince. Nekayah might have related her observations; but the reflections resulting from them should have been reserved for Rasselas. [...]

After further researches, the prince and princess meet with an astronomer, who imagined that for five years he had possessed the regulation of the weather, and the distribution of the seasons. This species of frenzy[2] gives room for a very sensible chapter on the dangerous prevalence of imagination.

The astronomer, however, is cured of his frenzy by intercourse with the world; and the tale draws to a conclusion, in which, as

---

1 To teach, instruct. *OED*.
2 Madness; distraction of mind; alienation of understanding; any violent passion approaching to madness. *Dictionary*.

the writer frankly acknowledges, nothing is concluded. They find that happiness is unattainable, and remain undetermined in their choice of life. As nothing is concluded, it would have been prudent in the author to have said nothing. Whoever he is,[1] he is a man of genius and great abilities; but he has evidently misapplied his talents. We shall only add, that his title-page will impose upon many of Mr. Noble's[2] fair customers, who, while they expect to frolic along the flowery paths of romance, will find themselves hoisted on metaphysical stilts, and born aloft into the regions of syllogistical[3] subtlety, and philosophical refinement.

## 2. From Sir John Hawkins, *The Life of Samuel Johnson, L.L.D.* 2nd ed. (1787)

[Sir John Hawkins (1719–89), music scholar and lawyer, was a friend of Johnson's and co-executor of his will. His was the first substantial biography of Johnson.]

In the beginning of the year 1759, and while the Idler continued to be published, an event happened, for which it might be imagined he was well prepared, the death of his mother, who had then attained the age of ninety; but he, whose mind had acquired no firmness by the contemplation of mortality, was as little able to sustain the shock as he would have been had this loss befallen him in his nonage.[4] It is conjectured that, for many years before her decease, she derived almost the whole of her support from this her dutiful son, whose filial piety was ever one of the most distinguishable features in his character. Report says, but rather vaguely, that, to supply her necessities in her last illness, he wrote and made money of his "Rasselas," a tale of his invention, numbered among the best of his writings, and published in the spring of 1759, a crisis that gives credit to such a supposition. No. 41 of the Idler, though it pretends to be a letter to the author, was

---

1  Johnson expected his authorship of *Rasselas* to be known even though his name did not appear on the title page and Ruffhead is likely being disingenuous here.
2  John and Francis Noble (d. 1797 and 1792), brothers, publishers, and proprietors of a circulating library. Their "fair customers" were the young women to whom such libraries particularly catered.
3  An argument composed of three propositions: as, every man thinks; Peter is a man, therefore Peter thinks. *Dictionary*.
4  Minority; time of life before legal maturity. *Dictionary*.

written by Johnson himself, on occasion of his mother's death, and may be supposed to describe, as truly as pathetically, his sentiments on the separation of friends and relations. The fact, respecting the writing and publishing the story of Rasselas is, that finding the Eastern Tales written by himself in the Rambler, and by Hawkesworth in the Adventurer, had been well received, he had been for some time meditating a fictitious history, of a greater extent than any that had appeared in either of those papers, which might serve as a vehicle to convey to the world his sentiments of human life and the dispensations of Providence, and having digested his thoughts on the subject, he obeyed the spur of that necessity which now pressed him, and sat down to compose the tale abovementioned, laying the scene of it in a country that he had before occasion to contemplate, in his translation of Padre Lobo's voyage.

As none of his compositions have been more applauded than this, an examen[1] of it in this place may be not improper, and the following may serve till a better shall appear.

Considered as a specimen of our language, it is scarcely to be paralleled; it is written in a style refined to a degree of immaculate purity, and displays the whole force of turgid[2] experience.

But it was composed at a time when no spring like that in the mind of Rasselas urged his narrator; when the heavy hand of affliction almost bore him down, and the dread of future want haunted him. That he should have produced a tale fraught with lively imagery, or that he should have painted human life in gay colours, could not have been expected: he poured out his sorrow in gloomy reflection, and being destitute of comfort himself, described the world as nearly without it.

In a work of such latitude as this, where nothing could be impertinent, he had an opportunity of divulging his opinion on any point that he had thought on: he has therefore formed many conversations on topics that are known to have been subjects of his meditation, and has atoned for the paucity[3] of his incidents by such discussions as are seldom attempted by the fabricators of romantic fiction.

Admitting that Johnson speaks in the person of the victor-disputant, we may, while he is unveiling the hearts of others, gain

---

1  Examination; disquisition; enquiry. *Dictionary*.
2  Swelling. *Dictionary*. Grandiloquent. *OED*.
3  Fewness; smallness of number. *Dictionary*.

some knowledge of his own. He has in this Abyssinian tale given us what he calls a dissertation on poetry, and in it that which appears to me a recipe for making a poet, from which may be inferred what he thought the necessary ingredients, and a reference to the passage will tend to corroborate an observation of Mr. Garrick's, that Johnson's poetical faculty was mechanical, and that what he wrote came not from his heart but from his head. [...]

In a following chapter the danger of insanity is the subject of debate; and it cannot but excite the pity of all those who gratefully accept and enjoy Johnson's endeavors to reform and instruct, to reflect that the peril he describes he believed impending over him. That he was conscious of superior talents will surely not be imputed to vanity: how deeply then must he have been depressed by the constant fear that in one moment he might and probably would be, not only deprived of his distinguished endowments, but reduced to a state little preferable, in as much as respects this world, to that of brutes! He had traced the misery of insanity from its causes to its effects, and seems to ascribe it to indulgences of imagination: he styles it one of the dangers of solitude; and perhaps to this dread and this opinion was his uncommon love of society to be attributed.

His superstitious ideas of the state of the departed souls, and belief in supernatural agency, were produced by a mental disease, as impossible to be shaken off as corporeal pain. What it has pleased Omnipotence to inflict, we need never seek to excuse; but he has provided against the cavils[1] of those who cannot comprehend how a wise can ever appear a weak man, by remarking, that there is a natural affinity between melancholy and superstition.

In characterizing this performance, it cannot be said, that it vindicated the ways of God to man. It is a general satire, representing mankind as eagerly pursuing what experience should have taught them they can never obtain: it exposes the weakness even of the laudable affections and propensities, and it resolves the mightiest as well as the most trivial of their labours into folly.

I wish I were not warranted in saying, that this elegant work is rendered, by its most obvious moral, of little benefit to the reader. We would not, indeed, wish to see the rising generation so unprofitably employed as the prince of Abyssinia; but it is equally

---

1    False or frivolous objections. *Dictionary*.

impolitic[1] to repress all hope, and he who should quit his father's house in search of a profession, and return unprovided, because he could not find any man pleased with his own, would need a better justification than that Johnson, after speculatively surveying various modes of life, had judged happiness unattainable, and choice useless.

But let those, who, reading Rasselas in the spring of life, are captivated by its author's eloquence and convinced by his perspicacious[2] wisdom that human life and hopes are such that he has depicted them, remember that he saw through the medium of adversity. The concurrent testimony of ages has, it is too true, proved, that there is no such thing as worldly felicity; but it has never been proved, that, therefore we are miserable. Those who look only here for happiness, have ever been and ever will be disappointed: it is not change of place, nor even the unbounded gratification of the wishes, that can relieve them; but if they bend their attention towards the attainment of that felicity we are graciously promised, the discharge of religious and social duties will afford their faculties the occupation wanted, and the wellfounded expectation of future reward will at once stimulate and support them.

The tale of Rasselas was written to answer a pressing necessity, and was so concluded as to admit of a continuation; and, in fact, Johnson had meditated a second part, in which he meant to marry his hero, and place him in a state of permanent felicity: but it fared with his resolution as it did with that of Dr. Young,[3] who, in his estimate of human life, promised, as he had given the dark, so, in a future publication, he would display the bright side of his subject; he never did it, for he had found out that it had no bright side, and Johnson had made much the same discovery, and that in this state of our existence all our enjoyments are fugacious,[4] and permanent felicity unattainable.

---

1 Imprudent. *Dictionary.*

2 Quicksighted; sharp of sight. *Dictionary.*

3 Edward Young (1683–1765), poet of the *Night Thoughts* (1742–46), published a long sermon-like discourse titled *A Vindication of Providence, or, True Estimate of Human Life* in 1727.

4 Volatile. *Dictionary.* Tending to disappear, of short duration; evanescent, fleeting, transient, fugitive. *OED.*

## 3. From James Boswell, *The Life of Samuel Johnson* (1791)

[James Boswell (1740–95), lawyer and writer, met Johnson in 1763 and carefully recorded the conversation and anecdotes that would become the basis of his massive biography.]

In 1759, in the month of January, his mother died at the great age of ninety, an event which deeply affected him; not that "his mind acquired no firmness by the contemplation of mortality;"* but that his reverential affection for her was not abated by years, as indeed he retained all his tender feelings even to the latest period of his life. I have been told that he regretted much his not having gone to visit his mother for several years, previous to her death. But he was constantly engaged in literary labours which confined him to London; and though he had not the comfort of seeing his aged parent, he contributed liberally to her support.

Soon after this event, he wrote his *Rasselas, Prince of Abyssinia*; concerning the publication of which Sir John Hawkins guesses vaguely and idly, instead of having taken the trouble to inform himself with authentick precision. Not to trouble my readers with a repetition of the Knight's reveries, I have to mention, that the late Mr. Strahan the printer told me, that Johnson wrote it, that with the profits he might defray the expense of his mother's funeral, and pay some little debts which she had left. He told Sir Joshua Reynolds that he composed it in the evenings of one week, sent it to press in portions as it was written, and had never since read it over. [...]

None of his writings has been so extensively diffused over Europe; for it has been translated in most, if not all, of the modern languages. This Tale, with all the charms of oriental imagery, and all the force and beauty of which the English language is capable, leads us through the most important scenes of human life, and shews us that this stage of our being is full of "vanity and vexation of spirit."[1] To those who look no further than the present life, or who maintain that human nature has not fallen from the state in which it was created, the instruction of this sublime story will be of no avail. But they who think justly, and feel with strong sensibility, will listen with eagerness and admiration to its truth and wisdom. Voltaire's *Candide*,[2] written

---

* Hawkins's *Life of Johnson*, p. 365. [Boswell's note. See Appendix B2.]

1 Ecclesiastes 1.14.
2 Published in February 1759.

to refute the system of Optimism, which it accomplished with brilliant success, is wonderfully similar in its plan and conduct to Johnson's *Rasselas*; insomuch, that I have heard Johnson say, that if they had not been published so closely one after the other that there was not time for imitation, it would have been in vain to deny that the scheme of that which came latest was taken from the other. Though the proposition illustrated by both these works was the same, namely, that in our present state there is more evil than good, the intention of the writers was very different. Voltaire, I am afraid, meant only by wanton profaneness to obtain a sportive victory over religion, and to discredit the belief of a superintending Providence: Johnson meant, by shewing the unsatisfactory nature of things temporal, to direct the hopes of man to things eternal. *Rasselas*, as was observed to me by a very accomplished lady, may be considered as a more enlarged and more deeply philosophical discourse in prose, upon the interesting truth, which in his *Vanity of Human Wishes* he had so successfully enforced in verse.

The fund of thinking which this work contains is such, that almost every sentence of it may furnish a subject of long meditation. I am not satisfied if a year passes without my having read it through; and at every perusal, my admiration of the mind which produced it is so highly raised, that I can scarcely believe that I had the honour of enjoying the intimacy of such a man. [...]

Notwithstanding my high admiration of *Rasselas*, I will not maintain that the "morbid melancholy"[1] in Johnson's constitution may not, perhaps, have made life appear to him more insipid and unhappy than it generally is; for I am sure that he had less enjoyment for it than I have. Yet, whatever additional shade his own particular sensations may have thrown on his representation of life, attentive observation and close inquiry have convinced me, that there is too much of reality in the gloomy picture. [...]

This I have learnt from a pretty hard course of experience, and would, from sincere benevolence, impress upon all who honour this book with a perusal, that until a steady conviction is obtained, that the present life is an imperfect state, and only a passage to a better, if we comply with the divine scheme of progressive improvement; and also that it is a part of the mysterious

---

1 This may be a reference to Hawkins's phrase "this morbid affection" in his biography. G.B.N. Hill and L.F. Powell, eds., *Boswell's Life of Johnson*, vol. I. (Oxford: Clarendon, 1934) 343 n.3.

plan of Providence, that intellectual beings must "be made perfect through suffering;"[1] there will be a continual recurrence of disappointment and uneasiness. But if we walk with hope in "the mid-day sun" of revelation, our temper and disposition will be such, that the comforts and enjoyments in our way will be relished, while we patiently support the inconveniences and pains. After much speculation and various reasonings, I acknowledge myself convinced of the truth of Voltaire's conclusion, "*Après tout c'est un monde passable.*"[2] But we must not think too deeply: "Where ignorance is bliss, 'tis folly to be wise,"[3] is, in many respects, more than poetically just. Let us cultivate, under the command of good principles, "*la théorie des sensations agréables*;"[4] and, as Mr. Burke[5] once admirably counseled grave and anxious gentlemen, "live pleasant."

The effect of *Rasselas*, and of Johnson's other moral tales, is thus beautifully illustrated by Mr. Courtenay:[6]

Impressive truth, in splendid fiction drest,
Checks the vain wish, and calms the troubled breast;
O'er the dark mind a light celestial throws,
And sooths the angry passions to repose;
As oil effus'd[7] illumes and smooths the deep,
When round the bark[8] the swelling surges sweep.

---

1   Hebrews 2:10.
2   The world is, after all, acceptable. This may be a reference to *Le Monde comme il va*. Hill and Powell 344 n.2. In *Le Monde comme il va*, an oriental tale by Voltaire published in 1748, a character named Babouc is sent by a congress of genii to investigate whether the city of Persepolis merits chastisement or destruction because of its luxury and corruption. See Voltaire, *Romans et Contes*, ed. Henri Bénac (Paris: Garnier freres, 1970).
3   Thomas Gray (1716–71). *On a Distant Prospect of Eton College* (1747), 1.99–100.
4   The theory of pleasant feelings.
5   Edmund Burke (1729–97), Irish-born politician and writer.
6   John Courtenay (1738–1816), Irish-born soldier and politician, was a friend of Boswell's and author of *A poetical review of the literary and moral character of the late Samuel Johnson, L.L.D.* (London: Charles Dilly, 1786).
7   The act of pouring out. *Dictionary*.
8   A small ship. *Dictionary*.

## 4. From Ellis Cornelia Knight, *Dinarbas* (1790)

[Ellis Cornelia Knight (1757–1837), author and eventually courtier to Queen Charlotte and her grand-daughter Princess Charlotte. She met Johnson and his circle through her mother, who was a friend of Sir Joshua Reynolds's sister Frances. She notes in her Introduction that she was inspired to write *Dinarbas*, a sequel to *Rasselas*, by Hawkins's claim in his biography that Johnson "had an intention of marrying his hero, and placing him in a state of permanent felicity."[1] *Dinarbas* was evidently a popular work; it went through at least ten editions by 1820, and was bound together with *Rasselas* throughout the nineteenth century.]

Chapter IX
Rasselas in confinement

[...] Rasselas, in the division of prisoners, fell to the share of the commander of the Arabs, and was esteemed a valuable prize, on account of his youth, his commanding figure, and his skill in various languages: but it was not convenient for the chief to carry him immediately to Cairo, the great mart for captives, as he would have been embarrassed[2] with him on his march: he therefore placed him with two slaves of approved fidelity, in a strong tower on the summit of an almost inaccessible mountain, and promised to return for him the next month. The slaves by turns descended into the valley to seek provisions for themselves and Rasselas, but, in compliance with what their master had exacted in proof of their fidelity, for some time never exchanged a word with their prisoner.

Rasselas, notwithstanding his former philosophy, daily lost all temper in his present situation: during his journey thither, and after his arrival, he had shewn so great an impatience of control, and so much desire of forcing his guard, that he was kept with uncommon strictness. However disagreeable and humiliating might be the fate which he expected after the return of the Arab, he anxiously counted the days allotted for his confinement: solitude appeared to him the worst of evils, and at the expiration of the month, he looked over the country for the arrival of the Arab

---

1  Hawkins. *The Life of Samuel Johnson* (London: 1787), 372–73.
2  To perplex; to distress; to entangle. *Dictionary.* To encumber, hamper, impede. *OED.*

with an eager expectation, equal to that with which he would have waited for the return of a friend. From the rising to the setting sun, he passed the day at the window of his prison, and would scarcely leave it to take his accustomed food: for several days following he remained in the same state of anxiety; his mind seemed absorbed in one idea, and could find no resources in itself. He endeavoured to substitute the thoughts of the past for those of the future: it was impossible—sleep fled from him by night, and repose by day; he interrogated the slaves and received no answer: at last, as they perceived his agitation to be violent, and feared it would endanger his health, they told him their master often came much later than he had designed, since his return depended on the success of his arms; that he might possibly be several months absent, but that in the mean time he himself should experience no other inconveniency than that of confinement.

Chapter X
The Resources of Solitude

The prince, far from being comforted by the answers of the slaves, was overwhelmed with affliction: he sunk hopeless on his mat, the only furniture of his prison, and gave himself up to all the melancholy of his reflections. "I am now," said he, "arrived at the evil I have always dreaded, and which it has been my constant study to avoid—why did I take such pains to quit the happy valley, but to emerge from a state of oblivion and inactivity? Why have I endeavoured all my life to improve in virtue and knowledge, but with the hopes of advancing the good of others and my own glory? To whom now can I communicate my thoughts? From whom can I gain applause or receive information? If the Arab should fall a sacrifice to his avidity,[1] than which nothing is more probable, who will be acquainted with my retreat? Shall I not be condemned to wear out my days in dreadful solitude, without any being to alleviate my woes? The guards, who are placed to watch me, are not only unwilling but incapable of affording me consolation: I have not the resource of conversing with the learned of former ages, since not a volume is to be found within these walls—the power of writing is denied me—I can gain no alleviation of my misery by setting down my thoughts and arranging

1  Greediness; eagerness; appetite; insatiable desire. *Dictionary*.

them with reflection—how poor is man when divested of external succour!"

Nor were these the only reflections of Rasselas: he was anxious for what might be the fate of Nekayah; he recalled to mind, with the most bitter regret, the happy moments he had passed in listening to the eloquence of Imlac, and the science of the astronomer: he often feared that Dinarbas had fallen a victim to his courage, and perhaps to his friendship for him. The image of Zilia was eternally present to him; every situation in which he had found himself with her, every smile, every tear, was fresh in his imagination: he often repeated the conversations he had held with her, and though the remembrance gave him inexpressible pain, he feared the images should decay, and strove to imprint them more strongly on his memory, lest he should lose the only satisfaction that was left him.[1] What gave him the greatest uneasiness, was the fear of being forgotten, and though he felt the improbability that his friends should discover the place of his retreat, his heart would sometimes accuse them of neglect.

In this state of weariness and affliction Rasselas passed near a fortnight; but at length he began insensibly to accustom himself to his situation, and to find amusement from the great objects of nature which alone presented themselves to his view. An awful[2] tempest, exhibiting the most noble contrast of light and darkness, first attracted his attention, and for a few moments made him forget his cares: he therefore pursued this new resource, and watched the various changes of the sky with their effects on the chain of mountains that surrounded him. A clear moonlight, which adorned the hemisphere some evenings after, gave him the first sentiment of pleasure which he had experienced since his captivity: he described his sensations in a small poem which he composed and addressed to Zilia: the pains he took to repeat and retain it in his memory employed the rest of the evening, and he slept that night better than he had done since his imprisonment. The following day he composed a description of the tempest, addressed to Imlac, and resolved, on the first occasion, that the absence of the moon should restore brilliancy to the stars, to dedicate an ode on that subject to the astronomer. At night, as soon

---

1  Dinarbas and Zilia, with whom Nekayah and Rasselas are in love, are the children of Amalphis, the governor of an Abyssinian fortress on the border with Egypt where Nekayah and Rasselas awaited permission from their father to re-enter Abyssinia.
2  That which strikes with awe, or fills with reverence. *Dictionary*.

as the lunar rays entered his chamber, he flew with rapture to the window, as to a situation that recalled to him more forcibly the image of Zilia; he made some changes in the poem addressed to her the former evening, added some descriptions of the prospect in his view, and retired to rest with more than usual tranquillity.

Nekayah was not forgotten in these ideal compositions, and from the time of his finding this employment, he was less wearied with expectation, and consequently more content with his present situation. He no longer spent hours at the window looking towards the only accessible side of the mountain, nor listened to the noise of the wind, in hopes it might be the trampling of horses. He felt applause in his own mind for this new acquired patience, as for a victory gained over himself, and the exultation of conscious merit gave new strength to his resolutions.

Chapter XI[1]
Resignation

Rasselas was not only resigned to his fate, but began to be persuaded that his confinement was rather a good than an evil. "How unthinking, and how ungrateful is man!" said he, "how could I prefer the thoughts of slavery and degradation to the life I am now leading! It is true that I am deprived of the amusements of variety, and debarred from the reciprocal communications of friendship, but I am equally saved from the mortifications so frequent in society, and from the malice of hatred and envy. If I am incapacitated from doing good, I am at least prevented from committing ill: it is true I am here useless to my friends, but I have the satisfaction of reflecting that it was in their defence, and in the service of my country that I lost my liberty.—Nekayah has sense and resolution, she can neither want friends to assist her with advice, nor prudence to follow their counsels. Imlac and the astronomer pursued their path in life long before they knew me: Dinarbas either perished nobly in the battle, or is engaged in the career of glory. Zilia—Zilia could never have been mine with honour to herself, and obedience to my father—I am saved from the pain of seeing her in the arms of another, or of destroying all the happiness of her life—Providence has certainly enclosed me here as a shelter from guilt, and I receive the benefit with gratitude.

---

1 This chapter deals with ideas in Chapters XI and XXI of *Rasselas*.

"The hermit whom we visited in his retreat, and accompanied back to Cairo, was not contented with a voluntary retirement, and yet I have accustomed myself to forced seclusion, even without many of the advantages which he enjoyed—whence arises so strange a difference? Perhaps, while the mind has a power of wandering, it can never sink into repose: perhaps, while choice is allowed us, inconstancy will attend our desires: how merciful is Heaven in allotting to man the part he is to act in this world! Did it depend wholly on himself, caprice would direct his actions, and remorse would follow them. Resignation should be the favourite study of the wise, and the principal virtue of the brave.

"How can a man think himself alone while surrounded with the noblest works of his Creator? while the planets, the stars, and that great luminary, whose general influence dispenses light and heat to the vast universe, afford a constant field for meditation and thankfulness? How can he consider himself as friendless and unprotected, when the hand of God equally supports the captive in his wretched dungeon, and the conqueror at the head of his triumphant army? when a moment may change the fate of either as his will directs, and when all their efforts, without his immediate assistance, can neither alter or continue their present situation? Uncertain as I am which is the most preferable of the various conditions of life, I am yet persuaded, that if there is much disappointment, there is likewise much comfort to be found in all. I will therefore form no other prayer to the Divinity, than to keep me from crime and error, and teach me to be wholly governed by his will. Would it not be presumption in a blind man to pretend to choose his path? All that he can do is to endeavour, as far as his strength will permit, to walk upright in that which is appointed him by his guide—and are we not all morally blind? What have the greatest sages discovered but that they knew nothing? And shall we not yield ourselves without reserve to the direction of that Divine Leader, who not only allots for us the path it is most fit we should pursue, but supports and consoles us amid dangers and difficulties that surround it."

Chapter XLIX
Marriages of Rasselas and Nekayah

[...] "To thee, Dinarbas, [said Rasselas] we owe the tranquillity of the empire; and in thy friendship I have found more than a recompense for all my searches after happiness; but how can I estimate the felicity that is promised me in the society of my Zilia! A felicity which was once beyond my hopes, but without which, I now could not exist. I remember that I had formerly with Nekayah a long debate on marriage, in which we could not decide whether early or late unions, whether sympathy or reason were most conducive to conjugal happiness: we have, by a singular course of events, been permitted to enjoy at once these opposite advantages: the warmest affection has been confirmed by the severest trials: surely we have before us the fairest prospect, a prospect to which neither interested[1] views, nor transitory passion can lay claim."

"In this," said the astronomer, "your virtues are rewarded; he who wants firmness deserves not success; reason can be no enemy to that love, which is founded on virtue, and supported by constancy."

The nuptials of Rasselas and Zilia, Dinarbas and Nekayah, were celebrated without ostentatious magnificence, but with a dignity becoming their rank. The poor had the greatest share in the rejoicings, because the superfluous treasures, consumed on similar occasions, were distributed among them. It was decided that Dinarbas should in a few weeks conduct back the army of the sultan[2] into his dominions; that he should, with Nekayah, fix his residence in Servia,[3] but that their visits to Abissinia should be frequent. Pekuah was to accompany the princess, and the astronomer, delighted in varying the scene, since he had tasted the charms of society, begged leave to visit the states of Dinarbas, who, with Nekayah, gladly acceded to his proposal: his knowledge and his virtues made them revere him as a father.

Rasselas concluded an alliance, offensive and defensive, with the sultan; repaid the expences of the troops, and graced the officers with distinguished marks of his favour.

Amalphis, honoured and beloved by his son and sovereign, applied all his care to form the Abissinian army. Imlac was no less attentive to the institutions of Rasselas,[4] for promoting learning in his dominions: both enjoyed the confidence of the monarch: but neither did Amalphis receive the memorials of the officers of the army, nor Imlac the dedications of the poets: every matter

---

1 Regard to private profit. *Dictionary.*
2 The Turkish emperour. *Dictionary.*
3 Now Serbia, a part of the Ottoman Empire when *Dinarbas* was published.
4 Rasselas is now emperor of Abyssinia.

was first referred to the emperor, who consulted those, whom he had appointed to be the heads of the several departments of the state, before he gave his answer, but did not always decide according to their judgment.

Zilia never interfered in public business; her voice often directed establishments of charity, and her taste frequently decided on the protection to be given to genius.

Innocent gaiety, and rational amusements, were introduced by her into the court of Abissinia; her dress was simple and elegant, and consisted of the manufactures of the country: she distinguished no woman as her favourite, but shewed peculiar regard to all those whose conduct was exemplary, without affectation, and whose minds were well informed, without vain pretensions to a display of learning. Her beneficence was extended to all, and if she shewed any partiality, it was to the orphans and widows of those who had served their country in battle; for she did not forget that she was the daughter of Amalphis: she knew the heart-felt misery of that disappointed hope and poverty, which honest pride forbids to own; the lot of many families, whose chiefs have bravely supported the honour of their prince and country.

Chapter L[1]
Visit to the Happy Valley

Before the departure of Dinarbas and Nekayah, Rasselas and his friends made a visit to the happy valley. The prince and his sister wished to review those scenes, which had been to them the objects of satiety at one time, and of uneasiness at another; they returned to every spot which remembrance had dignified, and rejoiced to contemplate those situations which were once irksome to their imagination.

Rasselas had only one brother left,[2] a youth whose education he recommended to the care of Imlac: he freed the princesses, his sisters, from the confinement of the valley, and gave them per-

---

1   Not only does Knight answer Johnson's inconclusive forty-ninth chapter with a conclusively happy marital ending in her forty-ninth chapter, but she also rounds out her tale with an additional concluding chapter, bringing her total to fifty chapters.

2   Rasselas learned in Chapter XVIII of *Dinarbas* that the second and third sons of the emperor escaped from the Happy Valley out of the tunnel Rasselas had dug and rebelled against the emperor. All three of Rasselas's elder brothers are killed in this civil war.

mission either to remain there, or return with him to Gonthar.[1] He commanded the massy gates that closed the entrance of the valley to be destroyed; the dancers, musicians, and other professors of arts, merely of amusement, to be dismissed with pensions, and liberty to be granted to all.

The prince, followed by his companions, led Zilia to the entrance of the cavern, through which he had first made his escape. "Consider this cavity," said he "and think what must be the grateful transports that glow in my breast—; Nekayah! Imlac! Pekuah! is not our search rewarded? Let us return thanks to Heaven for having inspired us with that active desire of knowledge, and contempt of indolence, that have blessed us with instruction, with friendship, and with love! It is true that we have been singularly favoured by Providence; and few can expect, like us, to have their fondest wishes crowned with success; but even when our prospects were far different, our search after happiness had taught us resignation: let us therefore warn others against viewing the world as a scene of inevitable misery. Much is to be suffered in our journey through life; but conscious virtue, active fortitude, the balm of sympathy, and submission to the Divine Will, can support us through the painful trial. With them every station is the best; without them prosperity is a feverish dream, and pleasure a poisoned cup.

"Youth will vanish, health will decay, beauty fade, and strength sink into imbecility; but if we have enjoyed their advantages, let us not say there is no good, because the good in this world is not permanent: none but the guilty are excluded from at least temporary happiness; and if he whose imagination is lively, and whose heart glows with sensibility, is more subject than others to poignant grief and maddening disappointment, surely he will confess that he has moments of ecstacy and consolatory reflection that repay him for all his sufferings.

"Let us now return to the busy scene of action where we are called, and endeavour, by the exercise of our several duties, to deserve a continuation of the blessings which Providence has granted, and on the use of which depends all our present, all our future felicity."

---

1 Gonder was the capital of Abyssinia from 1633 to 1845.

## 5. Elizabeth Pope Whately, *The Second Part of the History of Rasselas* (1835)

[Elizabeth Pope Whately (d. 1860), writer, wife of Richard Whately, Church of Ireland archbishop of Dublin. Her oeuvre was small, including religious essays, several pieces of religious fiction for young people, and a novel called *Reverses: or Memoirs of the Fairfax Family* (1833). *The Second Part of the History of Rasselas* is here printed for the first time since 1835. Whereas *Dinarbas* used marriage as the solution to Rasselas's choice of life inquiry, Whately's sequel makes Christianity the choice of life that leads to happiness.]

The History of Rasselas
Part II

Preface

The following little Sketch was published a year ago, in a volume of "Friendly Contributions,"[1] by a lady, with whose permission it is now (at the suggestion of some friends) reprinted by the Author, for the use of young persons, as companion to Dr. Johnson's Rasselas.

The History of Rasselas is interwoven with our earliest recollections of interest and delight; yet no one, perhaps, ever closed it, without a feeling of discontent and mortification.

This feeling has usually been referred to the unskilful management of the story; and attempts have been made to meet this defect, by supplying a more amusing and satisfactory conclusion. But the attempt has not been successful. However lively and entertaining, for instance, the story of Dinarbas may be, every one feels that it is a continuation, not so much of what it is, or ought to be, the moral design of the Work, as of the mere narrative:—that it professes only to supply the defect of the tale as a tale, not as an instructive work, drawing useful lessons from a view of human life.

It appeared to the writer of the Sketch, now appended as a Second Part to the History of Rasselas, that the fault lay deeper; and that whatever might be the defects of this interesting story,

---

1 *Friendly Contributions for the Benefit of Three Infant Schools in the Parish of Kensington*, ed. Lady Mary Fox (London: 1834).

its celebrated author had not failed to draw from it a just conclusion: that, in fact, his Abyssinian travellers, at the end of a pursuit, whose object (unenlightened and unaided by revealed truth) was to secure the greatest portion of happiness which life can afford, are left, just where we should expect to find them—under the dreary consciousness of a total failure.

It was felt, that in imparting to these interesting personages the light of Christianity,—in supplying them with christian hopes and christian motives,—the whole scene would change without effort, and a better and happier conclusion naturally arise.

It was also thought, that the young reader might derive more instruction, as well as interest, from the original story, by being led to compare the temper and feelings of the same persons employed in choosing their condition in life, first under the guidance only of natural religion, and afterwards under the influence of revealed truth.

To those young persons, therefore, who, having read the History of Rasselas, Prince of Abyssinia, are tempted to draw from it the conclusion, that every pursuit after happiness leads to disappointment; and that there is no way of avoiding the evils, or securing the blessings, of life;—this Second Part of his Memoirs is offered.

The Second Part of The History of Rasselas, Prince of Abyssinia

The first part of the History of Rasselas concludes with the determination of his pupils to return to their native country so soon as the inundations of the Nile should have ceased. But while they were awaiting this event, they had time to reflect on the rashness of attempting to re-enter their father's dominions, without first soliciting his pardon and consent. Instead therefore of returning themselves, on the retreat of the waters, they dispatched Imlac, under a guard, to the court of the emperor, to implore his forgiveness, with permission to return to Abyssinia, and reside there in personal freedom, under the protection of his government.

While they awaited, at Cairo, the success of their embassy, they employed themselves in drawing up a circumstantial account of their past life, from the time of their quitting the Happy Valley down to the present moment.

They had travelled through renowned countries, and had sojourned in celebrated cities—they had contemplated the wonders of nature and of art, scattered over that part of the world in which the earliest associations of men were formed; they had seen society in its various gradations, and under all the modifications of that social system which has for its chief aim, permanency and repose; they had acquired most of the languages of the East, and had applied themselves to the sciences, as far as their instructors were able to lead them. Yet the result of their labours was the conviction of their inability to form any scheme, which should secure to them the happiness of life, or exclude its evils.

A visit to the repositories of the dead, had indeed made Rasselas tremble at the shortness of life, and determined Nekayah "to think only of eternity." But eternity has no objects on which it can detain the mind. The bare belief that "that which acts, will continue to act," and "that which thinks, to think,"—and that "He who made the soul, will not destroy it,"—is calculated rather to appal the mind of man than to engage his hopes and win his desires. Yet this was the sum and substance of their belief—if such it might be called.—For though Christianity, under a very corrupt form, was professed in Abyssinia, our travellers, like the rest of their countrymen, looked on its ordinances as part of the laws of their country only, and never thought of inquiring into the truth or falsehood of the facts they related to; while Imlac, their guide and philosopher, was either unable, or unwilling to enlighten his pupils on the subject.

One fine evening, at the close of a sultry day, they walked forth into the public gardens, which at that time extended along the banks of the Nile, to enjoy the fresh breezes which were ruffling the waters of the Father of Rivers.

They seated themselves, with Pekuah, underneath a tree, and Rasselas read aloud the manuscript, which he had drawn up from his own notes, and those of his sister and Pekuah, of their common adventures. The scenes they had witnessed, the labours they had undergone, the knowledge they had gained, and the changes which had taken place in their minds, were all faithfully registered.

Pekuah drew a deep sigh as Rasselas folded up his manuscript. "I could wish to ask, O prince, did I not fear to displease you, what we have gained in exchange for the toil and anxiety we have undergone?"

"Liberty," replied Rasselas.

—"which you are about to renounce," said the lady.

—"and knowledge," added Nekayah.

—"which yet has not revealed to us the secret of happiness," replied Pekuah.

"It is true, lady," said Rasselas, after a few minutes' pause—"for it is not to you I would deny it—it is most true, and the inmost thoughts of my heart have this day compelled me to avow it. In looking over the past, I find that though much has indeed been attempted, little has been accomplished. Yet would I not recall the steps which have been taken. We have tasted of liberty, our minds have expanded under her genial influence; we have raised ourselves in the scale of beings; nay, if we have not learned the secret of happiness, we at least—"

"Alas," interrupted Nekayah—"Pekuah says too truly, we have rather learned where happiness is not, than where it is to be found. We have sought it in public and in private life, we have looked for it in the married and in the single state—with the philosopher, and the man of science—but it has flitted before us!"

"To me," said Rasselas, "the world seems yet in its infancy; perhaps we have lived too soon, perhaps it is reserved for future ages to enjoy the improvements of art, the extension of science, the development of a purer moral sentiment. Who knows but the Great Being who made the world, may intend its progressive improvement?—Who knows that he may not some day make known his will—and, freeing mankind from the superstitions which men call religion, teach us to know himself? Nekayah, I tremble while I say it, but I have prayed to the great Framer of the universe, that he would make me know him. I have scorned the superstitions which are taught and practised as coming from heaven, because they appear to me to have been framed by the folly and presumption of man.—I have not looked into them, it may be said—but I have judged them by their fruits. Imlac's silence on the subject has confirmed me in this view; but I cannot convince myself, that to desire a knowledge of the Creator's will, is unreasonable in the creature."

Nekayah and her friend bent their knees, and clasped their hands for some moments in silence.

The conversation was not renewed, for the attention of the princess was attracted by a person of singular appearance and deportment, who was sitting under some clustering shrubs, a few paces behind them, but whom they had not before noticed. The simplicity of his dress, with its peculiar form, pointed him out to Nekayah and her friend as a Frank,[1]—under which name, all

---

1  A name given by the nations bordering on the Levant to an individual of Western nationality. *OED*.

European nations were at that time included. He was talking, in Arabic, with a youth about sixteen years of age, who sat at his feet listening, with an air of attentive awe, to what he was saying, as he sometimes pointed upwards, sometimes turned to a book which he held in his hand.

The sun had now set, and the stars were beginning to show themselves on the blue vault of heaven. "He is an astronomer," said Rasselas; "how mild and benignant his look! It is as intellectual as Imlac's, yet it has all the gentleness of Pekuah."

The stranger's appearance was well calculated to interest such observers as the prince and his companions. He had not the appearance of being much advanced beyond middle life, though his hair was mingled with grey, and his face rather deeply lined. His form was erect, his eye penetrating, while goodness sat on his brow. The princess thought as he turned, and first caught sight of them, that his benevolent glance seemed to declare—"I love mankind."

They were about to move from their seat, that they might not molest[1] the interesting strangers, when a loud shriek from the youth, and a fainter one from his companion, made them hasten to the spot. Some venemous serpent had bitten the elder one, and he seemed to writhe with agony. The prince inquired of the youth, in the Arab tongue, where the stranger resided, that they might assist in his removal, and procure the attendance of a surgeon.

The youth said, that his kind friend was only just arrived in Cairo, and that his Greek servant had been despatched to look for lodgings, while they had wandered into the gardens.

On hearing this, the princess, with prompt benevolence, desired that he might be conveyed to their abode; and Rasselas, assisted by the young lad, carried him (for the suffering stranger had fainted,) to their home, which was near at hand.

Nekayah and Pekuah directed their women to prepare a room for the Frank; while Rasselas and the youth having laid him on a couch, sat down beside him, to await the arrival of the medical practitioner they had summoned.

The youth sank on his knees before his friend, whose consciousness seemed restored by his stifled sobs. He raised himself up. "It is probable," he said, turning to Rasselas, "it is more than probable that this accident will prove my death; I

---

1 To disturb; to trouble; to vex. *Dictionary.*

would fain know under whose benevolent roof I am likely to close my life."

Rasselas replied that he was an Abyssinian prince, at that time studying in Cairo. And he entreated to know the name and nation of his guest, that he might send an account of his situation to his friends.

"I belong to a nation of Franks, prince," replied the stranger. "I am a Briton: my name is Everard; I have friends, however, at Aleppo,[1] to whom, if I die, it is my request that this young man may be sent. My hand would now be unable to trace a letter, but in my pocketbook will be found an address."

He turned to the youth.—"Murad," he said, "I feel as if life were waning fast; O remember my words—rather," he added, "remember *His* words," and he drew from his bosom a small volume, which the youth received on his knees, and reverentially kissed. "Murad, hold fast to Him.—He has redeemed, and will never forsake you while you do His will." The stranger's hands were now clasped, he uttered only broken sentences, in an unknown tongue. "He prays," said Murad to Rasselas, in a low tone—"he prays in the tongue of his mother—he will go to his God—O, shall I ever go where he goes?"

Rasselas was wrapt in silent attention to the scene before him. But it was soon changed by the entrance of the surgeon, who, having exhorted the sufferer to patience, proceeded to take out the wounded part, and bind up the arm. He then assisted in conveying his patient to the room prepared for him; and having promised to return in a few hours, and give his opinion of the probable result of the case, he departed, recommending, meanwhile, perfect quiet.

Notwithstanding all the precautions which skill and care could devise, the stranger's situation was for some time precarious, and his sufferings great.

The ardent Murad, at first overwhelmed with grief, caught, by degrees, something of the mild and patient bearing of his friend. He sat on the ground by the side of the bed in mute anxiety; while Rasselas watched the sufferer with unremitting kindness, and an interest mingled with lively curiosity.

When Murad's spirits were raised, by a prospect of his friend's recovery, Rasselas and his sister drew from him some particulars

---

1 Halab, an important market city in northern Syria, site of a British trading station.

of his own history, and of his connexion with the stranger. He was by birth, he told them, a Hindoo.[1] His father had lost caste,[2] from what cause he did not explain, (for though he understood the Arab tongue, he spoke it imperfectly,) and he had, consequently, been deprived of his paternal property, and therefore, of all means of subsistence. He sold himself, accordingly, to an Arab merchant, who was journeying to Aleppo. This man ill-treated him in every possible way. But his sufferings happily attracted the attention of a Frank gentleman, who had joined the caravan, and who, on their arrival at Aleppo, bought him from the Arab. "He has delivered my body," said the youth, "from a hard bondage; but O, if I had words, or you could understand my language, I would tell you how he has set my mind free, and has taught me to know his God—our God—for there is none beside him; to know him is to live—and to live for ever!"

Rasselas and Nekayah felt their interest much excited by this slight history, told imperfectly, for want of words; but with a strength of feeling which was irresistably persuasive of its truth.

As soon as the stranger could bear the fatigue, he was removed, for some hours in each day, to one of the princess's apartments, and placed on a couch in a verandha filled with flowering shrubs, where, shaded from the intense heat of the sun, he could yet enjoy the coolness given out by the river beneath. Here the princess and Pekuah would engage him in conversation—for he spoke freely in the Arab tongue, with which they also were familiar. On the subject of his own peculiar views and feelings, they learned little more than they had gained from Murad. That he belonged to a nation of Franks called Britons,—that he was travelling, after severe domestic affliction, with a view to the improvement of his health and spirits,—when he met with Murad, in whose company he had intended to complete his travels, before he returned to Europe.

Perhaps the stranger felt too weak to excite his mind by further communication of his history; perhaps he wished to know more of his kind entertainers before he opened it further to them. On all other points, he was communicative. He was soothed by the persuasive gentleness of Pekuah, and delighted with the lively imagination and intelligent curiosity of Nekayah. While the anxious thoughtfulness of Rasselas—his extensive knowledge of

---

1 A native of northern India who practices the Hindu religion.
2 To lose social rank, to descend in the social scale. *OED*. *Jatis*, or castes, are hereditary endogamous groups that organize Hindu society.

the sciences, as taught in ages past, and directed to subjects of by-gone interest, together with his ignorance on other points, and especially of the world as it really is—his vigour of mind, with the paucity of the materials it had to work with—excited the interest of the stranger, and awakened his benevolent affections.

After a long conversation, which took place one day between them, on scientific subjects, the stranger retired to his own apart-ment with Murad. The party he left, remained for some time silent. At length Pekuah said:—"You sigh, prince; has the conver-sation of our friend disturbed you?—And yet it seemed that your mind not only seized on the truths announced, but followed them rapidly through all their consequences."

"Pekuah," said Rasselas, "when in the gardens of the Nile we reviewed the course of our life, from the moment we entered a world beyond the precincts of the Happy Valley, and began our patient pursuit of knowledge, as one of the means of attaining to happiness,—I consoled myself with the idea, that though we had failed in our end, I, at least, had acquired knowledge sufficient to raise me above the mass of mankind, and to make me, hereafter, useful to others. But my conversations with this stranger, by dis-closing my own ignorance, prove to me how much time I have lost. Man's years of vigour are soon spent, and I may be said to have wasted more than one half of mine already."

"Rasselas," replied Nekayah, "let us not despond; could we aspire to engage Everard as our friend and guide, might we not yet hope to retrace our steps? Might we not correct our views, misled as I suspect they have been by the false philosophy of Imlac, and confused by the wild theories of the astronomer?"

"The thought cheers me," said Rasselas, "but he is reserved. A mystery hangs about some of his views, and I suspect that it must be connected with superstition, since on all other points of liter-ature and science, he is communicative. Yet I am almost ashamed of my suspicions,—I believe him to be as *wise* as he is learned."

"And I am certain that he is as good," exclaimed Pekuah.

"Confiding in these two opinions," said Nekayah, "let us place the manuscript history of our life before him, and seek his guid-ance as our philosopher and friend."

"You are right, Nekayah," said Rasselas, "and I will begin this night to translate it into the Arab tongue."

Everard received from the prince, in a few days, the singular memoir, (the substance of which, written, as we have supposed, by Imlac, has some years since been given to the public) together with a detail of the thoughts and feelings which had occupied the travellers on the evening when his misfortune introduced the stranger to their sympathy and friendship.

Shortly after, Everard requested the company of his kind friends in the apartment where he used to spend the hours of study and retirement. They found him with the manuscript laid open before him. He held out his hands: "Dear friends," he said, "I perceive that we have been engaged in the same pursuit, though in different portions of the globe, and under very different circumstances."

"You too, then," said Pekuah, "have been engaged in this search after happiness—but have you been more successful?" she added, doubtfully, and with sadness in her glance at Everard.

"At least, dear lady," replied he, "I have discovered the way which leads to happiness; and pursuing it in that direction, have enjoyed—"

"O, tell us, happy mortal," exclaimed Nekayah; "if you have enjoyed it even in the approach—tell us more about this hidden treasure."

"He were more than mortal," said Rasselas, "if he could reveal that which the Deity has hitherto seen fit to conceal from man. I see, indeed, the elements of happiness around me, but they are like tools in the hands of a clown;[1] we want the knowledge to enable us to fit them for our use."

"Prince," said Everard, "the great Being who created the world has made that revelation of his will which your feelings and intelligence led you, as your manuscript declares, to expect. In this communication, the secret of happiness is contained; where your search is to begin, and when it is to be attained. But let me first ask you, whether among the pretended revelations which you appear to have looked at and discarded, you ever examined the christian faith, which being professed by your countrymen, is likely to have attracted a larger share of your attention than any other?"

"I was brought up professing, but utterly ignorant, even of this, the religion of my country," replied Rasselas, "and have since scarcely considered it worth examining. A religion suited to the ignorant inhabitants of Abyssinia, a religion of processions, and priests, and charms, cannot have proceeded from God, any more than that of our pagan, but more moral neighbours, the Gallas;[2] or the bloody and licentious visions of Mahomet."

---

1  A coarse ill bred man. *Dictionary*.

2  A pejorative name for the Oromo, the other major ethnolinguistic group in Ethiopia (Rasselas is of the Christian Amhara). Some groups of Oromo in southern Ethiopia still practice a religion centered on the worship of a sky god.

"Yet this degraded and dishonoured faith is mine, prince. And it contains, moreover, the substance of that shadow which you have been pursuing so eagerly and so vainly. Dishonoured it is indeed, even in my own country, where it has been received in its purest form,—shamefully dishonoured, by thousands of its professors,—but it contains the only revelations of his will, which God has made to man."

The whole party remained for some time silent. "Is it not very surprising," said Rasselas, "that if the Maker of the world has indeed revealed his will, mankind should remain uninfluenced by it, and the state of society unimproved?"

"That mankind has been powerfully influenced, and the whole state of society *changed*, by the christian faith, imperfectly as it has been received, and polluted as it soon became by human passion and ignorance, I hope to shew you hereafter, prince," replied Everard.

"But," said Nekayah,—"with humility I wish to speak it,—I should have expected a religion sent from God to have swept from the earth every thing opposed to its influence."

"The Founder of our faith taught us to expect no such thing, lady," replied Everard. "And is it not as unbecoming as it is useless in us, standing as we do on a point of the immense circle of his creation, and having only a very imperfect view of a minute portion of that circle, to argue as if we could comprehend the whole? No; let us not occupy ourselves with what God *might* have done; what he *has* done, is all we have concern with. If he has made any revelation of his will, then it is our business to understand, and make use of it. Now it is the belief of a great portion of the civilized world, that he has,—and it becomes therefore the business of every man to examine the grounds of this belief, with an honest and humble mind.

"You, dear friends, have prayed the great Being, of whose existence you had so imperfect a knowledge, that he would make known to you his will, and this is a prayer which was never, I believe, made in vain."

★ ★ ★ ★

The manuscript here breaks off—and then resumes.

———————————

Days, weeks, and months passed, during which Everard and his friends made excursions to the principal objects of interest which are scattered along the banks of the Nile, and which they were enabled to visit without undergoing the fatigues of a long land journey.

Rasselas and his sister found in Everard a guide and companion as acute and inquiring as Imlac, with a mind more enlarged, and knowledge more various and profound. Under his direction they examined for themselves the inspired records of our faith; and as truth makes a rapid progress in minds where she is neither distorted by prejudice, nor enveloped in the mist of unworthy passions, they were enabled in the course of this period to embrace Christianity, and to apply its spirit to the improvement of their lives.

They were accustomed to sit for hours under the awning of their vessel, as it glided down the Nile, and enjoy the conversation of their friend. It was during one of these tranquil hours, that they prevailed on Everard to relate some particulars of his own life.

"I am the eldest son," he said, "of a man of considerable influence in my country; he left me an untarnished name, with sufficient wealth to maintain the place he held in society. I passed with credit, along with an only brother, through the course of education chosen for us by our father. He died: we travelled together for some time; on our return, our paths diverged. My brother's profession led him into the country; I had a seat in one of the Chambers of our government, and was for many years actively employed in public affairs. I married; but though I married the woman of my affections, yet I was not so happy as I had expected. There was a difference in our views on the most important points, which I did not discover till after our marriage. My vanity had mistaken *assent* to my opinions on her part, for *conviction*; or perhaps I was not myself so strongly actuated by the principle which is now, I trust, become a part of my being. For your advantage, dear friends, I lay open my heart, and I deferred relating my history until I could do so without reserve. I lost my wife a few years ago, on which event I retired to the country, intending to devote myself to the education of my son and daughter, who were equally promising in mind and disposition. It pleased God to take them both away in the course of one year." Everard spoke calmly, with only a slight fall of voice.

Nekayah was affected by his history. "And you are alone; your affections without an object, your last pursuit cut off; unhappy friend!"

"Not unhappy, kind Nekayah," he replied; "there is one

pursuit yet remaining, which connects me with my fellow-creatures, and makes it still life to live—the service of my Master. It is the only pursuit in life which has never played me false; for, like you, dear friends, I have tried and enjoyed fame, pleasure, love, and friendship. I have also experienced the married and the single state; and, though I have found happiness in all, yet each has, at one time or other, proved insufficient. But the spirit of Christianity has never disappointed me. Entering into every concern of life, it fills up all those gaps and crevices in existence, of which the happiest life is conscious; and makes every event, whether agreeable or vexatious in itself, tend to the improvement of the whole being. But to conclude my story: by the advice of my kind brother, into whose family I had been received after my affliction, I determined to endeavour to mend my shattered constitution, by travelling in warmer climates. I undertook a mission connected with the promotion of Christianity in Syria. It failed; but soon after this disappointment, I became acquainted with my good Murad, whose situation first recalled me to myself. My complete recovery, dear friends, I owe to you, and to the pleasure your society has afforded me; with the belief that I have succeeded in pointing out to beings so intelligent, so kind, and so candid, the true end of their existence."

On the return of our travellers to Cairo, after one of their excursions upon the river, they found a messenger arrived from Abyssinia, bearing a packet from Imlac. The purport of it was to inform them that the emperor, their father, had issued a decree of banishment against them, and erased their names from the page on which they had been enrolled in the imperial genealogy. He transmitted to them, in his royal mercy, a portion for their future support, but forbad them, on pain of death, to re-enter Abyssinia. Imlac had found means of reconciling the emperor to himself; and having been offered a place at court, he took leave of his pupils, and resigned himself to the necessity of once more courting the great.

Rasselas and Nekayah were more shocked at the conduct of Imlac, than moved by the sentence of their father. Once a year they had been accustomed to receive a short and ceremonial visit from the emperor, celebrated by shows and banquets, indeed, yet little calculated to inspire any thing like filial affection. But Imlac they loved and confided in, as a friend warmly devoted to their interests; and though no longer blind to his deficiencies, they had taught themselves to look forward to the time when his mind would be enlightened by the society of

Everard, and his whole character expanded under the influence of Christianity.

Nekayah's affection, and also her pride, were severely wounded at the cool indifference with which he transmitted her father's edict, and left them to their fate. Her resentment was deep.

Everard, with judicious kindness, endeavoured to heal the wound, while he exposed to his young friend the evil tendency which it had laid bare.

After a long conversation one day on this painful subject, Nekayah arose, and taking the hand of Everard, she thanked him for his kindness. "Resentment is indeed," said she, "unworthy of one who bears the christian name; henceforth, I will think less of the ingratitude of Imlac, and more of the faults of Nekayah."

The wind, for which they had been waiting, at length proved favourable, and the whole party embarked on board a vessel bound for Syria. Our Abyssinian travellers were received at Aleppo by the English friends of Everard, with that affectionate confidence and ready sympathy which their circumstances claimed. They soon became endeared to each other; and Pekuah's delicate health induced Nekayah to accept the protection of these new friends, while Rasselas accompanied Everard and his young Arab through the remainder of their travels.

With interest unawakened before, Rasselas again traversed those beautiful regions in which the chosen people found their inheritance, and the Divine oracles were delivered. Here, his mind's eye was delighted to trace the footsteps of that divine Friend, whom he had lately learnt to love.

The travellers sought in vain for traces of the site of the temple, that honoured spot, in whose courts the tribes of Israel came up to worship. "Where now is the glory of Sion?" he exclaimed, with newly-awakened enthusiasm; "where the holy place once sanctified by the Divine presence?"

"It is here," said Everard, laying his hand on his breast; "you and I are living portions of that temple in which the Most Holy dwells. And wherever the meek follower of Jesus bows his head— it is there. May this temple of faithful hearts be enlarged, as I believe it will, till the whole earth is filled with 'the glory of the Lord!'"

With such reflections, and amidst such scenes, their evening glided away. The succeeding day was devoted to a less pleasing survey—to Jerusalem as it is.

It was not, however, the mosques, with their glittering minarets, these monuments of a false faith, which shocked our travellers so much, as the frippery with which christian superstition has contrived to overlay every trace of the past which she has commemorated. We cannot, however, follow up their researches, or accompany them through their subsequent wanderings.

A few months restored Rasselas to his sister and Pekuah. These few months had completed, in their minds, the work which Everard had so happily begun. But the period was also arrived, when he and Murad must bid them farewell.

"I leave you, dear friends," he said, "not without hope of introducing you one day to my native country. But it is still more probable that we may meet no more: have I redeemed the pledge I gave, of opening to your view the path of happiness, which you had sought in vain?"

"Nobly,"—replied Nekayah. "When Imlac led us from the Happy Valley, and introduced us into the world, we beheld evils for which he could offer no remedy, disappointments for which he had no consolation, and temptations from which there appeared no way of escape. It was for you, dear friend, to shew us, that under the support and cheering hope of christian faith, youth may be gay without immortality,* and age calm and cheerful, without the chilling aid of selfishness;† that prosperity may be enjoyed without trembling, and adversity endured without despair; that the happiness which we sought in vain through every station of life, is yet to be found *every where*, by a mind rightly disposed, and may be enjoyed without trembling, by beings who are looking forward to a happy eternity."

## Finis.

---

* In opposition to the opinion formed by Rasselas when he first mingled with young men of spirit and gaiety in Egypt. "The prince soon concluded, that he should never be happy in a course of life of which he was ashamed. He thought it unsuitable to a reasonable being to act without a plan, and to be sad or cheerful only by mere chance. 'Happiness,' said he, 'must be something solid and permanent, without fear, and without uncertainty.'"—Rasselas, chap. xvii. [Whately's note.]

† See the account given of himself by an old man to Rasselas and Nekayah.

"Every thing," said the princess to the old man, "must supply you with contemplation, and renew the consciousness of your own dignity."

"Lady," answered he, "let the gay and the vigorous expect pleasure in their excursions; it is enough that age can obtain ease." The rest of the old man's discourse in Rasselas, chap. xiv. [Whately's note]

# Appendix C: Orientalism in the Eighteenth Century

## 1. Joseph Addison, *The Spectator* no. 159 (1 September 1711): "The Vision of Mirzah"

[This is one of the first psuedo-oriental tales in an English periodical essay; one of the most popular of the *Spectator* numbers, it was frequently reprinted and became a model for short, free-standing oriental tales in the *Rambler*, the *Adventurer*, and other periodicals throughout the eighteenth century.]

[...] Omnem quæ nunc obducta tuenti
Mortales hebetat visus tibi, & humida circum
Caligat, nubem eripiam. [...]
Virg.[1]

When I was at Grand Cairo I picked up several Oriental Manuscripts, which I have still by me. Among others I met with one entituled, *The Visions of Mirzah*,[2] which I have read over with great Pleasure. I intend to give it to the Publick when I have no other Entertainment for them and shall begin with the first Vision, which I have translated Word for Word as follows:

"On the fifth Day of the Moon, which according to the Custom of my Fore-fathers I always kept holy, after having washed myself, and offered up my Morning Devotions, I ascended the high Hills of *Bagdat*,[3] in order to pass the rest of the Day in Meditation and Prayer. As I was here airing myself on the Tops of the Mountains, I fell into a profound Contemplation on the Vanity of humane Life; and passing from one Thought to another, Surely, said I, Man is but a Shadow and Life a Dream.

---

1 Virgil, *Aeneid* (translated by Dryden), 2.604–05: "While I dissolve/The Mists and Films that mortal Eyes involve:/Purge from your sight the Dross." Donald F. Bond, ed., *The Spectator* Vol. I (Oxford: Clarendon, 1965) 12.

2 "The title of Mirza or Mirzah, 'son of a Prince,' occurs frequently in Sir John Chardin's *Travels into Persia and the East Indies* (1686)." Bond 121 n.4.

3 Baghdad, today the capital of Iraq, was founded in 762 on the banks of the Tigris River. It is the setting for many tales in the *Arabian Nights*.

Whilst I was thus musing, I cast my Eyes towards the Summit of a Rock that was not far from me, where I discovered one in the Habit of a Shepherd, with a little Musical Instrument in his Hand. As I looked upon him he applied it to his Lips and began to play upon it. The Sound of it was exceeding sweet, and wrought into a Variety of Tunes that were inexpressibly melodious, and altogether different from anything I had ever heard. They put me in mind of those heavenly Airs that are played to the departed Souls of good Men upon their first Arrival in Paradise, to wear out the Impressions of their last Agonies, and qualify them for the Pleasures of that happy Place. My Heart melted away in secret Raptures.

"I had been often told that the Rock before me was the Haunt of a Genius;[1] and that several had been entertained with Musick who had passed by it, but never heard that the Musician had before made himself visible. When he had raised my Thoughts, by those transporting Airs which he played, to taste the Pleasures of his Conversation, as I looked upon him like one astonished, he beckoned to me, and by the waving of his Hand directed me to approach the Place where he sat. I drew near with that Reverence which is due to a superiour Nature; and as my Heart was entirely subdued by the captivating Strains I had heard, I fell down at his Feet and wept. The Genius smiled upon me with a Look of Compassion and Affability that familiarized him to my Imagination, and at once dispelled all the Fears and Apprehensions with which I approached him. He lifted me from the Ground, and taking me by the Hand, 'Mirzah,' said he, 'I have heard thee in thy Soliloquies, follow me.'

"He then led me to the highest Pinnacle of the Rock, and placing me on the Top of it, 'Cast thy Eyes Eastward,' said he, 'and tell me what thou seest.' 'I see,' said I, 'a huge Valley and a prodigious Tide of Water rolling through it.' 'The Valley that thou seest,' said he, 'is the Vale of Misery, and the Tide of Water that thou seest is Part of the great Tide of Eternity.' 'What is the reason,' said I, 'that the Tide I see rises out of a thick Mist at one End, and again loses itself in a thick Mist at the other?' 'What thou seest,' says he, 'is that Portion of Eternity which is called Time, measured out by the Sun, and reaching from the Beginning of the World to its Consummation. Examine now,' said he, 'this Sea that is thus bounded with Darkness at both Ends, and

---

1 The protecting or ruling power of men, places, or things. *Dictionary*.

tell me what thou discoverest in it.' 'I see a Bridge,' said I, 'standing in the Midst of the Tide.' 'The Bridge thou seest,' said he, 'is humane Life; consider it attentively.' Upon a more leisurely Survey of it, I found that it consisted of threescore and ten entire Arches, with several broken Arches, which added to those that were entire made up the Number about an hundred. As I was counting the Arches the Genius told me that this Bridge consisted at first of a thousand Arches; but that a great Flood swept away the rest, and left the Bridge in the ruinous Condition I now beheld it. 'But tell me further,' said he, 'what thou discoverest on it.' 'I see Multitudes of People passing over it,' said I, 'and a black Cloud hanging on each End of it.' As I looked more attentively, I saw several of the Passengers dropping thro' the Bridge, into the great Tide that flowed underneath it; and upon further Examination, perceived there were innumerable Trap-doors that lay concealed in the Bridge, which the Passengers no sooner trod upon, but they fell through them into the Tide and immediately disappeared. These hidden Pit-falls were set very thick at the Entrance of the Bridge, so that Throngs of People no sooner broke through the Cloud, but many of them fell into them. They grew thinner towards the Middle, but multiplied and lay closer together towards the End of the Arches that were entire.

"There were indeed some Persons, but their Number was very small, that continued a kind of hobbling March on the broken Arches, but fell through one after another, being quite tired and spent with so long a Walk.

"I passed some Time in the Contemplation of this wonderful Structure, and the great Variety of Objects which it presented. My Heart was filled with a deep Melancholy to see several dropping unexpectedly in the Midst of Mirth and Jollity, and catching at every thing that stood by them to save themselves. Some were looking up towards the Heavens in a thoughtful Posture, and in the Midst of a Speculation stumbled and fell out of Sight. Multitudes were very busy in the Pursuit of Bubbles[1] that glittered in their Eyes and danced before them, but often when they thought themselves within the Reach of them, their Footing failed, and down they sunk. In this Confusion of Objects, I observed some with Scymetars in their Hands, and others with Urinals,[2] who

---

1  Any thing which wants solidity and firmness; any thing that is more specious than real. *Dictionary*.

2  A bottle, in which water is kept for inspection. *Dictionary*, which uses this phrase from the *Spectator* to illustrate this meaning.

ran to and fro upon the Bridge, thrusting several Persons in Trap-doors which did not seem to lie in their Way, and which they might have escaped had they not been thus forced upon them.

"The Genius seeing me indulge myself in this melancholy Prospect, told me I had dwelt long enough upon it: 'Take thine Eyes off the Bridge,' said he, 'and tell me if thou yet seest any-thing thou dost not comprehend.' Upon looking up, 'What mean,' said I, 'those great Flights of Birds that are perpetually hovering about the Bridge, and settling upon it from Time to Time? I see Vultures, Harpyes,[1] Ravens, Cormorants, and among many other feathered Creatures, several little winged Boys, that perch in great Numbers upon the middle Arches.' 'These,' said the Genius, 'are Envy, Avarice, Superstition, Despair, Love, with the like Cares and Passions, that infect humane life.'

"I here fetched a deep Sigh; 'Alass,' said I, 'Man was made in vain! How is he given away to Misery and Mortality! tortured in Life, and swallowed up in Death!' The Genius, being moved with Compassion towards me, bid me quit so uncomfortable a Prospect: 'Look no more,' said he, 'on Man in the first Stage of his Existence, in his setting out for Eternity; but cast thine Eye on that thick Mist into which the Tide bears the several Generations of Mortals that fall into it.' I directed my Sight as I was ordered, and (whether or no the good Genius strengthned it with any supernat-ural Force, or dissipated Part of the Mist that was before too thick for the Eye to penetrate) I saw the Valley opening at the further End, and spreading forth into an immense Ocean, that had a huge Rock of Adamant[2] running through the Midst of it, and dividing it into two equal Parts. The Clouds still rested on one Half of it, insomuch that I could discover nothing in it: but the other appeared to me a vast Ocean planted with innumerable Islands, that were covered with fruits and flowers, and interwoven with a thousand little shining Seas that ran among them. I could see Persons dressed in glorious Habits, with Garlands upon their Heads, passing among the Trees, lying down by the Sides of Foun-tains, or resting on Beds of Flowers; and could hear a confused Harmony of singing Birds, falling Waters, humane Voices, and musical Instruments. Gladness grew in me upon the Discovery of

---

1 A fabulous monster, rapacious and filthy, having a woman's face and body and a bird's wings and claws, and supposed to act as a minister of divine vengeance. *OED*.

2 A stone, imagined by writers, of impenetrable hardness. *Dictionary*.

so delightful a Scene. I wished for the Wings of an Eagle, that I might fly away to those happy Seats; but the Genius told me there was no passage to them, except through the Gates of Death that I saw opening every Moment upon the Bridge. 'The Islands,' said he, 'that lie so fresh and green before thee, and with which the whole Face of the Ocean appears spotted as far as thou canst see, are more in Number than the Sands on the Sea-shore; there are Myriads of Islands behind those which thou here discoverest, reaching farther than thine Eye, or even thine Imagination, can extend it self. These are the Mansions of good Men after Death, who, according to the Degree and Kinds of Virtue in which they excelled, are distributed among these several Islands, which abound with Pleasures of different Kinds and Degrees, suitable to the Relishes and Perfections of those who are settled in them; every Island is a Paradise, accommodated to its respective Inhabitants. Are not these, O *Mirzah*, Habitations worth contending for? Does Life appear miserable, that gives thee Opportunities of earning such a Reward? Is Death to be feared, that will convey thee to so happy an Existence? Think not man was made in vain, who has such an Eternity reserved for him.' I gazed with inexpressible Pleasure on these happy Islands. 'At length,' said I, 'shew me now, I beseech thee, the Secrets that lie hid under those dark Clouds which cover the Ocean on the other side of the Rock of Adamant.' The Genius making me no Answer, I turned about to address myself to him a second time, but I found that he had left me; I then turned again to the Vision which I had been so long contemplating, but, instead of the rolling Tide, the arched Bridge, and the happy Islands, I saw nothing but the long hollow Valley of *Bagdat*, with Oxen, Sheep, and Camels grazing upon the Sides of it."

*The End of the first Vision of* Mirzah.

## 2. From Lady Mary Wortley Montagu, *The Turkish Embassy Letters* (written 1717; published 1763)

[Lady Mary Wortley Montagu (baptized 1689, died 1762) accompanied her husband Edward Wortley Montagu on his embassy to Constantinople from 1716–18. She revised copies of her letters written during this experience, which were published (over the objections of her children) after her death as *Letters of the Right Honourable Lady M—y W—y M——e: written, during her travels in Europe, Asia and Africa to Persons of Distinction, Men of Letters, &c. in different Parts of Europe. Which contain, Among other*

*Curious Relations, Accounts of the Policy and Manners of the Turks;*
*Drawn from Sources that have been inaccessible to other Travellers—*
this is now commonly known as *The Turkish Embassy Letters.*]

To Lady—
Adrianople,[1] 1 April 1717

I am now got into a new World, where everything I see appears to
me a change of Scene, and I write to your Ladyship with some
content of mind, hoping at least that you will find the charm of
Novelty in my Letters, and no longer reproach me that I tell you
nothing extraordinary. I won't trouble you with a Relation of our
tedious Journey, but I must not omit what I saw remarkable at
Sofia,[2] one of the most beautiful towns in the Turkish Empire,
and famous for its Hot Baths, that are resorted to both for diversion and health. I stop'd here one day on purpose to see them.
Designing to go incognito, I hired a Turkish Coach. These
Voitures[3] are not at all like ours, but much more convenient for
the Country, the heat being so great that Glasses[4] would be very
troublesome. They are made a good deal in the manner of the
Dutch Coaches, having wooden Lattices painted and gilded, the
inside being also painted with baskets and nosegays of Flowers,
entermix'd commonly with little poetical mottos. They are
cover'd all over with scarlet cloth, lin'd with silk, and very often
richly embroider'd and fring'd. This covering entirely hides the
persons in them, but may be thrown back at pleasure and the
Ladys peep through the Lattices. They hold 4 people very conve-
niently, seated on cushions, but not rais'd.

   In one of these cover'd Waggons, I went to the Bagnio[5] about
10 a clock. It was already full of Women. It is built of Stone in the
shape of a Dome, with no Windows but in the Roofe, which gives
Light enough. There was 5 of these domes joyn'd together, the
outmost being less than the rest and serving only as a hall where
the portress stood at the door. Ladys of Quality gennerally give
this Woman the value of a crown or 10 shillings, and I did not

---

1  Edirne, a city in the Ottoman Empire named for the Roman emperor
   Hadrian.
2  Today the capital of Bulgaria.
3  Carriage. *Dictionary.*
4  A pane of glass, *esp.* the window of a coach. *OED.*
5  A house for bathing, sweating, and otherwise cleansing the body.
   *Dictionary.*

forget that ceremony. The next room is a very large one, pav'd with Marble, and all round it rais'd two Sofas[1] of marble, one above another. There were 4 fountains of cold Water in this room, falling first into marble Basins, and then running on the floor in little channels made for that purpose, which carry'd the streams into the next room, something less than this, with the same sort of marble sofas, but so hot with steams of sulphur proceeding from the baths joyning to it, twas impossible to stay there with one's Cloths on. The 2 other domes were the hot baths, one of which had cocks[2] of cold Water turning into it to temper it to what degree of warmth the bathers have a mind to.

I was in my travelling Habit,[3] which is a rideing dress, and certainly appear'd very extraordinary to them, yet there was not one of 'em that shew'd the least surprize or impertinent Curiosity, but receiv'd me with all the obliging civillity possible. I know no European Court where the Ladys would have behav'd them selves in so polite a manner to a stranger.

I believe, in the whole, there were 200 Women and yet none of those disdainfull smiles or satyric whispers that never fail in our assemblys when any body appears that is not dress'ed exactly in fashion. They repeated over and over to me, Uzelle, pek Uzelle, which is nothing but charming, very charming. The first sofas were cover'd with Cushions and rich Carpets, on which sat the Ladys, and on the 2nd their slaves behind 'em, but without any distinction of rank by their dress, all being in the state of nature, that is, in plain English, stark naked, without any Beauty or deffect conceal'd, yet there was not the least wanton smile or immodest Gesture amongst 'em. They Walk'd and mov'd with the same majestic Grace which Milton describes of our General Mother.[4] There were many amongst them as exactly proportion'd as ever any Goddess was drawn by the pencil of Guido or Titian, and most of their skins shineingly white, only adorn'd by their Beautifull Hair divided into many tresses hanging on their shoulders, braided either with pearl or riband,[5] perfectly representing the figures of the Graces. I was here convinced of the Truth of a Refflexion that I had often made, that if twas the fashion to go naked, the face would be hardly observ'd. I perceiv'd that the Ladys with finest skins and most del-

1 A splendid seat covered with carpets. *Dictionary.*
2 A spout to let out water at will, by turning the stop. *Dictionary.*
3 Dress; accoutrement. *Dictionary.*
4 *Paradise Lost* IV.304–18.
5 A filet of silk; a narrow web of silk, which is worn for ornament. *Dictionary.*

icate shapes had the greatest share of my admiration, thô their faces were sometimes less beautifull than those of their companions. To tell you the truth, I had wickedness enough to wish secretly that Mr Gervase[1] could have been there invisible. I fancy it would have very much improv'd his art to see so many fine Women naked in different postures, some in conversation, some working,[2] others drinking Coffee or sherbet, and many negligently lying on their Cushions while their slaves (generally pritty Girls of 17 or 18) were employ'd in braiding their hair in several pritty manners. In short, tis the Women's coffee house, where all the news of the Town is told, Scandal invented, etc. They generally take this Diversion once a week, and stay there at least four or five hours, without getting cold by immediate coming out of the hot bath into the cool room, which was very surprizing to me. The Lady that seem'd the most considerable amongst them entreated me to sit by her and would fain have undress'd me for the bath. I excus'd myself with some difficulty, they being however all so earnest in perswading me, I was a last forc'd to open my shirt, and show them my stays,[3] which satisfy'd 'em very well, for I saw they believ'd I was so lock'd up in that machine that it was not in my own power to open it, which contrivance they attributed to my Husband. I was charm'd with their Civillity and Beauty, and should have been very glad to pass more time with them, but Mr W[ortley] resolving to persue his Journey the next morning early, I was in haste to see the ruins of Justinian's church, which did not afford me so agreable a prospect as I had left, being little more than a heap of stones.

Adieu, Madam. I am sure I have now entertained you with an Account of such a sight as you never saw in your Life, and what no book of travells could inform you of. 'Tis no less than Death for a Man to be found in one of these places.

To Lady Mar[4]
Adrianople, 18 April 1717

[...] I was conducted back in the same Manner I enter'd, and would have gone strait to my own House, but the Greek Lady

---

1  Charles Jervas (1675–1739), Irish-born fashionable portrait painter.
2  To embroider with a needle. *Dictionary.*
3  Boddice; a kind of stiff waistcoat made of whalebone, worn by ladies. *Dictionary.*
4  Frances (Pierrepont) Erskine (1690–1761), Countess of Mar, Lady Mary Wortley Montagu's sister.

with me earnestly solicited me to visit the Kahya's Lady, saying he was the 2nd Officer in the Empire and ought indeed to be look'd upon as the first, the Grand Vizier[1] having only the name while he exercis'd the authority. I had found so little diversion in this Haram[2] that I had no mind to go into Another, but her importunity prevail'd with me, and I am extreme glad that I was so complaisant. All things here were with quite another Air than at the Grand Vizier's, and the very house confess'd the difference between an Old Devote and a young Beauty. It was nicely clean and magnificent. I was met at the door by 2 black Eunuchs who led me through a long Gallery between 2 ranks of beautifull young Girls with their Hair finely plaited almost hanging to their Feet, all dress'd in fine light damasks brocaded with silver. I was sorry that Decency did not permit me to stop to consider them nearer, but that Thought was lost upon my Entrance into a Large room, or rather, Pavilion, built round with gilded sashes which were most of 'em thrown up; and the Trees planted near them gave an agreeable Shade which hinder'd the Sun from being troublesome, the Jess'mins and Honey suckles that twisted round their Trunks sheding a soft perfume encreas'd by a white Marble fountain playing sweet Water in the Lower part of the room, which fell into 3 or 4 basons with a pleasing sound. The Roof was painted with all sort of Flowers falling out of gilded baskets that seem'd tumbling down.

On a sofa rais'd 3 steps and cover'd with fine Persian carpets sat the Kahya's Lady, leaning on cushions of white Satin embroider'd, and at her feet sat 2 young Girls, the eldest about 12 year old, lovely as Angels, dress'd perfectly rich and almost cover'd with Jewells. But they were hardly seen near the fair Fatima (for that is her Name), so much her beauty effac'd every thing. I have seen all that has been call'd lovely either in England or Germany, and must own that I never saw any thing so gloriously Beautifull, nor can I recollect a face that would have been taken notice of near hers. She stood up to receive me, saluteing me after their fashion, putting her hand upon her Heart with a sweetness full of Majesty that no Court breeding could ever give. She order'd

---

1 The prime minister of the Turkish empire. *Dictionary*. Montagu visited the household of Grand Vizier Arnand Khalil Pasha (c. 1655–1733). Robert Halsband, ed., *The Complete Letters of Lady Mary Wortley Montagu* Vol. I (Oxford: Clarendon, 1965) 348 n.1.

2 The part of a Muslim dwelling-house appropriated to the women, constructed so as to secure the utmost seclusion and privacy. *OED*.

Cushions to be given to me and took care to place me in the Corner, which is the place of Honnour. I confess, thô the Greek Lady had before given me great Opinion of her beauty I was so struck with Admiration that I could not for some time speak to her, being wholly taken up in gazing. That surprising Harmony of features! that charming result of the whole! that exact proportion of Body! that lovely bloom of Complexion unsully'd by art! the unutterable Enchantment of her Smile! But her Eyes! large and black with all the soft languishment of the bleu! every turn of her face discovering some new charm! After my first surprize was over, I endeavor'd by nicely[1] examining her face to find out some imperfection, without any fruit of my search but being clearly convinc'd of the Error of that vulgar notion, that a face perfectly regular would not be agreeable, Nature having done for her with more successe what Apelles[2] is said to have essay'd, by a Collection of the most exact features to form a perfect Face; and to that a behaviour so full of Grace and sweetness, such easy motions, with an Air so majestic yet free from Stiffness or affectation that I am perswaded could she be suddenly transported upon the most polite Throne of Europe, nobody would think her other than born and bred to be a Queen, thô educated in a Country we call barbarous. To say all in a Word, our most celebrated English Beautys would vanish near her.

She was dress'd in a Caftan[3] of Gold brocade flowerd with Silver, very well fit to her Shape and shewing to advantage the beauty of her Bosom, only shaded by the Thin Gause of her shift.[4] Her drawers were pale pink, Green and silver; her Slippers white, finely embroider'd; her lovely Arms adorn'd with Diamonds; upon her Head a rich Turkish Handkerchief of pink and Silver, her own fine black Hair hanging a great length in various Tresses, and on one side of her Head some bodkins of Jewells. I am afraid you will accuse me of extravagance in this Description. I think I have read somewhere that Women always speak in rapture when they speak of Beauty, but I can't imagine why they should not be allow'd to do so. I rather think it Virtue to be able to admire without any Mixture of desire or Envy. The Gravest Writers have spoke with great warmth of some celebrated Pic-

---

1 Delicate; scrupulously and minutely cautious. *Dictionary*.
2 Renowned fourth-century BCE Greek painter.
3 A Persian or Turkish vest or garment. *Dictionary*.
4 A woman's linen. *Dictionary*.

tures and Statues. The Workmanship of Heaven certainly excells all our weak Imitations, and I think has a much better claim to our Praise. For me, I am not asham'd to own I took more pleasure in looking on the beauteous Fatima than the finest piece of Sculpture could have given me. She told me the 2 Girls at her feet were her Daughters, thô she appear'd too young to be their Mother.

'Her fair Maids were rang'd below the Sofa to the number of 20, and put me in Mind of the pictures of the ancient Nymphs. I did not think all Nature could have furnish'd such a Scene of Beauty. She made them a sign to play and dance. 4 of them immediately begun to play some soft airs on Instruments between a Lute and a Guitarr, which they accompany'd with their voices while the others danc'd by turns. This dance was very different from what I had seen before. Nothing could be more artfull or more proper to raise certain Ideas, the Tunes so soft, the motions so Languishing, accompany'd with pauses and dying Eyes, halfe falling back and then recovering themselves in so artfull a Manner that I am very possitive the coldest and most rigid Prude upon Earth could not have look'd upon them without thinking of something not to be spoke of. I suppose you may have read that the Turks have no Music but what is shocking to the Ears,[1] but this account is from those who never heard any but what is play'd in the streets, and is just as reasonable as if a Foreigner should take his Ideas of the English Music from the bladder and string, and marrow bones and cleavers. I can assure you that the Music is extremely pathetic. 'Tis true I am enclin'd to prefer the Italian, But perhaps I am partial. I am acquainted with a Greek Lady who sings better than Mrs. Robinson,[2] and is very well skill'd in both, who gives the preference to the Turkish. 'Tis certain they have very fine Natural voices; these were very agreeable.

When the Dance was over 4 fair slaves came into the room with silver Censors in their hands and perfum'd the air with Amber, Aloes wood and other rich Scents. After this they serv'd me coffée upon their knees in the finest Japan china with soûcoupes[3] of Silver Gilt. The lovely Fatima entertain'd me all this

---

1 Aaron Hill, *A Short and Just Account of the Present State of the Ottoman Empire* (London: 1709) 72–73. Halsband 351 n.1.
2 Anastasia Robinson (d. 1755), famous singer in London.
3 Saucers.

time in the most polite agreeable Manner, calling me often Uzelle Sultanam, or the beautifull Sultana, and desiring my Friendship with the best Grace in the World, lamenting that she could not entertain me in my own Language. When I took my Leave 2 Maids brought in a fine Silver basket of Embrodier'd Hand-kercheifs. She begg'd I would wear the richest for her sake, and gave the others to my Woman and Interpretress. I retir'd through the same Ceremonys as before, and could not help fancying I had been some time in Mahomet's Paradice, so much I was charm'd with what I had seen. I know not how the relation of it appears to you. I wish it may give you part of my pleasure, for I would have my dear Sister share in all the Diversions of etc.

# Select Bibliography

## Bibliographies

Clifford, James and Donald J. Greene. *Samuel Johnson: A Survey and Bibliography of Critical Studies*. Minneapolis: U of Minnesota P, 1970.

Fleeman, J.D. *A Bibliography of the Works of Samuel Johnson, Treating His Published Works from the Beginnings to 1984.* 2 vols. Oxford: Clarendon, 2000.

Greene, Donald J. and John A. Vance. *A Bibliography of Johnsonian Studies, 1970–1985.* Victoria: U of Victoria P, 1987.

Lynch, Jack., ed. *A Bibliography of Johnsonian Studies, 1986–ongoing.* 26 July 2005. <http://andromeda.rutgers.edu/~jlynch/Johnson/sjbib.html>.

## Primary Works

Boswell, James. *Life of Johnson*. Ed. R.W. Chapman and J.D. Fleeman. Oxford: Oxford UP, 1970.

Johnson, Samuel. *A Voyage to Abyssinia*. Ed. Joel J. Gold. *Yale Edition of the Works of Samuel Johnson* Vol. XV. New Haven: Yale UP, 1985.

——. *The Rambler*. Ed. W.J. Bate and Albrecht B. Strauss. *Yale Edition of the Works of Samuel Johnson* Vol. III. New Haven: Yale UP, 1969.

——. *Rasselas and Other Tales*. Ed. Gwin J. Kolb. *Yale Edition of the Works of Samuel Johnson* Vol. XVI. New Haven: Yale UP, 1990.

Mahdi, Muhsin, ed. *The Arabian Nights*. Trans. Husain Haddaway. New York: Alfred A. Knopf, 1992.

Mack, Robert L., ed. *Oriental Tales*. Oxford: Oxford UP, 1992.

——. *Arabian Nights' Entertainment*. Oxford: Oxford UP, 1995.

Meloccaro, Lynn, ed. *The History of Rasselas; Dinarbas*. London: Everyman, 1994.

Redford, Bruce, ed. *The Letters of Samuel Johnson*, 5 vols. Princeton: Princeton UP, 1992–94.

Richardson, Alan, ed. *Three Oriental Tales*. Boston: Houghton Mifflin Co., 2002.

Whately, Elizabeth Pope. *The Second Part of the History of Rasselas, Prince of Abyssinia*. London: B. Fellowes, 1835.

## Secondary Works

Ali, Muhsin Jassim. "*The Arabian Nights* in Eighteenth-Century English Criticism." *Muslim World* 67 (1977): 12–32.

Aravamudan, Srinivas. *Tropicopolitans*. Durham: Duke UP, 1999.

——. "In the Wake of the Novel: The Oriental Tale as National Allegory." *Novel* 3.1 (Fall 1999): 5–31.

Basker, James G. "Dancing Dogs, Women Preachers and the Myth of Johnson's Misogyny." *The Age of Johnson* 3 (1990): 63–90.

——. "Myth upon Myth: Johnson, Gender, and the Misogyny Question." *The Age of Johnson* 8 (1997): 175–87.

Berland, Kevin. "The Paradise Garden and the Imaginary East: Alterity and Reflexivity in British Orientalist Romances." *The Eighteenth-Century Novel* 2 (2001): 137–59.

Bronson, Bertrand H. *Johnson Agonistes and Other Essays*. Berkeley: U of California P, 1965.

Chico, Tita. "*Rasselas* and the Rise of the Novel." *Johnsonian News Letter* 56.1 (March 2005): 8–11.

Clifford, James L. *Young Sam Johnson*. New York: McGraw-Hill, 1955.

——. *Dictionary Johnson*. New York: McGraw-Hill, 1979.

Clingham, Greg. *The Cambridge Companion to Samuel Johnson*. Cambridge: Cambridge UP, 1997.

Conant, Martha Pike. *The Oriental Tale in the Eighteenth Century*. New York: Columbia UP, 1908. New York: Octagon Books, 1966.

DeMaria Jr., Robert. *The Life of Samuel Johnson: A Critical Biography*. Cambridge, MA: Blackwell, 1993.

Deutsch, Helen. *Loving Dr. Johnson*. Chicago: U of Chicago P, 2005.

Folkenflik, Robert. "The Tulip and its Streaks: Contexts of *Rasselas* X." *Ariel: A Review of International English Literature* 9.2 (1978): 57–71.

Greene, Donald. *The Politics of Samuel Johnson*. 2nd ed. Athens: U of Georgia P, 1990.

Grundy, Isobel. "Samuel Johnson as Patron of Women." *The Age of Johnson* 1 (1987): 59–77.

Hansen, Marlene R. "Sex, Love, Marriage, and Friendship: A Feminist Reading of the Quest for Happiness in *Rasselas*." *English Studies* 66 (1985): 513–25.

Hawes, Clement. "Johnson's Cosmopolitan Nationalism."

*Johnson Re-visioned: Looking Before and After*. Ed. Philip Smallwood. Lewisburg: Bucknell UP, 2001. 37–63.

Heffernan, Teresa. "Feminism against the East/West Divide: Lady Mary's *Turkish Embassy Letters*." *Eighteenth-Century Studies* 33.2 (Winter 2000): 201–15.

Hinnant, Charles H., ed. *South Central Review: Special Issue: Johnson and Gender* 9.4 (1992).

Hudson, Nicholas. "'Open' and 'Enclosed' Readings of *Rasselas*." *Eighteenth Century: Theory and Interpretation* 31.1 (1990): 47–67.

Johnson, Claudia L. "Samuel Johnson's Moral Psychology and Locke's 'Of Power.'" *SEL: Studies in English Literature* 24 (1984): 563–82.

Jones, Emrys. "The Artistic Form of *Rasselas*." *Review of English Studies* 18.72 (Nov. 1967): 387–401.

Kernan, Alvin. *Samuel Johnson and the Impact of Print*. Princeton: Princeton UP, 1990.

Knipp, C. "The *Arabian Nights* in England: Galland's Translation and its Successors." *Journal of Arabic Literature* 5 (1974): 44–54.

Kolb, Gwin J. "The 'Paradise' in Abyssinia and the 'Happy Valley' in *Rasselas*." *Modern Philology* 56.1 (Aug 1958): 10–16.

——. "The Structure of *Rasselas*." *PMLA* 66 (September 1951): 698–717.

——. "The Reception of *Rasselas*, 1759–1800." *Green Centennial Studies*. Ed. Paul J. Korshin and Robert Allen. Charlottesville: U of Virginia P, 1984. 217–49.

Lew, Joseph W. "Lady Mary's Portable Seraglio." *Eighteenth-Century Studies* 24.4 (Summer 1991): 432–50.

Liu, Alan. "Toward a Theory of Common Sense: Beckford's *Vathek* and Johnson's *Rasselas*." *Texas Studies in Literature and Language* 26.2 (Summer 1984): 183–217.

Lockhart, Donald M. "'The Fourth Son of the Mighty Emperor': The Ethiopian Background of Johnson's *Rasselas*." *PMLA* 78 (December 1963): 516–28.

Lowe, Lisa. *Critical Terrains: French and British Orientalisms*. Ithaca: Cornell UP, 1991.

Lynch, Jack. "Samuel Johnson." 26 July 2005. <http://andromeda.rutgers.edu/~jlynch/Johnson/>.

MacKenzie, John M. *Orientalism: History, Theory, and the Arts*. New York: Manchester UP, 1995.

Mayhew, Robert J. "Nature and the Choice of Life in *Rasselas*." *SEL: Studies in English Literature* 39.3 (1999): 539–56.

Messenger, Ann. "Choices of Life: Samuel Johnson and Ellis Cornelia Knight." *His and Hers: Essays in Restoration and Eighteenth-Century Literature*. Lexington: UP of Kentucky, 1986. 197–221.

Metzdorf, Robert F. "The Second Sequel to *Rasselas*." *The New Rambler* 16 (January 1950): 5–7.

Miquel, André. "*The Thousand and One Nights* in Arabic Literature and Society." '*The Thousand and One Nights' in Arabic Literature and Society*. Ed. Richard C. Hovannisian and Georges Sabagh. Cambridge: Cambridge UP, 1997. 6–13.

Nussbaum, Felicity. *Torrid Zones: Maternity, Sexuality, and Empire in Eighteenth-Century English Narratives*. Baltimore: Johns Hopkins UP, 1995.

Parke, Catherine N. *Samuel Johnson and Biographical Thinking*. Columbia: U of Missouri P, 1991.

Potkay, Adam. "The Spirit of Ending in Johnson and Hume." *Eighteenth-Century Life* 16 (1992): 153–66.

Power, Stephen S. "Through the Lens of *Orientalism*: Samuel Johnson's *Rasselas*." *West Virginia University Philological Papers* 40 (1994): 6–10.

Rawson, Claude. "The Continuation of *Rasselas*." *Bicentenary Essays on Rasselas*. Ed. Magdi Wahba. Cairo: Société Orientale de Publicité, 1959. 85–96.

Richard, Jessica. "'I Am Equally Weary of Confinement': *Rasselas* and Women Writers from *Dinarbas* to *Jane Eyre*." *Tulsa Studies in Women's Literature* 22.2 (2003): 335–56.

Rogers, Pat. "Johnson, Samuel (1709–1784)." *Oxford Dictionary of National Biography*. Oxford: Oxford UP, online edn. May 2006. <http://www.oxforddnb.com/view/article/14918>.

Rousseau, G.S. and Roy Porter. *Exoticism in the Enlightenment*. New York: Manchester UP, 1990.

Said, Edward W. *Orientalism*. New York: Vintage Books, 1979.

Sherburn, George. "Rasselas Returns—to What?" *Philological Quarterly* 38 (1959): 383–84.

Tillotson, Geoffrey. "'Rasselas' and the 'Persian Tales.'" *Essays in Criticism and Research*. Ed. Geoffrey Tillotson. Hamden, CO: Archon Books, 1967. 111–16.

Uphaus, Robert W. "Cornelia Knight's *Dinarbas*: A Sequel to *Rasselas*." *Philological Quarterly* 65.4 (Fall 1986): 433–46.

Wallace, Tara Ghoshal. "'Guarded with Fragments': Body and Discourse in *Rasselas*." *South Central Review* 9.4 (1992): 31–45.

Weinbrot, Howard D. "The Reader, the General, and the Particular: Johnson and Imlac in Chapter Ten of *Rasselas.*" *Eighteenth-Century Studies* 5 (1971): 80–96.

Weitzman, Arthur J. "The Oriental Tale in the Eighteenth Century: A Reconsideration." *Studies on Voltaire and the Eighteenth Century* 58 (1967): 1839–55.

——. "More Light on *Rasselas:* The Background of the Egyptian Episodes." *Philological Quarterly* 48.1 (January 1969): 42–58.

Whitley, Alvin. "The Comedy of *Rasselas.*" *ELH* 23.1 (1956): 48–70.

Using 911 lb. of Rolland Enviro100 Print instead
of virgin fibres paper reduces your ecological footprint of:

Trees: 8
Solid waste: 492lb
Water: 4,6444gal
Suspended particles in the water: 3.1lb
Air emissions: 1,081lb
Natural gas: 1,126ft$^3$